W9-BWK-691

*This special signed edition
is limited to 1000 copies.*

LEWIS SHINER

DARK

TANGOS

BOOKS BY LEWIS SHINER

NOVELS

Dark Tangos (2011)

Black & White (2008)

Say Goodbye (1999)

Glimpses (1993)

Slam (1990)

Deserted Cities of the Heart (1988)

Frontera (1984)

COLLECTIONS

Collected Stories (2009)

Love in Vain (2001)

The Edges of Things (1991)

Nine Hard Questions about the Nature of the Universe (1990)

DARK TANGOS

A NOVEL BY

LEWIS SHINER

SUBTERRANNEAN PRESS 2011

Interior design by Lewis Shiner
Set in Bembo

First edition

ISBN 978-1-59606-396-9

Subterranean Press
PO Box 190106
Burton, MI 48519

www.subterraneanpress.com
www.lewisshiner.com

For Orlita:

Vamos a bailar

I have used «guillemets» throughout to indicate dialogue originally spoken in Spanish. A glossary of Spanish and tango terms appears at the end of the book.

T HE FIRST TIME I saw her was in the chrome and cracked-plaster lobby of Universal's Buenos Aires office. From where I stood, on the other side of the glass wall that separated our servers from the noise and dirt of the city, I got an impression of power and grace from the way she held herself, saw long dark hair and a flash of gold at her ears and wrists.

She was one more beautiful woman in a city full of beautiful women, and young, not much past thirty. Yet something made me look again. Maybe her nose, which was long and slightly crooked, as if it had been broken in the distant past and never properly set.

She was deep in conversation with the receptionist, a young guy with a dark suit and a permanent five o'clock shadow. It seemed like he was not giving her what she wanted, though I couldn't hear their words through the glass.

She glanced up at me and I thought she would look away, bored or even annoyed by another wistful male gaze. Instead she let me see something else, a question, an urgency.

I found myself, to my surprise, mouthing words to her in Spanish: «Can I help?»

She gave me a rueful smile and a small, tilted shake of the head that said no, thanks. Then she turned back to the receptionist and I forced myself to walk away.

IT WAS MY FIRST full day on the job. I'd been in the city for a week, moving into my tiny apartment, opening a bank account, putting a local chip in my cell phone, contacting old friends. I also called my favorite of the tango teachers I'd worked with on previous trips and scheduled some private classes. I drifted from one thing to the next as if in a dream, sometimes looking up to realize I didn't remember the last ten minutes.

In terms of time zones, Buenos Aires is only an hour ahead of North Carolina. What I was feeling was not jetlag but culture lag, life lag. I could focus my brain on no more than one thing at a time, and my feelings had shut down entirely. There had been too many shocks in a row, more than I could bounce back from.

The Buenos Aires office existed in another era from Universal's vast campus in Research Triangle Park. My cubicle had gray metal walls instead of taupe fabric. Bare fluorescent bulbs hummed from stained fixtures on tile ceilings instead of being tucked away in recesses. The background sounds came from cars and buses six floors below and not from piped-in white noise.

I'd lost most of the morning tracking down a laptop and a port replicator, a mouse and monitor and keyboard, and I spent the afternoon getting my email ID and installing software. By suppertime I had managed to connect to the repositories in our upstate New York headquarters, check out my programs, and write exactly three lines of new code. I felt as pleased with myself as if I'd won a marathon, and about as exhausted.

But that night, on the edge of sleep, I thought of her again.

MY FIRST TRIP to Buenos Aires had been in 2003, three years before. Universal had flown me down to meet the local programmers assigned to the governance software project. They would report to me in North Carolina, and I would get my choice of the most interesting parts to write myself.

I arrived at the end of September, as spring was lighting up the monochrome streets. In what spare time I had, I wandered the city and let the strangeness settle on my skin like the dust and grit in the air. It reminded me of Paris, but a younger Paris, sprawled across wide avenues dotted with plane trees and purple jacarandas and the swollen trunks of palos borrachos. Most of the grey stone buildings had gone up between 1875 and World War II, when Argentina was one of the ten richest nations on the planet. The architectural style was massive and European, with wrought-iron grilles and balconies full of flowering plants, arches and domes and the occasional red-tiled roof that gave everything a Spanish accent. And now primary-colored storefronts erupted from the ground floors, even as sprays of black graffiti on the endless corrugated metal security doors provided a reminder that the days of first-world status were long gone.

The sidewalks swarmed with pedestrians, men in dark suits and women in black dresses and heels. Despite the formality of the clothes, it was a city where both sexes greeted each other with a hug and a kiss on the cheek. It was a city with one of the highest literacy rates in the world, where newspaper kiosks sold the novels of Borges and Cortázar, and bookstores lined Avenida Corrientes. It was also a city where the homeless slept in doorways and the weight of 13 million people stretched the city's resources to the breaking point. Cartoneros went through the trash on the streets for scrap cardboard and plastic to recycle, and crafters in the plazas made stunning art from cans and bottles and folded subway tickets. And it was a city of tango music, bandoneones and violins and pianos, the heart-wrenching melodies that evoked the giant, echoing ballrooms of the 1930s, and the insistent rhythms that whispered of seduction.

My first morning in the city, groggy and stale from ten hours on an airplane, I wandered into the flea market at Plaza Dorrego and saw an older man dancing tango, not in the clichéd fedora and ascot, but bareheaded in a loose white shirt, his long gray hair slicked back, a dark-skinned and eagle-beaked son of indigenous Americans named Luis Ortega, though everybody called him Don Güicho. I saw the joy in his dancing and the pleasure in the eyes of his partner and I was hooked.

Back in the States, I found out that there had been tango all around me without my knowing it. I convinced Lauren to take classes with me, and while the first months were frustrating, there were milongas once or twice a week where I could glimpse the grace and sensuality that had spoken to me in Buenos Aires. Like all principiantes, we started with open embrace, looking like teenagers at a junior high school prom. But it was close embrace that held the magic for me, where tango became a three-minute love affair, intense, passionate, hypnotic—if I could get past my self-consciousness enough to enjoy it.

I took Lauren with me to Buenos Aires the next September. We went directly to Plaza Dorrego, where we found Don Güicho and convinced him to give us private lessons.

Unfortunately, the second life it gave our marriage didn't last. Lauren dropped out of the classes, though she came to Buenos Aires again with me in 2005. After that she was through with dancing entirely and by the next summer she was through with me.

That had been in June, three months before I arrived in Buenos Aires to stay. She came home from work one day and informed me that she was putting our marriage "on hiatus." I was reasonably sure she was having an affair, though somehow that issue failed to come up in the polite negotiations that followed. Lauren was the director of Durham Regional Hospital, making twice what I did, so logic dictated that she keep the house and the mortgage payments while I found a place over a friend's garage. I took only a few favorite pieces of the furniture I had repaired and refinished over the years because that was all I had room for. I kept half the savings in case of emergencies and she agreed to pay for Sam's last year of college. The rest of what was mine, including my books and my woodworking tools, went into storage.

The dislocation had been profound. I'd been moving all my life, and when we'd bought that house I'd sworn that this was it, that the only way I would leave would be feet first. Some days I missed the house more than I missed the marriage.

I was three weeks into the separation when my manager at Universal called me into her office to tell me that my job had "relocated" overseas. It was as if she'd come in that morning and been unable to find it, or discovered a farewell note next to the coffeemaker. I had the option of moving to Buenos Aires with it, or I could quit, which meant I couldn't even collect unemployment. If I chose Buenos Aires, I would be paid the same number of Argentine pesos that I was currently making in dollars, coming to somewhat less than a third of my US salary.

The timing was remarkable, in that way disasters have of finding each other. Even without my telling her about Lauren, she seemed to know how little I had left to lose. I said that I needed a couple of days to think about Argentina, but in truth I'd known all along that I would go.

MY SECOND DAY on the job, Bahadur Singh invited me to lunch. He was my immediate boss and the manager for all the sixth floor programmers. We were fellow outsiders to the easygoing Latin attitude toward time and deadlines, and over years of long distance phone calls we'd found enough other things in common to sustain a friendship.

Bahadur was from the Punjab via Bangalore, a Sikh with lineage going back to the eighteenth century. For him, the move to Buenos Aires had been a promotion too substantial to refuse, though now that he was here he regretted it. There were not many Indians in Buenos Aires and fewer Sikhs. The winters were far colder than he had anticipated and the meat-and-leather culture of Argentina took a constant toll on his sensibilities. He was still struggling with his Spanish and was relieved to be able to speak English with me.

I told him about the woman I'd seen in the lobby. "I don't know why she made such an impression on me."

"You had a darshan of her," Bahadur said. "That's when you don't just passively observe someone, you really see into them, yes?" He pointed his index and middle fingers at his eyes. "It's a gift from the Divine."

"It was just that there was some kind of mystery there."

"Yeah, right, Rob. That and the fact that she was a knockout." Bahadur loved US slang, which he picked up by watching too many DVDs alone in his apartment.

I shrugged and looked at my plate and he laughed.

We were sitting in a hole-in-the-wall café on the ground floor below the office, little more than an oven and a few tables on a linoleum floor. There was a glass case with cold cuts, bread, empanadas, and fresh fruit.

Through the windows I could see Avenida 9 de Julio, the widest street in the world. The cars, most of them taxis, ignored the painted lines and swarmed into any available space. A few blocks to the right was el Obelisco, the city's best known symbol, so blatantly phallic that the year before, the city government had covered it with a 200-foot pink condom for the duration of World AIDS Day.

El Obelisco sat on a concrete island in the intersection of 9 de Julio and Corrientes. Corrientes was the aorta of Buenos Aires, running from the heart of the microcentro, where I sat, past theaters and bookstores and nightclubs and restaurants, past the US-style Abasto shopping mall, dying out finally near the huge Chacarita cemetery. It was always red in my mind, red for the illuminated plastic signs for Linea B of the subway that runs beneath it, for the neon lighting up the gray buildings, for the taillights of the cars headed east «hacia el bajo,» toward the Rio de la Plata that forms the northeastern border of the city and the country.

Spring had come again, though the overdressed porteños that I could see on the sidewalks were slow to admit it. They'd insulated themselves with long scarves and high boots, sweaters and cashmere overcoats. I myself had compromised with the dressier Buenos Aires standards, wearing a long-sleeved soft cotton shirt, khakis, and a knit tie. Bahadur tended toward jeans and rugby shirts. He was tall and lean and fit, with a curly black beard and gentle eyes. He'd had on a different colored turban every time I'd seen him and that day he was in navy blue.

He was eating a slice of the tarta de verduras, a pie stuffed with hard-boiled eggs and acelga, the Swiss chard that Argentines used in place of spinach. I had gone for the empanadas de choclo, filled with a corn and cream sauce that had a famous tango named after it.

A woman's voice said, «Mind if I join you?»

I looked up and saw Isabel, the director of the Buenos Aires office. She was in her early fifties, a few years older than me, compact, olive-skinned, with a scattering of white in her short black hair. Her eyes sat close together and it gave her a certain intensity of expression. She had a generous mouth and an easy smile, and she made it clear that I didn't want to know what happened when the smile went away. Her nickname, which she encouraged, was La Reina, the Queen.

«¿Como no?» I said, and stood up so she could squeeze past me.

«You settling in okay?» she asked. «Bahadur isn't trying to talk you into any of his crazy chanting shit, is he?»

«It's not crazy, it's kirtan,» Bahadur said. «It's quite beautiful, some of it. If you have the patience for it.»

Isabel had a big laugh, not something you heard much from Universal's upper management in the US. We talked about the governance project, and then about my apartment in the old San Telmo district, which she considered a dangerous part of town. She brought up the Boca Juniors futbol team and I had to tell her that I was not a sports fan, my father having forced me to play games I had no aptitude for as a kid.

After a silence, she said, «Tell me, Beto, how bad is it in the US?»

I'd told everyone to call me Beto, short for Roberto, rather than my English name. It was one more way to put distance between me and my old life in the States.

«It's hard to know the truth,» I told her. «They don't keep statistics on everyone who's unemployed, only on the ones who are getting benefits, and those run out after six months.»

«It's the same here,» Bahadur said. «They had an official unemployment rate of twenty percent not that long ago and you know it was really twice that. Now they say it's gone down, but you still see the homeless everywhere.»

I said, «All I know is a lot of my friends are out of work and not finding anything. And Universal is laying people off, like everyone else.»

«Which is why you're here, no?» Isabel said.

I shrugged. «It was a good opportunity for me. I love Buenos Aires. I always wondered how it would be to live here.»

«I think maybe you're being diplomatic. That's not a bad thing. Still, you wonder where all this is going to end up. I know Jim would not be laying people off if there was any other way. You never met Jim, did you?»

I shook my head. She was talking about James W. Watkins, the Senior Vice President for Software Development at Universal, one of the most powerful men in the company. It was a little-known fact that Watkins' first assignment for the company was in Buenos Aires, back in 1975. He spent seven years as director, doubling the size of the staff as well as the revenue, before getting promoted to the Anaheim office. He was at the top of the chain of command that included the three of us, and he had a reputation for being a decent guy who kept his door open to his employees.

«I was just a secretary when I started here,» Isabel said. «Somehow Jim noticed me. He paid attention to everyone. He saw something in me, I don't know what. God knows I wasn't that cute, but he helped me get promoted. I still hear from him now and then. I think he would take an interest in everybody in the company if he could, but with half a million people, what can you do?»

I smiled and nodded. I suspected you couldn't be that selfless and still claw your way to the top of a global giant like Universal Systems, though I liked Isabel's loyalty.

Isabel had sat down with a large chunk of bread stuffed with ham and cheese, and she had worked at it with steady concentration while she listened to us, to the point that she was finished and drinking off the last of her Diet Coke while Bahadur and I were still eating.

«Hope you guys write code faster than you eat,» she said, standing up.

«No one can keep up with you, mi reina,» Bahadur said. «This is well known.»

She laughed again and put both hands on my shoulders as she squeezed past. «Believe everything everyone tells you, this has always been my philosophy. See you.»

When she was gone, Bahadur said, "She's a ball of fire, yes? Always has been."

"With Jim behind her, I would think she could transfer to the States and really move up."

"She doesn't seem to want it. She gets offers sometimes, but she doesn't want to leave Buenos Aires."

I looked outside again. The scruffy trees on the median showed new leaves, the hands of the people on the sidewalks danced as they talked, and the very air seemed to glow.

"I can understand that," I said.

Bahadur shook his head. "Then you are as crazy as she is. It's just a big, dirty city. Finish up and let's go back to work."

OFFICE HOURS IN THE CITY run from nine in the morning until seven or eight at night. People take long lunches, sometimes go home for a nap and work into the evening. Dinner is anywhere from eight to eleven PM, and then the fun starts.

I once asked Don Güicho when people were supposed to sleep. He smiled happily and said, «Nunca.» Never.

At 7:30 I locked my desk, slung my bright orange shoe bag over my shoulder, and left for my class.

Bahadur was right that Buenos Aires was dirty, but wrong about it not being special. The animated neon signs surrounding the Obelisk hung from old buildings by flimsy scaffolding, yet the effect at night reminded me of the energy and excitement of Times Square— except for the way the wide avenue made everything feel so open and spacious, and the warmth and sociability of the crowds that was the antithesis of New York.

I turned my back on el Obelisco and walked south through the cool evening. The air smelled of car exhaust and the spiced peanuts the vendors sold on the street, of perfume and grilling meat. I heard laughter and sales pitches and music pouring out of the brightly lit ies, tango and electronica, ballads and rap and the Rolling Stones.

I took the stairs down into the Subte and shoehorned myself ito the crowd on a hundred-year-old car on the A line. I rode three stops to El Once, an older neighborhood west of the central business district, where Don Güicho taught classes in the Saverio Perre studio.

When I got back to street level it was fully dark. I walked south past a park full of barking dogs to Avenida Belgrano, turned right through a neighborhood of high-end furniture stores to a corroded metal door in the middle of the block, and rang the bell. A motorcycle roared past, trailing rapid-fire Spanish from its radio. After a second the buzzer sounded and I climbed a flight of steep, worn marble steps to the studio.

Saverio himself greeted me at the top, porteño style, with a hug and kiss on the cheek. I'd been a little nonplussed the first time it happened, despite warnings in the guidebooks, and then I'd quickly taken to it. There hadn't been a lot of physical affection in my family and a part of me hungered for it.

Saverio was small, aristocratic, with long white hair and a neatly trimmed goatee. He had a kind of radiance that made his age impossible to guess. He asked after my health in Italian, the second language of the city, a language I only wished I spoke, and offered me the same cup of coffee that I always refused. He had these sorts of running jokes with everybody. There had apparently been some back sacada that he'd tried to teach Don Güicho twenty years before and Saverio would ask him how it was coming along, or whether he planned to teach it to me that day.

In his long life, Saverio had been an actor, singer, and dancer, and taught all those things. The walls were covered with posters and photos of him and the celebrities he'd taught and the films and festivals and shows and awards they'd all been part of. Some of the biggest names in tango were on those walls and Don Güicho's was among them.

It was one more thing about Buenos Aires that moved me, the sense of history that the US so badly lacked. There were a few modern shopping centers in the city, including the massive Abasto mall that literally cast a shadow over the childhood home of Carlos Gardel, the world's most famous tango singer. But there was not much new development, and even renovations of existing buildings were likely to provoke storms of protest, especially in my San Telmo neighborhood.

As usual, Don Güicho was late and I was early. I changed my shoes and talked to Saverio, and at ten past eight Don Güicho came

running lightly up the stairs, followed by Brisa, his latest in a long
line of dance partners. Though Don Güicho himself must have been
past 60, his energy seemed infinite. He was my height, six feet, thinner even than I was, with a wiry strength I'd never had. I felt it in
his abrazo there at the top of the stairs.

«One of my students saw you at Salon Canning last night,»
Saverio said to Don Güicho. «He very much admired your sacada
por atrás.»

«You should teach it to him,» Don Güicho said.

Saverio shook his head sadly. «Apparently I lack the skill to teach
that step.»

There was a sense of haste even in Don Güicho's small talk.
Saverio pointed us to the nearest studio and Brisa led the way in.
The floor was a worn, intricate parquet, a hundred years old. The
high walls were powdery white stucco, covered with still more
posters and photos. Two battered steel and black vinyl chairs were
pushed against the wall, and a small triangular shelf in one corner
held a vintage boom box. Brisa sat down to change into her four-
inch heels.

She was a college student, smart and ambitious, with fair skin and
dark brown hair, the sort of Northern Italian good looks that had
prompted then-President Sarmiento to flood Argentina with Italian
immigrants in the 1880s. It was part of a policy that included the
elimination of virtually the entire black population. Blancificación,
Don Güicho had called it when he explained it to me. The results
were obvious walking down any street in Buenos Aires. Many blacks
had been cannon fodder in a bloody war with Paraguay and there
were rumors of concentration camps and forced marches across
the Brazilian border. By the 1920s, the few remaining blacks in
Argentina had simply stopped having children.

Don Güicho shrugged out of the backpack that he carried everywhere, opened a set of French doors that let onto a tiny balcony,
and folded back the ubiquitous steel shutters to let in the night air
and the sounds of traffic. He put on a CD of D'Arienzo tangos, spare
and staccato, and as soon as Brisa got to her feet, he wiggled his
fingers at us and said «dale,» the all-purpose Argentine equivalent of
"let's go."

Brisa smiled. I reached behind her with my right arm, gripping
her lightly outside her right shoulder blade and drawing her gently

into me. Her left arm went around my neck and she sighed—anticipation, pleasure, acceptance—a thrilling sound. We breathed together for a moment and I felt the warmth of her body against me. Then I reached for her right hand with my left and pointed our forearms upward. I found my place in the music, shifted her onto her left foot, and led a slow step to my left.

I had been rehearsing in my mind the move he'd shown me in our last class and as I thought about it, I felt my shoulders start to creep up around my neck. I forced them down, breathed again, focused on the beautiful woman in my arms and tried to think about the steps I wanted her to take and not my own.

Tango, at some level, is simple. There are only three steps: forward, backward, and the so-called open step to the side. The lead comes from the torso. The arms, relaxed, merely extend the torso and add clarity. The hands are still.

The steps come only at specific intervals in relation to the music. On the beat, or tiempo. Double time, or doble tiempo, and half time, or medio tiempo. Then there is contratiempo, the skipping heartbeat of the habanera rhythm, the African ancestor who will not be denied, da-DUM dum dum.

Yet for every rule, tango finds a loophole. The leader can pivot the follower, or himself, before taking any of those three steps. Leader and follower do not have to step at the same time, or in the same direction, or take the same number of steps. The complexities multiply exponentially until hope of mastering even the bare essentials of the dance recedes into an improbable future.

«Don't think so much,» Don Güicho said. «Just dance.»

I gave up on replaying the move I had not quite learned and tried instead to dance the music. Brisa was a marvelous partner, needing only the smallest cues to execute anything I asked for, but my brain was floodlit with self-consciousness, straining for something appropriate to lead for each new phrase of the music, to keep the leads subtle and clean, to keep my feet close to the floor without dragging, to keep my posture straight yet relaxed, to make my arms and shoulders a perfect circle from my eje, my axis, my center.

After less than a minute, Don Güicho said «bueno,» not as praise but as a signal to stop.

I stepped away from Brisa and said «Gracias,» and Don Güicho stepped in. He took her through a sequence of moves that involved two changes of direction, blocking her right foot in a parada, and swinging her left leg around the back of his right in a gancho, and we were off.

For the next hour I struggled to keep up, to stay focused, to take the same steps he took without losing the fundamentals of the dance. Brisa gave me a gentle correction or a nod of encouragement here and there, while Don Güicho stayed impassive and intent, with an occasional «ahí va» or «eso» when I got something right, and more often a «¡no!» with a wagging finger, followed by a demonstration—sometimes he would take me by the arm and walk me through it side by side with him, sometimes he would take me by the elbows or into close embrace and lead me through the follower's part. Only at the very end did I get a «Muy bien, Beto, bien hecho.»

I used my cell phone to film Don Güicho going through everything we'd done, then Brisa had to rush off for a dinner date. I paid Don Güicho for the class and Saverio for the room and changed my shoes, feeling deeply tired.

Don Güicho walked me down to the street and said, «Can we change your lesson to Thursdays? My class at the Sexto Kultural starts up again next Wednesday.» It was a public cultural center in a run-down building across from the Federico Lacroze railway station. I'd been to a few of his classes there on previous trips.

«Sure, no problem.»

«Bueno,» he said, about to take his leave, and then he said, «Where are you going now?»

«Back to my apartment, I guess.»

«A friend of mine is opening his new café tonight. I'm going over there now if you're interested. Good food, tango music, there's a little dance floor. I'm teaching a beginner's class there later.»

«Sure.» I hadn't spent a lot of time with him outside of class, so I was flattered by the invitation.

He took off at a fast pace and I had to hurry to keep up. After a block or so he said, «Do you know this neighborhood? El Once?» I shook my head. «It used to have a big Jewish population, lots of stores, synagogues, textiles. During the Crisis there was a lot of emigration to Israel, so it's different now.»

The Crisis started in the late 1980s with hyperinflation and ended in 2002 with a staggering devaluation that wiped out most people's savings. Though the peso had been stable since 2003, the resentment and protests continued.

Carlos Menem had been President for most of the Crisis years. Menem had pushed the so-called "neoliberal" program of privatization, cutting social programs and letting the IMF and World Bank set the agenda for foreign investment.

«Everything changing,» Don Güicho said, «so much of it not for the better.» He stopped to look in the window of a stationery store. Though it was closed and dark, we could see wooden cabinets and floors and wainscoting through the iron bars. «There are still a few old stores like this one. We lose more of them every year.»

«It's beautiful,» I said. «You don't see anything like this in the US anymore.»

We were walking a zigzag course, north then east then north again. As we turned right onto the avenue that would eventually take us past El Congreso, the National Congress building, I heard the noise of a crowd. The closer we got to El Congreso, the louder and angrier the voices got.

I looked at Don Güicho. «What's going on?»

«Una manifestación,» he said. A demonstration. «Over Jorge Julio López.»

I shook my head. «I think I heard the name somewhere. Did I miss something?»

I HAD.

I of course knew about the military dictatorship that ruled Argentina from 1976 to 1983. Their euphemistic "National Reorganization Process," el Proceso, included the kidnapping, torture, and murder of tens of thousands of civilians. The victims were accused of having liberal sympathies, or being related to someone who did, of being a teacher or a student or a writer, or being pro-union. The usual estimate was 30,000 dead. It was hard to be sure because so few of the bodies were ever recovered. This was the regime that gave us the word "disappeared" as a noun.

Tens of thousands were also tortured and set free as a warning. One of them was Jorge Julio López, who spent close to three years in various detention centers.

When the regime finally fell, only nine men were tried. They were found guilty of human rights violations and sentenced to life in prison, then pardoned a few years later by Carlos Menem. The rest of the architects and henchmen of el Proceso were pardoned under what became known as La Ley de Punto Final, named for the period at the end of a sentence.

It wasn't until June of 2005 that the Argentine Supreme Court finally declared the law unconstitutional. A year later, the first defendant, Miguel Etchecolatz, was brought to trial. Etchecolatz was 77, sick and feeble. During his year and a half as Director of Investigations for Buenos Aires Province at the start of el Proceso, he had been responsible for a record number of kidnappings and detentions. The main witness for the prosecution was Jorge Julio López.

López was ill with Parkinson's and the experience of reliving his torture on the stand had been traumatic for him. He was to make his final court appearance on Monday, September 18, 10 days ago. On the night of the 17th, the day I'd arrived again in Buenos Aires, he had been at home in La Plata, south of the city, and that was the last anyone had seen of him.

Etchecolatz's supporters suggested that López had gone into hiding, or that the stress of the trial had left him befuddled and that he'd wandered off into the countryside. The suggestions were demolished as fast as they were made and none of them explained the recordings of torture sessions that had supposedly been left on his answering machine before he vanished.

Etchecolatz himself denied any involvement and claimed that the trial was nothing but a political exercise, that he was being punished for doing only what was necessary to protect his country from Communism. The judges sentenced him to life imprisonment, though the verdict was strictly pro forma. Under Argentine law, convicts over 70 years old can't be sent to prison, so he got off with house arrest.

During el Proceso, the repression had been so fierce, so absolute, so widespread, that there had been no organized attempt to fight back. The montoneros, the guerillas whose assassinations had provided the junta's excuse for their reign of terror, had been all but wiped out before the coup and no one emerged to take their place.

The only substantial protest had been by Las Madres de la Plaza de Mayo, the women who marched in front of the Presidential Palace, demanding the return of their children with the refrain, «Aparición con vida,» let them appear alive, and even Las Madres had been subjected to beatings and murder attempts.

Those years had cost the people of Argentina their tolerance for silence. During the Crisis they invented the cacerolazo, a protest march to the banging of pots and pans, pieces of metal pipe, anything that would make noise, and they attacked the bank buildings with hammers, paint, urine, and bonfires. Buildings were covered with political graffiti, from scrawled slogans to elaborate murals to something I'd never seen before: small, detailed paintings done with stencils and multiple layers of spray paint, showing a woman's face with her mouth taped shut and her eyes bulging in fear, or an anarchist about to hurl a bouquet of flowers, or a portrait of Mexico's Subcomandante Marcos. And when something particularly outrageous happened, they took to the streets by the hundreds—men, women, children, and grandparents.

That was what had happened in front of El Congreso.

THE MOB OF PROTESTERS had massed across the street from the Palacio. They carried a twenty-foot banner that read APARICIÓN CON VIDA: JORGE JULIO LÓPEZ and individuals in the crowd held signs that showed his face and a question mark. They chanted «¡Dijimos nunca más!» again and again, and the sheer quantity of anger in those voices was both thrilling and frightening. I couldn't imagine being on the other end of that much collective rage, or what kind of repercussions they might bring down on themselves.

Literally translated, the chant meant, «We told you never again,» but the «nunca más» was a loaded reference, deliberately evoking the title of the 1984 report published by the national commission that had investigated the abuses of el Proceso. It was nearly 500 pages of fine print that included account after firsthand account of kidnap and torture, photos of the detention centers, lists of the missing.

Dozens of police encircled the demonstrators. The cops were in black uniforms, black billed caps, and orange bulletproof vests. Parked conspicuously nearby were black vans, police cruisers, and a flimsy-looking tank with a pair of machine guns mounted on the roof. The threat of violence was palpable and everything about the scene screamed that I was not in the US anymore. It had all the makings of one of those overseas bloodbath photos that would be everywhere for a couple of days and leave privileged white middle class US citizens like me feeling sickened and at the same time grateful to be a continent away from it.

Don Güicho might have been watching a slow, elegantly played futbol match. He stood with his hands in the straps of his backpack and smiled and nodded and said, «Bien, bien.»

As I had learned to do in the last few weeks, I made a quick estimate of my anxiety level. I surreptitiously found the pulse below my left thumb and counted the beats, a cognitive therapy trick I'd picked up on the Internet. I tried to sound casual as I said, «How dangerous is this?»

«Not so much, I think. The government is on their side in this. They would like nothing better than for Lopez to suddenly show up, alive and well. This makes everybody look bad. The cops will let them work off their anger and keep anybody from getting hurt.»

«You think López is dead?»

«Of course he is. The junior officers from Etchecolatz's day are the ones in charge now. I'm sure he's got connections still. Maybe they even found a green Falcon to pick him up with.»

Green Falcons—supplied to the government by the Ford Motor Company—were the vehicles of choice for the euphemistically named grupos de tarea, the "task groups" who did the actual kidnapping back in the seventies. It was part of the branding. Just the sight of a green Falcon in those days would clear the streets. The task group, usually in plain clothes, always heavily armed, would approach its victims in the street, in their apartments, at their jobs. The kidnappings took place in broad daylight, at suppertime, in the dead of night. The victims were immediately tied up or handcuffed, hooded, and dragged to the car. They were thrown on the floorboards and the car would scream away from the scene, a calculated process of disorientation that would culminate in the sadistic application of electric shock at the detention centers.

«It's hard to believe,» I said. «That it could happen again, after all these years.»

«That's what they're saying.» Don Güicho pointed to the protesters. «For those of us who lived through it, this is our worst nightmare, that it could all start again. Because it never really ended for us. There was no justice, the guilty were left to walk the streets, you could look over some night and see the man who tortured you sitting at the next table at the café. There are all those tens of thousands of people who disappeared and we'll never know what really happened to them. So the ones left behind can't even mourn properly, can't ever get past it.»

I nodded, not wanting to say anything that might distract him. In all the time I'd spent in Buenos Aires, no one had ever volunteered anything about those days, and anyone I asked about it would quickly change the subject. It was Argentina's Holocaust, literally unspeakable.

«But the world is catching up to us, no?» he said. «They openly steal elections even in the United States now, and torture and terrorize civilians in Iraq. Where are the human rights in Russia and China? After Videla and the rest, we had Menem, who was even worse in some ways. So why not more kidnappings? López and now maybe this guy Suarez, too.»

«Suarez?»

Don Güicho shrugged. «There's a guy named Marco Suarez that disappeared last week. He's not like López, he wasn't kidnapped and tortured during el Proceso. There's nothing obvious to connect him to the dictatorship, so he didn't make the news. The thing is, I heard from one of my contacts that he was on a list of witnesses for another trial, the trial of Emiliano Cesarino. Cesarino was an officer under Videla and he was the one in charge of coordinating the detention centers. So one night last week Suarez told his wife he was going out to get some oranges. Apparently he loved oranges, they made him think of the tropics. He never came home.»

There was another roar from the crowd and I felt the sweat break on my forehead. «We should go,» I said. «We don't want you to be late.»

Don Güicho gave me a curious look and then nodded. We started walking again and I tried not to hurry. A line of cops stood at the edge of the sidewalk to keep people from blocking the street and we had to pass within a few feet of them. I felt their eyes on me, profiling me as foreign, possibly trouble.

«You seem different from last year,» Don Güicho said. «More nervous or something.»

There were a lot of things I hadn't told Don Güicho. This was not the time to start. «Things are different now,» I said. «I'm separated, I'm not on vacation anymore.»

«You shouldn't think of it that way. Now you're on vacation all the time.»

«Tell that to my boss,» I said. The police were behind us, the crowd noises fading. The moment had passed and I felt the coolness of the sweat drying on my forehead.

«Speaking of your job,» Don Güicho said, «did you know that Suarez worked for your company?»

«For Universal? You're kidding me.»

«No, he was there most of his life. He used to be a handyman, you know, change the light bulbs, fix a broken chair. He was smart, taught himself how to work on computers. He was supposed to retire, but he liked the work and he was still there until he…disappeared.»

It made me feel strangely vulnerable that Isabel and Bahadur and the developers under me had been touched so directly by the cold, dead hand of the dictatorship. As sad and obvious as the sentiment was, the personal connection made his disappearance more real and more disturbing.

«They really think Suarez was kidnapped? And murdered?»

«The police say no. But my friends? My friends think yes.»

Don Güicho had never been specific about who his friends were. I knew he leaned toward the left and that in Latin America the left was far more radical than what I was used to, generally meaning strong anti-US sentiment and socialist ideology.

Don Güicho stopped in front of a shop window with the words «El Caburé» painted in the gaudy style of the souvenir plaques that were for sale on every street corner. It was both a transliteration of "cabaret" and the name of a famous tango. «Here we are,» he said.

Inside, the place was not much larger than the shop where I'd had lunch. A tiny hardwood dance floor filled the back, leaving room for a few tables in the front and a bar down the left side. There was a man on the dance floor, dark and handsome, late thirties, wearing a charcoal pin-stripe suit over an open white shirt. He broke off the introductory tango lesson he'd been giving to an older woman with unrealistically yellow hair to greet Don Güicho. She seemed irked as the two men ignored her.

«Beto, this is Miguel Autrillo,» Don Güicho said. «He was a student of mine a long time ago, but now I should be studying with him.»

«Never,» Autrillo said. «You're the maestro.» He recognized me as a foreigner and so shook my hand rather than embracing me. «A pleasure. Where are you from?»

«Igualmente. I'm from the US.»

He switched to English. "Really? I thought maybe Paris or Rio."

I acknowledged the compliment with a tilt of the head and a smile. He was impossibly charming.

"I'm practicing my English because I want to tour the US next year. I have an agent setting up some dates now. I've tried for years to get Don Güicho to go, but he won't learn English."

«*Eeenglish,*» Don Güicho smiled. «You can't teach tango in *Eeenglish.*»

«You can if you want to make money at it,» Autrillo said.

I got out one of my business cards and on the back I wrote the email address of a tango instructor in Durham who put on a lot of workshops. «Tell him I recommended you.»

Autrillo was effusively grateful and gave me his own card and finally begged off to return to his lesson.

«Are you hungry?» Don Güicho asked me.

I nodded. «My treat. Since you are doomed to poverty for your lack of *Eeenglish.*»

Don Güicho ordered a hamburger and I got a plate of gnocchi. One of the consequences of the blancificación was the abundance of superb Italian food at most of the restaurants in the city, making it easy for me to be a vegetarian in a nation of beef eaters.

When the food came, Don Güicho said, «Argentina has the best beef in the world. You're crazy not to at least try it. How did you come by this eating disorder of yours?»

«I quit eating meat when I was a kid.»

«But why?» He was smiling, to excuse the rudeness. There was a side of Don Güicho that liked to tease, and it could be ruthless, like when he imitated me with my shoulders hunched and stiff.

«I was eight and my dog got hit by a car. It was bad, a lot of blood, and I saw the whole thing. That night my mother was cooking and I connected the meat in the kitchen with my dog and I told my mother I wasn't going to eat it anymore. She thought it would just be for a day or two, but I never backed down. For a while I went on eating chicken and fish, but really, it was the same thing for me and I didn't want to eat animals anymore.»

«You were a sensitive kid.»

«Yeah,» I said. «Sensitive.» His willingness to press opened the door for me to do the same. «So tell me. What was it like for you during el Proceso? You were never arrested, were you?»

Don Güicho shook his head. «For most people, things were not that different. It was a very quiet, very serious time. Especially during the Videla years. He was a very strict Catholic, very religious, so there was this enforced morality. They banned Carnival, they banned dancing, including tango. People mostly stayed home.

«There would be secret milongas, the information passed by word of mouth, and we would gather in a deserted building, in an inside room with no windows, late at night. For light we would only have flashlights and candles. Someone would bring a record player that worked on batteries, people would bring records, and we would dance. We would take turns keeping watch. Once the police came and I had to run down an alley carrying a phonograph. Somebody else had the speakers and somebody else had the records, all of us running in different directions.

«We were all angry about it, and scared, but in a way it made the tango more...intense. Because it was at risk. That was when I really came to understand tango for the first time. The music is full of despair and yet you dance to it. To me that says everything.»

I WAS TIRED and left after we finished eating. On my way back to the apartment, I stopped at the locutorio down the street to call Sam. I had never seen Skype before this trip, though everyone in Buenos Aires seemed to know about it and all the computers had headsets. Sam had scoffed at my ignorance when I first brought it up, and now it was our standard mode of communication.

"D!" he said when he made the connection. He claimed "D" was short for Dad, though I suspected it was "Dawg" in his head. He kept his dorm room dark and I could barely make him out in the square of video on the screen.

"Studying hard, are we?"

"D, if I'm not on the Internet, where am I going to find stuff to plagiarize for my papers?" He had been a beautiful child, getting Lauren's looks with a masculine edge, and girls followed him around long before he was interested. He hadn't lost the looks or the female interest now that he was nearly grown. He was the consolation for all the bad luck in my life. He'd never seemed unhappy for long stretches, had never gotten into serious trouble, had tried pot and ecstasy and not cared for them and told me so, had always hated cigarettes and never developed much of a taste for alcohol.

It had always been music for him, piano early on and then guitar starting in high school. Now he was on his way to a music degree at Berklee in Boston.

We talked for a while about his band and my job and then he said, "So, are you and Mom talking?" He'd been as hurt by our separation as I'd ever seen him and he refused to believe it was permanent.

"In theory," I said.

"Which means you're not, but if you had to, you could probably be civil?"

"We haven't been less than civil in any of this. We just don't have a lot to say to each other at the moment."

"You could talk about how wonderful I am."

"Preaching to the converted."

"Call me this weekend?"

"If I can track you down. I love you, Sam."

"You too, D. See ya."

I GOT IN at 11:30 and took a shower. The way I felt, there was no point in trying to sleep. I was able to put up a good front for Isabel and Don Güicho and the others, and most of the time I bought into it myself. Only sometimes, after a long day, did I sink into thoughts about the way I'd let everyone do what they wanted with me, let myself get hounded out of my marriage and my house and my stateside job and backed into this tiny apartment in a foreign city, left to fester, forgotten and alone in the middle of the night.

By objective standards, maybe my marriage had not been ideal, but I'd been happy enough. I'd always been drawn to smart, powerful women, and if Lauren was a little cold, a little distracted, I accepted it as part of the package. We both had demanding jobs and we'd both been good about making time for Sam, if not for each other. As Sam needed less of us, I'd spent more time in the workshop and Lauren's job had expanded to fill all the gaps.

Sex had been an infrequent occurrence for many years, but when Lauren did put it on her schedule, it was worth the wait. Her anatomical knowledge matched her complete lack of inhibitions, and on top of that she had a beautiful body that she maintained, like the expensive machine it was, in the hospital gym. As I stood there in my darkened kitchen, leaning out over the airshaft, I could picture that body, every square inch of it.

I thought of the demonstration for Jorge Julio López and my political perspective was swamped in a tidal wave of pettiness and self-pity. Where was *my* justice? What exactly had I done to wind up here?

I reached my hand up to my brow line, to push back my hair and ease the burning in my scalp that was one of my headache symptoms. I was careless, and a potted cactus that my landlady had left behind put a long scratch in my forearm.

I lashed out at the pot and watched it sail off into the darkness of the airshaft, then make a satisfying crash on the cement floor 20 feet below. Immediately my downstairs neighbor's dog began to bark furiously and lights came on and the patio door flew open.

«Lo siento,» I called down to her. «I'm sorry. An accident.»

She was in her sixties and lived with her daughter and three noisy grandchildren. She knelt by the mess I'd made. «The pot is broken,» she said, «but the plant is okay, I think. I will put it in a new pot for you tomorrow.»

I wanted to tell her to throw the damned thing away, then I felt ashamed. «Thank you,» I said.

«No, no, ¿por qué?»

I retreated to the kitchen. Her kindness should have helped my mood. Instead I felt smothered, ineffective, and sour.

THE NEXT DAY at work I asked Bahadur about Marco Suarez.

"Sure I know him," Bahadur said. "He does most of our IT. He's kind of a tough guy, you know, lower class upbringing and all that. He didn't go to college, he learned about computers on the job. He's nice enough, if you play it straight with him. He's got a desk in the corner of the hardware lab and he's there pretty much every day, though he's supposed to be retired. I haven't seen him in a few days, I hope he's okay..."

"He was kidnapped," I said.

"What? Kidnapped?"

"I heard he was on a witness list for the Emiliano Cesarino trial."

"No," Bahadur said, "nobody told me. Where did you hear that?"

"From somebody I trust."

I watched the anger come over him. It started in his eyes and ended up in his clenched hands. He looked away until he had himself under control. "Bastards," he said. "That's the thing that makes you crazy. That there is no punishment. No justice. Human evil, it's always been around. Only here it's never punished."

I HAD BEEN WAITING to go out dancing, mostly because of nerves. Without Lauren there, I wasn't sure if I'd be able to find anyone to dance with. The time had come to try.

Thursday was the early milonga at El Beso, "the kiss," a very traditional venue near El Congreso. It was on the second floor of a beautiful old building on Riobamba, a decent-sized dance space by local standards, with tiny, tightly packed tables on three sides. Single women sat on the side nearest the door, single men at right angles to them, couples on the far side of the dance floor. Invitations to dance were strictly by cabeceo, the tango tradition of eye contact followed by an inquiring tilt of the head from the leader. The follower then accepted with a nod or quickly looked away.

On my first two tango expeditions to Buenos Aires, between the less than stellar technique I was able to show on the dance floor and my having Lauren with me, I never once met a stranger's eyes at a milonga. Somehow every woman I looked at was looking somewhere else.

The year before—at El Beso, in fact—my luck had finally changed. It was our last night out before coming back to the States. Lauren had complained that her feet hurt and we'd hardly danced. The crowd had thinned after 11:00 and suddenly I was looking into the eyes of a woman all the way across the floor. I inclined my head, she nodded, and I felt like I'd hit my number at roulette.

The next challenge was passing muster. Tangos are played in sets of three or four and you are expected to dance the entire tanda with the same partner. If you don't live up to the follower's expectations and she doesn't care about hurting your feelings, she will murmur a quiet «gracias» after the first tango and there is nothing to be done but nod graciously, escort her back to her table, and walk away. After that you might as well go home, as the chances of getting another cabeceo are virtually nonexistent.

Fortunately it had gone well for me. I'd gotten compliments on both my Spanish and my dancing, we'd made the expected small talk between one dance and the next, and when I got back to Lauren she'd said, "Well, it looks like you don't need me anymore." At the time I'd thought she was kidding.

A tanda ended as I settled in at my table, and as soon as the next one started, I saw the woman I'd danced with the year before. I nodded toward the dance floor, she smiled, and I was off. She remembered me and I remembered her name and she told me I was dancing even better than the year before. Argentina is a very polite country.

After that, it was like those years of failure had happened to someone else. I didn't dance every tanda, but when I was ready, or the DJ played an orchestra I liked, I was able to find a partner. And the partners were amazing. One woman must have been 70, in great shape and showing it off with a low cut bustier, slit skirt over fishnet stockings, and luminous yellow hair, as light on her feet as a shadow. Another was heavyset and short, with perfect control of her body and the apparent ability to predict what I was about to lead, and another, with severe gelled hair and a gray business suit that smelled of cigarettes, flirtatiously caressed my leg with one foot.

It was easy enough to confuse the sensuality of tango with more primal feelings. "The vertical expression of a horizontal desire," was one of the clichés. And while none of the serious dancers I knew mistook tango for sex, I had come to realize that the dance satisfied many of the same desires that sex did—the need for physical closeness, the joy of moving together in rhythm, the ebb and flow of command and surrender. A night of dancing well could quiet my demons, and it was looking to be one of those nights.

Then, suddenly, in the middle of a dance, she was there.

I didn't see her come in. She showed up in my peripheral vision, seated near the back of the women's section, and at first I couldn't be sure it was her. There were twenty or thirty other couples on the floor, with only a few centimeters at best separating us, and we moved with painful slowness counterclockwise around the room. As we finally came around again I saw that it was her—there was no mistaking the slightly crooked nose and the intensity of the eyes. As I watched, she saw me and recognition lit her face.

I forced myself to look away and concentrate on the partner in my arms. When the song ended, we were on the far side of the room from her with at least one more tango to go. I had no idea what I said to my partner, except that I must have seemed rude and distracted. Another song started and everyone ignored it for the customary thirty seconds or so, then, slowly, the couples reconnected and began to move. As we came around, I saw that her chair was empty and I had a moment of alarm before I realized that she must be dancing now too.

I was on the outer edge of the floor, as I'd been taught, with the slower and more experienced dancers. Never hurry, Don Güicho told me, leave the big, showy moves for those too young to know better. At that moment I wanted little more than to cruise into the fast lane and look for her. I was paying more attention to the couples around me than I was to my own dancing.

It occurred to me that she could be watching me, that I needed to focus on dancing my best. The orchestra, unfortunately, was Biagi, with stuttering, staccato arrangements that I had never been able to anticipate. I tuned out everything but the music and my partner and did what I could.

After that was still another tango. As the music crashed around us and I discussed the weather with my partner, whose name I no longer remembered, I saw a woman facing away from me, ten feet away, who might have been her. I told myself not to look and I looked anyway.

Then it was time to dance again.

There are people who believe that there is a reason for everything, that things happen because they're meant to. Not me. I believe in eternal vigilance, in doing everything I can to boost my odds, in answering the phone every time it rings. As I waited for the endless dance to finish, I began to sweat.

Finally it was over. I thanked my partner, apologized, and told her I wasn't feeling quite right. She nodded and smiled, already thinking about the next dance. I walked her to her table and tried not to hurry back to mine.

Between the tandas there's a short piece of music they call la cortina, the curtain—usually instrumental, anything from jazz to rock to flamenco, as long as it's clearly not another tango—a signal that the tanda is over and it's time to clear the floor. This time it was the opening riff from the Who's "Baba O'Riley" and it seemed to go on forever. It's bad form to look for a partner before the next tanda starts and you know what the orchestra and the style are going to be. I stared at the red linen tablecloth in front of me and waited.

The music faded. The sound system crackled and then the rather martial violins and piano of "Pavadita" by Alfredo De Ángelis

echoed across the club. It was one of my favorite tangos, with swirl-
ing melodies and sudden pauses and dramatic tempo shifts.

I looked up. She was already watching me. I gave her the cabeceo
and we both headed for the floor.

«I'm Beto,» I said as I took her hand. «I saw you at Universal on
Monday.»

«Yes, yes, I remember you.» She was laughing and it made her
even more beautiful. «What a crazy coincidence. My name is Elena.
I love this tango. Can we dance?»

Part of what drew me to tango was the formality, the elaborate
codes and traditions. There were even tango colors, which I had
honored in my black shirt and red tie. Elena wore black knit trousers, tight around the curvature of her hips, wide and loose where
her long legs met her four-inch heels. She had a matching black
bolero jacket with 3/4 sleeves and long, crocheted fingerless gloves,
and under the jacket was a red silk blouse cut hypnotically low.

Elena, I thought. Elena, Elena.

«Dale,» I said.

I reached for her and she simply melted into me. The connection
was perfect, electric. She had some kind of perfume or essential oil
in her hair with a sweet citrus smell that I instantly loved. I took a
deep breath of her into my lungs and she settled her right cheek
against mine and the fingers of her right hand against the back of
my neck. We breathed out together and in together and I settled her
weight on her left leg. There was a moment of weightless anticipation and then we stepped forward into the music.

MY TEACHERS HAD hammered at me over and over about el eje,
the axis, the center, how all the steps had to start there. They attacked
my slouching posture and showed me again and again how to stand,
how to step, gave me complex moves to execute and showed me
the moods and rhythms and structure of the music. Yet in the end,
nothing really mattered to me in tango but the connection. There is
nothing like it in any other dance. When it works, a stranger comes
into your arms and you are immediately as close as lovers.

Elena was not a flawless dancer. She missed at least one fairly
clear lead. She led herself into a couple of risky boleos and even
ended up on the wrong foot once. As for me, I still struggled with
those moments when my brain went white and I couldn't think of

anything to lead, and I still got flustered when the couples around me stopped moving for too long.

None of that made any difference. She knew every note of the music and when we sped up with it, there was a catch in her breath like mounting passion, urging me on. When "Pavadita" spiraled up to its silences, it left us wrapped tight in our embrace, our breathing suspended. It was the feeling that made me want to learn tango in the first place—that I was no longer an isolated, solitary creature, but half of something greater and more graceful. In tango, when you're in sync with the entire floor, moving and breathing and pausing together, there is no longer any distinction between your body and the music and the very concept of loneliness ceases to exist.

When the song ended, she didn't let go. I didn't know if it was artifice or genuine emotion, I only knew that I didn't want to let go either. A second passed, and another, and another. Dancers on both sides of us were conversing. The next song began and finally her arms began to relax. We slowly moved apart and when I could see her face, it reflected what I was feeling: confusion, longing, amazement.

Then she saw me looking and smiled. The smile had a rueful quality, as if she hadn't meant me to see her like that. «So you know de Ángelis too. Clearly.»

«Yes, I love him. He's probably my favorite. Next to Pugliese.»

«Yes, yes, Pugliese, of course, always. How do you know all this? Your Spanish is good, but you're not from here.»

I gave her the short version: studying in the States, trips to Buenos Aires, living here now. Before I could ask her about herself, we were well into the next song and the floor was starting to move. It was de Ángelis again, a vocal this time, "Para qué te quiero tanto," why do I love you so much?

We made fewer mistakes this time and the connection was just as electrifying. Halfway through the dance she began to sing along, softly. Her voice was high and clear and beautiful, and I was perfectly willing to pretend that she was not just lost in her love of tango but was singing to me.

At the end she clung to me again, and like before she quickly shifted into idle conversation. «What is it that you do for Universal?»

«It's very boring to talk about. I write programs to help bosses create a lot of paperwork for their employees to waste their time

with. I want to know about you. What do you do? Where did you
learn to dance like that?»

«No, no, it's my life that's really boring. I work in a shoe store.
In Abasto Mall. The dancing, I don't know. Two years ago I heard
a tango in the street, I must have heard it a thousand times before,
only this time it was different and I had to dance. So that night I
took my first class. Mostly I come to milongas.»

I realized how completely out of practice I was at this. How did
you ask the real questions, the important ones? Are you with someone? Did you feel what I felt when we were dancing?

I said, «I want to dance with you again,» shocking myself with my
lack of discretion.

She laughed. «That's easy. There's already another tango started
and you will dance it with me, no? 'La Brisa.' It's beautiful.» She
sang along, «...so warm and soft in the rose garden...»

I felt my face heat up. It was clear enough what I'd been asking and
she had laughed it off. I put my arms around her and took her into
the thick of the other dancers. What had I been thinking, anyway? I
was too old for her, and with her looks and ability she could have her
pick of younger men, better looking, better dancers than me.

It was a classic tango moment. From the ecstasy of the first two
dances I fell into despair in an instant, and there was no better dance
than tango to express it. I knew there was a chance I would never
dance with her again, so I gave it everything I had.

When it was over the DJ played the opening of the Doors' "Break
On Through" for the cortina. She turned the end of our tango
embrace into a hug and kissed me on the cheek. «Thank you,» she
whispered. «It was marvelous.»

I walked her toward her table, so full of emotion that I couldn't
speak at first. «I've never—» I started, then shook my head and let it
go. «You're an incredible dancer.»

At her table I hesitated a moment longer than was proper, finally
forcing myself to take a step backward and start to turn away.

«Just a second,» she said.

She got a business card out of her purse and wrote a phone
number and an email address on it, and as she slipped it into my
shirt pocket she held the back of my neck with her other hand and
kissed me again on the cheek.

•

I SAT OUT the next tanda and pretended I was not watching her as she danced with another man. She caught me doing it once and looked at me and laughed. The rest of the time she had her eyes closed and she seemed to give her new partner all the intensity she'd given me.

He was one of the milongueros viejos, the old paunchy guys in suits who never seem to do anything fancy, yet hit every break in the music, never get hung up in traffic, and make all their partners look good. I envied him his skill and his carelessness, and I hoped to be able to dance like that one day if I lived long enough.

It was a set of vals, tango in waltz time, using many of the same steps with a different feeling: more continuous, more turns, more forward momentum. It was a dance I loved, but not one I wanted to be dancing just then. Instead I sat and held onto all the contradictory feelings raging inside me—joy over the card in my pocket, jealousy of the man she was dancing with, the knowledge that I was reading too much into too little, that I was making a fool of myself.

When the next tanda started, I didn't look for another partner. Though it was too soon to ask Elena again, I looked in her direction anyway and saw her changing her shoes.

I was mystified. Who goes to a milonga to dance three tandas and then leave? She didn't look at me, or look back at all, just took her shoe bag, her purse, and her sweater and headed out the door.

I probably would not have noticed the next thing if my emotions hadn't been in such turmoil, with Elena at the center. Within a few seconds of her leaving, a man got up behind me and followed her out. He was at least six foot four and extremely thin, older than me, with a lined face and receding jet black hair. He wore rimless glasses and a threadbare suit over a black T-shirt. His left leg didn't bend properly, giving him a slight limp. He was so remarkable looking that I was sure I hadn't seen him dance all night, and certainly not with Elena. There was something alarming about him and I had an urge to go after him, to watch Elena's back. I didn't because the doorman downstairs made sure everyone got safely into their cabs, and because I was out of my element, if I had an element, and a long way from the country where I was born.

ONE OF MY DANCE TEACHERS used to tell a story about seeing one of his students leave a milonga after less than half an hour. My teacher stopped him to ask what was wrong and the student said, "Nothing. I just had the best tanda of my life. I'm done."

I decided I was done too.

I HAD ELENA'S CARD in my wallet at work the next day, though to be on the safe side, I had already emailed myself all the information on it. I didn't yet know what I wanted to say to her.

The front of the card featured the logo of the New Diqui shoe store, along with her full name, Elena Maria Lacunza, and I had to fight the impulse to go to the Abasto mall on my lunch hour and look for her. She already had one stalker and I doubted she would appreciate another.

Then, at 11 AM, the police arrived.

I heard them before I saw them. The receptionist was telling them, in a frightened voice, that they had to wait for the director, and the detective was insisting that he needed to see «the computer.» Then Isabel's voice joined in, demanding to know what was going on.

I got up to look, as did three or four other people, our heads sticking up over the tops of the cubicle dividers. Prairie dogging, the wits back in the States called it. We were all in a single room that had once been a warren of offices. Some decades ago they'd knocked out the walls and replaced them with supporting columns. It was a mark of the esteem they had for me that there was no column through the middle of my cubicle. All the other programmers kept their heads down, having spent their lives staying as far away from the police as possible.

There were three cops, a detective in a suit and two black-uniformed officers with automatic weapons. Each of the uniforms carried an empty cardboard box. The cops, plus Isabel, plus the receptionist, plus a uniformed Universal security guard, all stood at the edge of the cubicle farm. «You're in charge?» the detective asked Isabel.

«I'm Isabel Salcedo. I'm the director. What's this about?»

«I need to see the office of Marco Suarez.»

«He had no office. He was retired.»

«Did he continue to work here?»

Grudgingly, Isabel nodded. «Sometimes.»

«He had a desk?»

«Yes.»

«A computer?»

«Yes.»

He saw he'd won the high ground and visibly relaxed. He was a small man with a thick moustache and a shaved head, probably in his mid-thirties. «I am Sublieutenant Bonaventura.» He opened a passport-sized leather folder long enough for her to glimpse the contents. «I am looking into the disappearance of Sr. Suarez. I am required to bring his computer to our technicians to help with the investigation.»

«Our computers contain confidential trade information. I can't let you simply walk out of here with one.»

«I assure you I have no intention of letting Microsoft get their hands on it. We'll return it to you in a couple of days. You understand that I am not asking your permission? Good. Can you show me the computer?»

My curiosity was not strong enough to risk a confrontation with Isabel or the police, so I sat down again and stared at my monitor without seeing anything.

I got the story later from Bahadur, who had been in the lab running tests.

Isabel worked the combination on the keypad outside the lab to let the cops in. It was a big room, 60 feet across to where Suarez's desk sat, 40 feet wide, with racks of test computers and long tables end to end down the middle. Bonaventura had apparently received very clear instructions. He went to the desk that Isabel pointed out to him, sat down, and immediately opened Suarez's laptop.

«I'll need the password,» he said.

«I don't know any of my employees' passwords,» Isabel said.

«Can we skip the games, Sra. Salcedo? We actually have computers, you know. I'll tell you what, I'll look the other way while you put in the administrator password, then I can change the logon password myself.»

He got up and offered Isabel the chair. Bahadur told me he could see her brain working furiously and failing to get traction. She sat down and typed the password and got up again.

Bonaventura took care of his business, shut down the machine, then pointed to the cable lock that held the laptop to the desk. «You have the key for this?»

«That only Marco has. Or I suppose I should say 'had.'» If she was
expecting a reaction from Bonaventura, she was disappointed. She
shook her head and said, «I would have to get the number of the
lock from our records and have the locksmith make a new key.»

He apparently believed her. He raised a hand, fingers pointed up,
and tapped the thumb against the fingertips. One of the uniforms
took off his backpack, rummaged around, and came up with a pair
of heavy-duty bolt cutters the length of his forearm. He stepped
up and cut the cable and then took a step back, ready for the next
assignment.

Bonaventura tugged at the center drawer of the desk. «I don't
suppose you have the key for this either?»

Isabel shook her head again. Bahadur told me he'd never seen her
so frustrated before. She looked like she might start to cry.

Bonaventura held out his hand and the uniform went into the
backpack for a small pry bar. The lock offered no more resistance
than Isabel had. He didn't find much in any of the drawers: a candy
bar, some loose change, pens, printouts, a few recordable CDs. They
all went into the boxes.

«Anything else?» Isabel asked.

«Not today.»

«You don't want to talk to anyone? You don't want to take state-
ments from the people who knew him?»

Bonaventura straightened up and looked into her face. «Do you
wish to make a statement?»

Isabel was the first to look away. «No. But I need a receipt for
everything you take out of here.»

«I will send you one,» Bonaventura said. He put Suarez's laptop
under his arm, made the fingers-up gesture with his hand again,
and the two uniforms followed him out, carrying the boxes on
their shoulders.

I ASKED BAHADUR if we would ever see the computer again.

"Not a chance," he said.

He was telling me the story while we ate sack lunches in the "caf-
eteria," a disused meeting room with worn carpet, a long, dark table
whose top veneer was coming loose, a matching microwave, and a
half-sized refrigerator.

"The Buenos Aires police department is famous for corruption.

Even if this guy Bonaventura is clean, that laptop will disappear out of the property room inside a week. You know what those things are worth down here. I was just surprised by all the bullying, given the history."

"What history?"

Bahadur seemed embarrassed. "Well, you know. Universal has always gone to bed with the government."

"I think you mean 'been in bed with.' Come on, Bahadur, you don't have to be coy with me."

"Don't I? Even liberal people of good faith sometimes have surprising loyalty to their countries."

"I don't feel especially loyal right now. We're bogged down in a war nobody wanted, the rich are looting the country, and nobody seems to care about anything but a thinner TV and a longer SUV."

"The looting is nothing new, yes?" Bahadur said. "It was big business from the US that helped finance the dictatorship here. Companies like Ford and ITT and Universal Systems."

"Why would they risk that kind of bad publicity?"

"There wasn't any bad publicity. They were helping to fight communists. At least that was the public version. The real story is that Peron had nationalized everything, so the government still had all these tremendous resources. The deal they made was that the junta would privatize the country's wealth and sell it off to foreign investment. In return the World Bank and International Monetary Fund would loan the government more money than they could ever hope to repay. Putting the country into permanent debt and destroying the economy for all time, while giving them all the money and weapons they needed to wage their war on liberals."

"How come nobody knows this?"

"Everybody knows it. At least everyone here. I guess if people in the US don't, it's because they don't want to."

Bahadur looked at his Tupperware dish of rice and dal. "Sometimes I just want to go home. But home is no better now. We've been colonized again, this time by big business."

I WAITED UNTIL LATE Saturday afternoon to call Elena, a feat of superhuman patience. I'd spent Friday night watching an Argentine movie on DVD and much of the day Saturday in grocery shopping and cleaning the tiny apartment. I dropped off my dirty clothes at the laundry around the corner—the idea of self-service had never taken hold in a country where labor was so cheap—and then went back to the apartment and made the call.

I got her answering machine. Every answering machine in Buenos Aires that I had ever talked to had the same software and the same prerecorded woman's voice. It was one of the mysteries of the city I doubted I would ever solve.

«Hi, it's Beto, from El Beso on Thursday. I was thinking about going to Confitería Ideal tonight. If you're interested, give me a call.» I left my cell number, added, «Un beso—chau,» and hung up.

I'd done well, I thought. Short, to the point, very casual. My hands didn't start to shake until I put the phone down.

THE MILONGA STARTED at 10:30, leaving me empty hours to fill. I called Sam, who was out. I walked down Humberto Primo, dodging the barreling colectivos on every side street, to Plaza Dorrego, where the big flea market would be the next day. Don Güicho would be there, as he had been every Sunday for ten years, dancing with Brisa between the stalls full of old books and clothes and jewelry and coins. There would be mimes and puppeteers, young tango orquestas and old tango dancers passing the hat, artisans with silver and macramé spread on blankets. Lauren had spent all day there every Sunday we were in Buenos Aires.

It seemed to me then that I was kidding myself, chasing a thirty-year-old. What did I have in common with Elena besides tango? What possible interest could she have in me? It was desperation talking, the emptiness of being alone in all these places that were saturated with memories of Lauren.

I turned right on Calle Defensa, crossed the eight lanes of Avenida San Juan, and walked under the elevated expressway. Two blocks later I was in Parque Lezama. Grass was in short supply in Buenos Aires and I'd made a habit of going there when Lauren was at the flea market. I always brought a book and rarely managed to read.

Artisans had set up booths in the high ground around the monument to Pedro de Mendoza, a statue and massive white marble slab commemorating the site of the founding of Buenos Aires in 1536. A band played hardcore in the amphitheater where the park sloped steeply downhill toward the river, and vendors pushed carts full of ice cream around the paths. Kids played futbol with their fathers, lovers kissed on blankets under the trees, and an old man put handfuls of kibble through the chain link fence that surrounded a cat sanctuary in this city of dogs. After rain on and off all week, the sky was finally clear. It was hot in the last of the sun, cold in the shade, and I opted for the heat.

My phone rang and I nearly jumped off the bench.

«¿Hola?»

«Hi, is this Beto?»

I knew her voice immediately, hushed and musical, always seeming on the verge of laughter.

«Hi, Elena, how are you doing?»

«¡Barbaro! I'm going dancing tonight. That always makes me happy.»

«Sounds like fun. Going anyplace special?»

«I heard La Ideal was the place to be tonight.»

«I believe you heard correctly.» I closed my eyes and jumped. «Would you be interested in some dinner first?»

«Oh, Beto, I'm sorry, no, I can't. But I'll see you there. Save me a tanda, okay?»

«For you, I might manage to save two.»

«Perfecto. See you later—chau.»

«Chau, Elena.»

I switched off the phone and watched two teenage girls—closer to Elena's age than Elena was to mine—walk by, arm in arm. I breathed in and out, tasting dust and trampled grass and distant cigarette smoke.

I never liked roller coaster rides and this one was already making me sick—and excited and dizzy and afraid.

LA CONFITERÍA IDEAL is near el Obelisco and the Universal offices, in the heart of the microcentro. The downstairs is still a functioning confectioner's with tiny wooden tables. Porteños love their sweets and it's hard to go more than a few blocks without seeing a pastry shop or a heladeria with designer ice cream. Upstairs at La Ideal there's a milonga nearly every afternoon and night. The place draws tourists and serious dancers alike and is probably the most beautiful tango setting in the city: lofty ceilings, stone columns, ornate chandeliers, carved mahogany paneling ten feet high. Everything gleams there, including the marble floor.

I arrived at 10:50. I was dressed very milonguero viejo in a white shirt, no tie, and a dark jacket and trousers. I had prepared myself emotionally in case Elena was not there, but still felt let down when I didn't see her. I spent a couple of tandas at my table, getting the lay of the land—who was hooked up and not interested in dancing with strangers, who was visiting royalty from some tango show, who was just there to watch.

Then a nice Di Sarli tanda came up and I connected with an older, heavy-ish woman that I liked because I had seen her mouthing the words to the songs as she danced with her eyes closed. The way Elena did, I couldn't help thinking.

I sat out a tanda of milongas, the faster and more rhythmic cousin of the tango, because it was too early to sweat through my jacket. Then I landed a beautiful red-haired woman from Germany, very swank in a long, cream-colored gown that showed a great deal of cleavage. She was overly athletic, but she made me look good and even as I was starting to enjoy myself, a part of me thought, this would be a great time for Elena to walk in.

Which she proceeded to do, during the second song. She was by herself, dispelling another worry that had been eating at me, and dressed dramatically in a black leotard and a long black skirt slit halfway up her thighs. I hadn't realized until then how tense I'd been. I felt my shoulders come down and my embrace relax into a more natural circle, and my partner said, "Ahh."

I caught Elena's eyes once as I danced, long enough to trade smiles with her as she put on her shoes. I led a leg wrap at the end of the last song of the tanda and my German rewarded me by throwing her leg all the way up around my waist, only the second time that had ever happened to me. I took it as a good omen.

"Danke schön," I said as we exchanged a ritual kiss on the cheek, using up nearly my entire German vocabulary. She ran back to her table, eager for her next conquest, and I returned to mine. I was directly across the long, narrow floor from Elena and as soon as the next tanda started—by Miguel Caló, a great romantic orquesta—I looked up. She was already watching me, and she smiled mischievously and arched one eyebrow and nodded toward the floor.

Her small defiance of tradition charmed me, like everything else about her. I thought then that the night was already perfect and I would ask no more of it than this.

I myself stuck to the rules and took the long way around the perimeter of the floor to meet her. She flowed into my arms for a hug and a kiss on the cheek. She was freshly scrubbed, perfumed, and oiled, smelling of honey and citrus and vanilla.

«You look very handsome tonight, Beto. Muy porteño.»

«And you,» I said, «look like a goddess.» Spanish is the language of inflated compliments and she would not have to know that I meant it.

The DJ played four Caló tangos, including the heart-rending "Que falta que me hacés," how much I need you, which she sang as we danced. The connection was as phenomenal for me as it had been before, if not better. She gave me the sense that the instant she began to dance, all the laughter and mischief went away and she opened herself to a darkness and longing and passion so powerful that it took complete control of her body, so much so that at the end of the song she needed those clinging seconds to recover.

Clearly she was not completely unconscious, because she was now anticipating the moves that had tripped her up on Thursday, adding adornments instead of merely following, reading me and reacting to me with a sensitivity that undoubtedly went beyond the dance floor.

The cortina was Dave Brubeck's "Take Five." I felt like an accident victim, called back from my rush toward the white light to find myself on an operating table.

When the gifts were handed out, the one I got was stubbornness. It had gotten me through a computer science degree despite a lack of math skills, kept me in my basement workshop late into the night sanding away my mistakes, pushed my stiff, ungainly body onto the dance floor until it finally began to exhibit a little grace. And it kept me smiling and casual as I led Elena to her table, because I believed that was my best shot with her.

«Don't forget,» she said. «You promised me another tanda.»

«How could I forget a goddess?» I said, and kissed her hand before I made myself turn and walk away.

The place was filling up. There were probably a hundred people in the room, and the dance floor was as crowded as a rush hour subway car. When I first started to learn, the packed floors in Buenos Aires had frustrated me nearly to tears—to stand in one place for so long, searching for things to occupy your partner, then having to move instantly when space opened up, all while keeping some

semblance of connection to the music, was beyond me. Dance is
a language and I didn't have the vocabulary. Over the years I had
learned to relish the challenge. A few bumps and kicks were inevi-
table and there were always reckless drivers to avoid, but the crowds
helped create the whole out-of-body experience.

I threw myself into the middle of it, making a brave show to
Elena that I didn't need her, for close to an hour. Then a new tanda
opened with Pugliesi's "Gallo ciego," and as I started to look for her
she was turning to look for me.

Pugliesi is deeply revered in Bueno Aires, as much for his
defiance of authority as for his complex and romantic tangos. I
didn't know how much of the emotion I felt was mine alone and
how much was Elena's and how much came from the dozens of
bodies wedged in around us, but there was enough of it to reach
the twenty-foot ceilings and burst out the windows into the cool
spring night.

Between tangos we hardly talked—a smile, a «qué lindo,» a re-
mark about the crowd or the heat, and then more dancing. I knew
the music well, still I listened with fierce attention to every note,
trying to slow time, to free my body to experience Elena without
my brain getting in the way.

AFTERWARD I TOOK HER to her table. I had been through a
dozen lines in my head and rejected them all. Be cool, I told myself.

She said, «Come sit with me a minute, can you?»

«Of course.»

I held her chair for her, worked my way to the other side of the
table, and squeezed into the other seat.

«So, tell me, is Beto short for Roberto?»

It was a common nickname, also short for Alberto, Humberto,
and others. I told her yes and gave her a business card, writing my
land line number and email on the back.

She asked what it was like to dance tango in the States and I
told her about the comparative wealth of teachers and milongas in
North Carolina. «The problem is most people want to learn show
tango, with the ganchos and high kicks. People mostly dance in
open embrace. And there's no place like this.» I waved one hand at
the room. «In the United States everything is new. There's no history, everything's made to fall apart.»

«In school, my friends talked about the 'Yankee imperialists,' and now all of them want to go there, where the economy is better.»

«Not so much better now,» I said. «Since 2000, everything has been going downhill. We're having a, what's the word, *recession* they say in English, and no one will admit it.»

«The government lies here too, about unemployment and crime and cost of living, but here we all take the lies for granted.»

Something in the words stung her and she was quiet for a few seconds. I took the opportunity and said, «I've been meaning to ask you. The other day, when I saw you at Universal, what were you doing there?»

The smile fell off her face so suddenly, it was like I'd caused her physical pain.

«Look, I'm sorry, that was rude,» I said. «Please forgive me, it's not any of my business.»

She still didn't say anything.

«Elena?»

«Beto,» she said at last. She picked up my hand from the table and studied it. «I could lie to you, but I'm not going to do that, for reasons that I will tell you one day, maybe one day soon. And I can't tell you why I was at your company right now either, though I will someday. Is that okay?» She looked into my face. «You don't want lies, do you?»

I told her no, of course not, even as I was thinking that there were any number of lies she could tell me that I would love to hear.

«Good,» she said. The smile came back, not entirely without effort, but still dazzling. «So are you here in Buenos Aires by yourself?»

It seemed too good to be true, first the implied promise of "I will someday," and now she had opened up our personal lives for inspection. «Yes. I'm separated. It happened three months ago.»

«I'm sorry, Beto, that's so sad. How long were you married?»

«Nineteen years.»

«Were you happy?»

«More or less. Yes, I think so. It was her decision, not mine. And you? Can I ask you...?»

«If I have a boyfriend? It's okay, you can ask, and the answer is no, no one special, not right now.»

She still had hold of my hand.

I knew so little about her, I didn't know where to start. «You don't seem to care about your job,» I said. «What is it you really want to do? If you could do anything.»

She smiled, for real this time. «I think I would like to be very rich. Not to own things, I don't need anything but a few tango clothes and a place to sleep. And books, lots of books. I would like to not worry about money and just do what I wanted. I would like to learn Arabic and Chinese and take dance classes and see other countries. Uruguay doesn't count.» Montevideo, on the other side of the Rio de la Plata, was a popular day trip. «I would like to do good for others too, don't misunderstand. To help animals and the cartoneros and political prisoners. What a waste to have to work when there is so much to do. But you, you like your job, I think.»

«I do. I like to make things. And when you get a program to run and watch it come to life...it's very satisfying.»

«Do you make anything besides programs?»

«Food. I'm an okay cook.»

«This is a good sign.»

«And furniture. I like to work with wood.»

She seemed excited by that, said she loved to go to flea markets and estate sales, that all her furniture was antique, though not all of it was in good shape. «You will have to come fix it for me sometime.»

She was easy to talk to—except for the weird, forbidden zones. She was careful not to speak too fast or use a lot of slang, having quickly and accurately sized up my Spanish skills. She was a good listener and animated when she talked, bubbling over with energy.

We talked through an entire tanda and then she said, «Here is what I would like. There are a couple of friends here who have been trying to catch my eye and I really should dance with them. And then I would like to dance another tanda with you and then I must go home. Do you think that sounds reasonable?»

«Completely.» I squeezed her hand, which was still holding mine, and got up. I felt dizzy. I went back to my table and drank some agua con gas and danced a tanda with an older woman who had been sitting out much of the night. She was unhappy about that, and not terribly happy with me as a partner, as I couldn't seem to do much with her. I sat out the next tanda of milongas and then Elena was ready for me.

We danced to a set of Anibal Troilo, complex, rhythmic, with lush strings. I let myself get lost in the intensity of the music, the heat of her body, the sound of her breath. As long as she was in my arms, I had no trouble convincing myself that she felt the same way I did.

AFTERWARD SHE SAID, «Beto, if I ask you something, will you just say yes or no and not ask me any questions?»

«Okay.»

«Will you walk me downstairs and stay with me until I get a cab?»

«Of course. I'm tired too. I'll just get my things.»

«Thank you.»

I changed my shoes and left enough pesos on the table to cover my water and a tip. Elena was ready by the time I got to her table, and I knew there were men watching me, wondering how I had landed a woman like her. If only, I thought.

She took my arm as we walked down the marble stairs, gossiping about the characters that showed up at the famous milongas—like the elderly couple who had a set of ballroom-style choreographed moves that they would do over and over in the opening hour of the dance, while there was room enough to get away with it. I'd seen them the year before and remembered their spins and pirouettes. Elena's laughter felt forced and I remembered that she'd said no questions.

At the bottom of the stairs, my glance went automatically into the confitería and I froze. The tall, sharp-faced man with the limp sat drinking a cup of coffee at one of the tables.

«Keep walking,» Elena said quietly.

We went out onto Suipacha, a narrow street squeezed between office blocks. My shirt was completely soaked with sweat and the night air was cold and damp-smelling.

«That man,» I said. «He was at El Beso too.»

A Radio Taxi waited at the curb and Elena waved to get the driver's attention. He switched off his LIBRE light and reached to open the back door for her.

Elena turned to me. «I know.»

«Is he dangerous?» My head began to hurt, the bad way, behind my right eye.

«I don't think so. Anyway, I'm safe for now. Thank you.»

«Elena...»

«I know. This is not fair. Call me tomorrow. At noon, okay? We'll talk.»

«Okay.»

Then she was in my arms. It was not a tango abrazo, it was a kiss, the real thing, on the mouth. I don't know how long it lasted. Not terribly long, certainly not long enough. Her lips were open, warm and soft, I smelled her perfume, musky now from dancing, I felt her tongue flick gently against mine and then she was running for the cab. «Chau, Beto,» she called, and laughed, genuinely this time. «Chau, Beto, mi Betito.»

She got in, and just before she closed the door, the smile dropped away again and her eyes burned into mine and she mouthed the word «gracias,» and then she shut the door and the cab shot away.

I CONSIDERED GOING BACK into the confitería and confronting the man, asking him what he wanted. It was more than self-preservation that stopped me. Elena had some idea of what was going on, which made it a bad idea to meddle until I knew more.

And my head was seriously hurting, for the first time since I'd left the States.

Another cab had already pulled up. I got in and said, «San Telmo, por favor. Humberto Primo con Tacuari.»

I still felt her lips on mine.

I ATE SOME FRUIT and showered and did some stretches and yoga to help the head. It was important not to panic because the headache was back. Panic would make it worse. Better to accept it with a certain bitter sense of inevitability and keep going.

It was after 4 AM. I set the alarm for 11:30 and went to bed.

The headaches had started the night after the job ultimatum. I woke in the night with a shooting pain in my head, but managed to get back to sleep. That went on another night or two, then I woke up one morning and the headache was still there. It felt like a hot poker jammed into my right eye.

Within a week it was so bad that I had to leave work and lie down in the darkness of my bedroom and call Lauren to take me to the hospital.

When she got to the apartment she did a few preliminary tests: had me squeeze her thumbs, tugged on my feet, looked into my eyes with a flashlight. There was no indication of a stroke, so she packed me off to Durham Regional, where they X-rayed my sinuses and my chest, did CAT scans and MRIs, and couldn't find anything wrong. The consulting neurologist diagnosed "men's cluster head-aches," a migraine-like mystery ailment, even though he admitted I didn't fit the symptoms.

It was a typical hospital nightmare. I never got more than a few minutes' sleep at a time; the experimental meal plan delivered food late or cold or not at all; my IV infiltrated the surrounding tissue and pumped my arm up to twice its size. I went in on a Thursday night and on Friday they ran tests. By Saturday I was a complete wreck.

That was when they gave me oxygen and Imitrex, the recom-mended treatment for cluster headaches, which sent me into a full scale panic attack.

People had told me they would rather be in a car wreck or an earthquake than have another panic attack. I had no idea what they meant until that moment. I was hyperventilating, shaking, vomit-ing, claustrophobic, pacing frantically around the room. I ended up screaming at the nurse until he gave me Ativan to bring me down. If the window had opened, I would have jumped through it.

It was a life changing experience. Once I calmed down, I saw that what the Imitrex had unleashed was different only in inten-sity, but not in kind, from feelings I had been holding in all my life, holding in since my parents' divorce and those long, lonely, cross country trips. The symptoms suddenly seemed obvious: the need for control that had made Lauren complain about my inflexibility, the day job where I built small, structured worlds on the computer, the aching, constant fear when I'd spent five months on unemploy-ment in 2002 before I landed the job with Universal. The physical discomfort I felt in roller coasters or in heavy traffic, the islands of order I had created in the chaos of Lauren's clothes and books and papers and CDs.

I made them let me out of the hospital on Sunday, against Lauren's advice. She took me back to my apartment and I slept around the clock, then made a series of appointments with acu-puncturists and chiropractors and massage therapists. For the first week, when I couldn't drive myself, I had to take taxis. Lauren re-fused to help, telling me I needed to stick with the neurologist until he found something that worked.

I saw then how far we'd grown apart and how slim the chances were that we would ever reconcile. Hospitals and western medicine were her life and her parents' lives before that. I was so traumatized that I couldn't let myself think about the possibility of going into a hospital again.

Within two weeks I was able to go back to work part time. My various therapists had worked out a "perfect storm" scenario of bad diet, bad posture, repetitive motion from my mouse and keyboard, and stress from the separation and pending relocation, all of which had collected in my upper back, where it inflamed the occipital nerve that went up over the top of my head and into my right eye.

In headache land, you constantly rate your pain on a scale of one to ten. I was at nine when I went into the hospital. The night after La Confitería Ideal I peaked at five and was down to three by bedtime.

It helped that I knew what it was and that I'd beaten it before. What helped the most was the prospect of answers from Elena and the memory of her kiss.

IN THE MORNING my headache had faded until it was more threat than reality. I ate and brushed my teeth and counted the minutes until I could call Elena.

I waited until 12:15 because too strict a punctuality is not polite in Buenos Aires. I dialed quickly, hands trembling, and as I listened to the phone buzz on the other end, I wondered how it was possible to stand this kind of constant suspense, not knowing whether she would answer, not knowing what to expect.

It was her voice mail. I said, «Elena, it's Beto. Call me when you can.» I took too long to find the next thing to say and her phone cut me off.

I went to the bedroom to make the bed. The window was open on an airshaft where I heard the kids downstairs yelling. I had barely started when the phone rang.

«¿Hola?»

«Beto, I'm sorry, I never answer the phone when it rings, I should have told you that. So how are you? What a beautiful day it is. Was it wonderful last night?»

«Yes,» I said, «Yes, it was wonderful last night.»

«Well, so here I am. Is this a good time for you? Do you want to talk?»

«Yes, I want to talk very much. But I would rather do it face to face.»

She hesitated. I let the silence go on rather than back down. Finally she said, «Okay. Yes. We can do that. You said you live in San Telmo, no? We could walk around. I think Orquesta Tipica Imperial is playing on the street.»

«I would love that,» I said.

«Where should we meet?»

«If you're taking the Subte you should come here. I'm right by the San Juan station.» I gave her the address. «Just ring and I'll come down.»

«Perfecto,» she said.

It was one of the things I loved about Buenos Aires. In Buenos Aires, things aren't just okay. They're perfect.

SHE WORE JEANS, a rugby shirt with green horizontal stripes, a pink baseball cap, and big sunglasses. She hugged and kissed me, and even in that quick kiss there was a tenderness that turned me inside out.

She held my hand as we walked down Humberto Primo. It took concentration because the sidewalks were narrow and, like all the sidewalks in the older parts of town, dogs had crapped on them, an average of once per block. Our tango skills helped.

The spring had intoxicated her. The temperature was in the 70s and she'd pushed her sleeves up past her elbows. The first leaves were out on the few slender trees, invisible birds sang, and a few lacy clouds streaked the sky. The neighborhood was in the process of gentrification, the old two and three story stucco and stone build- ings being sold to overseas investors and retrofitted for the tango tourist subculture. There were flowers and ivy on the balconies and music playing through open windows.

At the bottom of the three-block incline was Calle Peru and the first of the crowds. Once inside the plaza it was shoulder to shoul- der, belly to back. Tourists from all over the world pushed past visi- tors from all over Argentina and locals from all over the city. Elena moved closer and slipped her arm around my waist.

At the outer edge of the square I saw a Peruvian silversmith that I knew. He was in his twenties, with black hair to his collar and a high-necked black sweater with a zipper. I angled us toward him and said, «Hola, Dani, it's Beto.»

«Beto!» He hopped down from the wall and hugged me, then looked hesitantly at Elena.

«I'm separated now,» I told him. «This is my friend Elena.»

He reached across to shake her hand, then asked how I was doing. I gave him the short version, while Elena looked at the jewelry spread out on his blanket.

«These are beautiful,» she said, fascinated.

«They're really special,» I said. «Nobody else does work like this.»

The pieces were made of silver or alpaca alloy wire twisted into rosettes and complex asymmetrical patterns, usually with a crystal or cabochon at the heart. She held up a pendant centered around a rough cut piece of turquoise. «This is wonderful. How much is it?»

Dani quoted her a price that I knew was much too low. He threaded a chain through it and offered her a mirror. I saw the longing in her eyes.

«Let me get it for you.»

«Beto, no, you can't possibly—»

«You have no idea,» I told her, «how happy it would make me.»

She left it on and as we walked away she stopped me and kissed me, slowly and sweetly, both hands on my face. «Thank you, Beto. You have very talented friends.»

We turned right and went up the steps into the square itself. A loud, distorted D'Arienzo tango told me that my luck was holding and Don Güicho was in the middle of a performance. We wormed our way toward the front of the audience.

The moves were showier than anything he would ever teach me, yet more graceful than any other show tango I'd seen. Part of it was the ecstatic look on his face, part of it was the gentility of it. His tango was about displaying his partner rather than dominating her, and Brisa, in tourist-ready costume of black slit skirt, fishnets, and red bustier, made quite a display. He ended with her arched backward across his left arm, and Elena and I joined in the applause.

As he brought around an old felt hat for donations, I reached out to drop a two-peso note in it. «Beto!» he said, and wrapped me in an abrazo. I introduced Elena and he looked at me again, this time with theatrical admiration. «You've been keeping secrets from me. What a beauty!» He asked Elena, «I've seen you, no? Maybe at Salon Canning? Do you dance?»

She blushed and looked at her feet, so I answered for her. «Like a dream.»

«Once the crowd goes, come over and say hello to Brisa. She'll be unhappy with me if you don't.»

He continued his rounds and Elena gave me a crooked smile. «So, was that supposed to impress me?»

I shrugged and failed to look repentant.

«Well, it did,» she said. She hugged me, and with her head in my chest she said, «How do you know the famous Don Güicho?»

«He's my teacher.»

«Ah. That explains a lot, actually.»

We walked over to the trees to say hello to Brisa, who was excited to see me. I felt ridiculously pleased at the way my home court advantage was paying off.

«Are you coming to the milonga tonight?» Don Güicho asked. Every week that the weather permitted, he hosted an open air milonga after the flea market broke up. «It's going to be a beautiful night for it.»

«I don't know what I'm doing tonight,» I said, careful not to look at Elena. «We'll have to see.»

After a few minutes we walked on. «I'm afraid if I admire anything else, you'll buy it for me,» Elena said.

«No more presents, I promise.» I stopped her and held her by both hands. «I wanted you to have the necklace because you clearly loved it and because my friend Dani made it. And because...people who believe those things say that turquoise is good for the throat, uh, *chakra,* in English.»

«It's the same in Spanish.»

«They say the throat chakra is what helps you to speak the truth.»

I had apparently blindsided her. Tears came up in her eyes so fast that they surprised both of us. I took a clean handkerchief out of my back pocket and handed it to her. «I like a man who always has a clean handkerchief,» she joked as she dabbed at her eyes. «He's good to have at a chacarera.»

The chacarera is a folk dance that they sometimes do at milongas. The men wave handkerchiefs and clap rhythmically and stomp their feet in zapateos as they circle their partners. Don Güicho loved it and sometimes did it in the square. Elena fluttered the handkerchief at me and the very pathos of it made me smile.

«So,» she said, «I will tell you some truth.»

•

WE STROLLED PAST the rows of vendors, Elena looking down, arms folded protectively across her chest. I touched her back now and then to guide her.

«There's only so much I'm willing to say, I told you that,» she said.

«I understand.»

«Until this past fall, I lived with my parents. I was on my own after college for a few years, but I never, you know, got into a really serious relationship. So I moved back home. I was saving money, they liked my being there, I had my own entrance to the house and I could come and go as I wanted. My father is...he's a man of very strong principles, or so he always told my mother and me. He's a director at Citibank, very rich, very powerful. He is also very Catholic, very conservative, and he was very strict with me, growing up. And continued to be, even after I was grown. Like, for example, he was very upset that I wanted to dance tango. Beto, I'm sorry, can I have the handkerchief again?»

«Keep it,» I said.

«I learned something about him, something he'd done, that he'd never told me. This is the part I can't tell you about. It was bad, really bad. I moved into an apartment. I quit my job at the bank and took the first thing I could get, which was the job at the shoe store.

«I didn't tell him or my mother where I was going. I got new credit cards and a new phone. I didn't change my name because that would be a lie, and because of what he did, I can't stand liars.»

It took her a few seconds to collect herself. «So it wouldn't be hard for him to find me. And then a few weeks ago I noticed that man that you saw last night.»

«You think he works for your father.»

«Yes. I don't think he would ever hurt me. But I think my father is watching me, through that man. And I don't want my father's eyes on me anymore, not even secondhand.»

«What about the police?»

«I don't know what the police are like in your country, but here the police do what men like my father tell them. People like me, we try not to attract their attention.»

She turned to me, arms still folded. «So you see, I have all these things I can't talk about. And what I want most of all is to forget them, to be some other person completely. That's what tango gives me.»

«I understand,» I said. «If you ever want to tell me the rest, I want to hear it.»

«I know you think that, Beto. But there are things you don't want to know. Please believe me.»

We had passed completely through the square, oblivious to the booths and the people around us. I turned her left onto Defensa, where the high end antique stores were open all afternoon and the performers had staked out their small territories.

Elena stopped and held up her hand. «Listen!»

I heard only the noise of a hundred rapid-fire conversations in Spanish and the voice of the puppeteer next to me, whose drunken marionette clung to a miniature lamppost.

«Come on,» she said, and pulled me by the hand through the crowd, walking fast. Then I heard it too, the creak of the bandoneón and cry of the violin.

Orquesta Tipica Imperial had set up against one of the metal-shuttered storefronts in the middle of the next block. They'd rolled an upright piano onto the street and they had a cello, double bass, two violins, and three bandoneones. They were part of the new breed of tango orchestras, kids in T-shirts and blue jeans, some with long hair and beards. One of the violinists and one of the bandoneonistas were women. The tango they played was in the classic style, but was new to me.

Elena dropped her purse and baseball cap in front of the female bandoneonista and opened herself to me. I took my time, happy just to look at her, to feel the first touch of her body, to smell her hair, to let my left hand dance out the length of her right arm.

I had never danced on cobblestones before. Calle Defensa is the real thing, paved in big, rounded, slick stones, and we were both in sneakers, making it hard to pivot. Elena seemed not to care. In Argentina, the word for cobblestone is adoquín, and they use it to refer to the quality of dance that you can acquire only in Buenos Aires—to say «tiene adoquín» is to give the highest compliment for the authenticity of someone's tango. Elena had it.

They played for twenty minutes. We inspired a few other couples to join us and the band applauded us all. I felt the happiness inside me, filling my entire body, and at the same time I felt like something subtle had changed between us.

I knew that I lived too much inside my own head. Dancing was supposed to be my way out of that. Still I managed to find a trace of sadness in that perfect moment. I felt like her opening up to me had frightened her, made her self-conscious in a way she hadn't been before. The height of happiness is the start of the decline.

I call it the Sunday Effect. Sunday was a day off for me, just like Saturday, except that it felt different, tarnished, because I could feel Monday coming.

Tango is all about the light in the darkness and the darkness in the light. And so we danced.

THE BAND BEGAN to pack up. We threw money in the open violin case and Elena reclaimed her hat and purse. Unwilling to let the afternoon end, I convinced her to let me buy her lunch at one of my favorite restaurants there on Defensa. She had a glass of wine. Over feta ravioli we finally got to some of the conversation that would normally have happened earlier. I had to be careful with my questions, especially about family and childhood. I mostly let her choose the way.

She was an only child, like me. She'd grown up with a lot of time to herself and escaped into books, like I had. She still loved to read, especially Jorge Amado and Isabel Allende. She'd studied business in college because her father was paying for it, while taking as many literature courses as she could. She loved cats and dogs both, but didn't have room for either where she lived.

She loved old buildings, old tangos, old clothes, old movies.

She'd had lovers, not many, because she needed to feel more than physical attraction. She said again that there was no one in her life right now.

There was a silence after that.

We spent an hour and a half over lunch and as we left she said, «Beto. I should go home now. I have work tomorrow.»

Climbing back up Humberto Primo, I told her about the Sunday Effect. Yes, she said, she knew exactly what I was talking about.

We stopped in front of my building. «Can you come in for a few minutes?» I asked. My heart was pounding. I worried that she could see me tremble.

«I wouldn't mind a glass of water,» she said. «The wine has gone to my head a little.»

I let her in and we climbed the curved concrete stairs to the first floor. She pretended not to notice the trouble I had working the key to my apartment.

The place was tiny. A closet-sized kitchen on the right as we came in, a living room with a dining room table against one wall, then a short hallway that led to the bedroom. The floor was yellow parquet, polished to a high gloss. That was what had finally sold me on the place, knowing that I could practice tango there.

«Beto, it's lovely,» she said. She put her hat and purse and sunglasses on the table.

«Thanks. Let me get your water.»

When I came out of the kitchen, she was standing by the bookshelf. «Cortázar, Sabato, Casares—and Galeano,» she said. «Very nice.»

«That's more of a wish list, not what I've actually read. I still read slowly in Spanish, especially when there's a lot of idioms.» I handed her the water and she took a long drink. Her eyes were closed. I reached up slowly and let my fingers trail down her cheek.

She opened her eyes and smiled. She looked for somewhere to put the glass and there was only the dining room table. She walked to it and set the glass down and then stood there, both hands on the table.

I went to her and touched her shoulder. She turned and the smile was gone and instead she had the other look, the intense tango look. Very slowly I reached for her and took her in my arms and kissed her.

It had been nineteen years since I had kissed anyone other than Lauren that way. I couldn't remember the last time Lauren and I had kissed like that, if ever. Elena was trembling and her breath was ragged. I was shaking too.

I led her to the couch and sat next to her and kissed her again. She didn't resist me or pursue me, she followed my lead as she did on the dance floor, eagerly, passionately.

I didn't rush her and I didn't back away. Gradually the kisses got more urgent. I put my hands under her shirt so that I could feel her skin. I ran my hands over her back and hesitated with my hands on the clasp of her bra. She laughed and reached behind her and unfastened it. I raised her shirt and lifted her bra and kissed her breasts. They filled my hands perfectly and her skin was warm and fragrant. I felt delirious. Her fingers were in my hair and she was kissing the top of my head, both of us breathing hard.

I lifted my face and looked into her incredibly dark eyes. «Elena...» I said.

She looked back at me and it was like she was searching for something. There was a question on her face and suddenly it was a much bigger question than the one I was asking, and infinitely sadder, and then it was like watching a piece of glass fall from my hands to shatter against the floor.

«Elena?»

She was crying.

She stood up and refastened her bra and brushed at her shirt.

«Elena, what's wrong?»

«I made a mistake, Beto, a really terrible mistake.»

«Elena, I'm sorry if I—»

«No, not you. Nothing you did.» She knelt on the couch and kissed me fiercely, one hand on my neck, the way she'd held me at El Beso, the first time. «This was my fault. I can't let you get involved with this business. It is so much worse than you can possibly imagine.»

«What business?»

She pulled back and gathered her things from the table. I got up and started toward her and she held out one hand to push me away. «No, Beto, please. I'm begging you now. Please don't call me, don't look for me.»

«This is crazy. How can I just let you walk away?»

Her eyes went cold. There was something like contempt in her voice when she said, «You can't understand this, Beto. You don't have the history.»

«At least tell me what this is about.»

«I can't do that.» She opened the apartment door and stood in the hallway, looking at her feet, holding herself as if she were cold. «Can you let me out?»

I nodded numbly. There was no dramatic storming out of an apartment building in San Telmo, where everything was double locked, needing keys inside and out.

I heard her footsteps running down the stairs and I went after her, leaving my apartment door standing open. By the time I got downstairs, she was across the lobby and standing by the front door, crying, holding my handkerchief to her face. I couldn't think of the magical thing to say that would stop her and turn her around, open her up and make her talk to me.

I put my key in the lock and turned it and she pushed past me onto to the sidewalk. «Goodbye, Beto,» she said, and ran across the street, a taxi honking at her as she disappeared around the corner.

I WENT BACK UPSTAIRS. The apartment was now utterly desolate. Her half-finished glass of water was still on the table. I drank the rest of it and ran my tongue around the edge where her lips had been.

I went to the bathroom and washed my face. "She's crazy," I said to the mirror. "She's absolutely right. You can't handle this. Let her go."

I had never wanted anyone so much in my life.

I sat on the couch and replayed everything that had happened since we walked in the apartment. Then I replayed the entire day. Then I went back to the first time I saw her at Universal and went through it all again.

Then it was just the highlights, bits and pieces of conversation, moments. Mostly the feel of her, the smell of her, the taste of her.

I used up an hour that way, time enough for her to get home. I called and left a message that said, «Elena, don't leave me hanging like this. Please, just call me and tell me what's going on.»

I tried to read, tried to eat a little. The sun went down. I called again. At 8:30 I walked back to Plaza Dorrego in the pathetic hope that she might show up for Don Güicho's milonga. Or maybe hoping to feel the ghost of her presence still in the square.

I found Don Güicho setting up his ancient, patched-together sound system, into which he had plugged his new iPod. He jiggled a wire, a few seconds of scratchy tango blared through the speakers, then there was silence again.

Brisa watched from the sidelines. «Hola, Beto, did your friend have to go?» She read something in my face and said, «Oh, Beto, did she hurt you? What happened?»

Don Güicho did something and suddenly there was music. A single violin, infinitely sad, mocking me.

«I don't know what happened,» I said. «We danced a few times, I thought we really liked each other. Then...» I opened my empty hands.

Brisa hugged me. «These young girls are so shallow. I should know!» She laughed at herself and said, «Come on, dance with me a little, while the old man finishes with his toys.»

The dance floor was a thin canvas sheet that Don Güicho unrolled for his Sunday performances. The Buenos Aires dancers didn't care that it was not a particularly good surface. I changed into my dance shoes and Brisa led me onto the floor. Though I was touched by her concern, having her in my arms only reminded me of what I was missing. The first song ended immediately and the next was Miguel Caló, "Qué falta que me hacés." I was on the verge of tears. Even with Brisa covering for me, my dancing was an embarrassment. We were the first couple on the floor, I was with Don Güicho's partner and I was practically stumbling. At the end Brisa thanked me and said, «Poor Beto, it'll be okay.»

I retreated to where Don Güicho was pouring hot water into a yerba mate cup made from a carved gourd. He offered me a sip and I declined it, as I did Saverio's coffee.

«So who is this woman?» he asked. «She looked familiar.»

«I met her at El Beso. She goes to a lot of milongas.»

«Her name is Elena, you said?»

«Elena Maria Lacunza.» I was nearly 50 years old. I thought I was long past that kind of hurt.

«Lacunza. That name is familiar. Not from tango, though, from something else.»

I shrugged.

«Beto, you should do as Brisa says. Tango is the remedy for what you're feeling now. The tangos oscuros, the dark tangos, they understand how you feel.»

«I don't think so. I tried dancing just now and I was terrible.»

«Are you the teacher now? Do you think I don't know what the hell I'm talking about? Dance.»

He turned away. I looked past him and recognized one of the women from his Sexto Kultural class, a short, tough girl named Patricia. I caught her eye, gave her the cabeceo, and we met at the edge of the floor.

I gave it my best shot. The crowd was full of older couples, tourists, cliques. I sat out a lot of tandas. But when I thought about going back to my empty apartment, I started searching the crowd for someone who would meet my eyes. My dancing, eventually, got better. My partners were polite, some of them even kind. I felt like I was dancing through quicksand.

I MANAGED TO SLEEP, on and off, until 5:30. I lay in darkness for 15 minutes, then called Elena, hoping to catch her off guard. She didn't answer and I didn't leave another message.

At work I nodded off a few times during the day, split second lapses of consciousness that made my body jerk and left me with muddled dream images superimposed on reality. I left early and stopped by my apartment to change clothes, in the futile hope that she might have come by and left a note. Then I started looking.

My first stop was the Monday practica at the Club Deportivo Villa Malcolm far out on Corrientes. No one there recognized Elena's name or description. I stayed and danced a while, remembering how intimidated I'd been my first time there with Lauren, surrounded by teachers and professional performers, despairing that I could ever learn.

At ten, dizzy with fatigue, I wandered out and found some fruit and bread at a market, then took a cab to Salon Canning, where the milonga started at 11:00. The building is located in an innocuous, tree-lined residential neighborhood. Inside, the main room is like an airplane hangar, the music that night echoing hollowly because of the sparse crowds.

It was a city full of slender, beautiful, dark-haired women and my heart stopped two or three times as the host led me to a table in the men's section. I stayed until two, dancing a few tandas here and there, until exhaustion overwhelmed me and I took a cab back to San Telmo for a few hours of restless sleep.

TUESDAY WAS THE SAME. After an endless, numb day in front of the computer, I called Elena from my apartment, then immediately called again, hoping for a busy signal, any sign of life. I forced myself to eat a little before I took to the streets.

I was obsessed with the idea that if I found her, she would not refuse to dance with me. And that once we danced, everything would be all right. Magical thinking, crazy thinking, but the only thinking I had.

El Beso first, because they started at 9:00. After 11, I walked to Porteño y Bailarin, a block away on the other side of Corrientes, a famous milonga with two tiny dance floors and its own regular clientele. I stayed less than half an hour, long enough to convince myself she wasn't there.

WEDNESDAY AT LUNCH I took Linea B of the Subte to the Abasto Mall. An exit on the north side of the station led down a hallway and into the lower level of stores. It was cleaner than any-place else I'd been in the city, shining and perfume-scented. It was like walking through a secret passageway into the suburban US, a world of bright plastic and chrome and glass. The difference was the customers in Buenos Aires were better dressed and vastly more fit.

I found New Diqui on the directory. I took some deep breaths as I walked counterclockwise past the shops full of leather and elec-tronics and dresses. The place was in a cluster of shoe stores, most of them selling women's shoes, a couple of others with the latest odd-ball designs from Nike and Converse. I brushed my fingers through my hair, straightened my jacket, and went in.

A woman with blonde hair and black roots was helping a custom-er. A woman my age with cat-eye glasses was behind the counter near the register.

I had worked up an elaborate story about being there the week before with my wife, then I heard Elena in my head saying, «I hate liars.»

I said hello to the woman in the glasses and asked how she was and said, «There's a woman who works here, I think her name is Elena. She was very kind to me last week. I wondered if she was working today.»

«Not today, I'm afraid.»

«Is something wrong?»

She sighed. «I may as well tell you. She doesn't work here anymore.»

«Oh.» I felt my shoulders slump.

«She quit on Monday. All very sudden, I must say.»

«I hope there's nothing wrong. She seemed very nice.»

«She *was* nice. Everyone loved her, customers, management, the other salesgirls. She was the best employee I've ever had. And she called and quit over the phone, didn't even do it in person.»

«Well,» I said. «Maybe she'll change her mind.»

«We can hope, can't we?»

I CALLED BAHADUR and told him I needed the rest of the after-noon off.

"You sound terrible," he said. "Is everything okay?"

I told him I wasn't feeling well, which was certainly true, and he told me to get some rest.

I found an Internet place a block from the mall and spent an hour writing an email, then rereading it and rewriting it and reading it again.

> Dear Elena,
> Please understand just one thing: I don't care.
> Whatever your secret is, it won't change how I feel about you. I don't care about your past. I care about what your father did only because it hurts you so much.
> I don't care about the difference in our ages or in our cultures. If you do, okay, I will live with that. If I can't be your lover, I want to be your friend. If I can't be your friend, I at least want to dance with you again.
> Dancing with you is like nothing I have ever felt before. All I want is to feel that way again.
> —Beto

I clicked Send. It was my last idea.

WEDNESDAY WAS a big night for milongas. La Nacional, very traditional, a long, narrow, smoke-darkened room with cracking plaster. La Viruta and Salon Canning again and El Beso and at least half a dozen others I'd never been to.

I went back to my apartment for a few hours' sleep. When I woke up, the light was fading and I had the momentary conviction that my consciousness had inhabited a corpse. My body lay like an inert slab of meat and my brain was dark and empty as a shuttered nightclub. I managed to roll my legs off the bed and sit up, which made my head throb.

I splashed water on my face and freshened my deodorant. I hadn't shaved since Monday morning and I decided it gave me a certain grizzled porteño authenticity.

It was only 7:00. The idea of staying in the flat was unbearable. I put on a dress shirt and a jacket, grabbed my dance shoes, and went down the street to call Sam. He told me I looked like hell, "in a degenerate, Mickey Rourke kind of way." I couldn't talk to him about Elena, though he knew something was wrong and kept pushing for an explanation. After I hung up, I caught the Subte to Federico Lacroze and Don Güicho's class.

The building was run down, the tiny elevator tired and barely willing to climb the six floors. The Sexto Kultural was a long, empty loft with improvised décor, the walls covered with graffiti-style art, the furniture third-hand and losing its stuffing.

The class was already underway. Don Güicho was breaking down a doble tiempo change of direction step. He went through it twice, put on some music, and came over to me. «You look like shit, Beto,» he said as he hugged me. «No luck with your friend yet?»

I shook my head.

«Well, I found out something interesting. I talked to a guy I know who's been following the trials. He works at La Biblioteca Nacional and he's done a lot of research on the dictatorship. He said there was a guy named Osvaldo del Salvador who worked for Cesarino, you know, the guy who ran the detention centers? This guy del Salvador was a torturer at the Club Atlético.»

I'd heard about it. It was on Avenida Paseo Colón, under the elevated highway that led to the airport. The detention center, one of the worst, was in the basement. They said the noise of the cars overhead helped drown out the screams.

«He got off under La Ley de Punto Final, changed his name, got a civilian job.»

I saw it coming, wanted to put my hand over Don Güicho's mouth to keep him from going on. I didn't have the strength to lift my arm.

«My friend said he was living under the name Osvaldo Lacunza. The same as your girlfriend. Maybe it's just coincidence, but...»

«No,» I said. «It's no coincidence.» What had Elena said? I couldn't understand her because I didn't have the history.

«Beto, my friend, welcome to Argentina. You want to know why we have more psychiatrists than anywhere else on earth? This is what I tried to tell you at the demonstration, we deal with this every day. These people are walking among us.»

«Thanks for finding this out. You're a good friend.»

«It wasn't anything. Come and dance, they're waiting on me.»

«In a minute.»

I FELT THE FEAR in my shoulders and neck, in the itching of my scalp and the burning in my right eye.

Elena's father hadn't betrayed her with a mistress or a crooked business deal. He'd betrayed her by not telling her that he was a monster. Conservative, she'd said, deeply religious. What would he think of some godless Yanqui corrupting his daughter?

I danced for a while. I took a turn with Patricia, who found plenty of things to correct me on, as usual. «Are you paying attention?» she asked.

«Trying,» I said.

I left at 10:15 to get to El Beso by 10:30. If Elena had gotten my email, if I'd touched her at all, El Beso would be the place she would go.

Visualization, they say, is the key to getting what you want. I pictured her walking in, seeing me at my front row table, me rising to take her in my arms as she ran to me...

Then I pictured the tall, sharp-faced man, who was probably one of del Salvador's torturers, following us outside and putting a pistol to the back of my neck, firing a single shot through my brain and disappearing into an alley.

SHE WASN'T at El Beso. She wasn't at La Ideal. I went by the office to check my email. Nothing from Elena. I fell asleep in my chair, woke up at 1:00 AM not knowing where I was, and dragged myself off to bed.

LATE THURSDAY MORNING, I called Don Güicho and canceled my class for that night. It was one week from my first dance with Elena. I told myself that if she had a trace of desire for me to find her, that if she were remotely open to leaving things to Fate, she would be at El Beso. I had been telling myself things all day. Not to check my personal email, for example, which I continued to do every five minutes. I told myself to give up. That I was an idiot, that she was crazy, that her father was a murderer, on and on, until I had made myself thoroughly sick of myself.

The milonga started at 6:00 on Thursdays and I was there by seven.

Superstition is the last refuge of the hopeless. I wore my red tie and freshly laundered black shirt. The woman who'd accepted my first-ever cabeceo was there again and we danced a tanda. I told myself that it would all play out the same way as the week before and any minute Elena would walk in.

I danced with two or three other women. Mostly I watched. Time crawled. I wanted it to go even more slowly because suddenly it was after ten, and then it was eleven, and Elena was still not there.

I stayed until 12:30, until they played "La cumparsita" to end it, and I walked down to the street with the last of the diehards and waited in the street for a cab. The weather had turned cold again, the wind coming straight from Patagonia and the South Pole, and it chilled me to the center of my chest.

I was not going to find her.

FRIDAY WAS UNBEARABLE. I couldn't remember my last good night's sleep. The weekend yawned before me, empty and endless.

I didn't bother to go out that night. A steady, cold, determined rain fell on the city, spattering noisily on the floor of the airshaft next to my bed. I sat there in the dark in my work clothes and when the voices in my head started in on me I told them to shut up.

Eventually I fell asleep.

SATURDAY MORNING.

I ate the last food in the apartment and made a grocery list. The rain still fell relentlessly. I put on an extra layer of clothes and a pair of old shoes and went downstairs with my umbrella. I had the key in the inside lock when something caught my eye across the street, in the sheltered overhang of the technical school.

It was the glow of a cigarette. A car hissed past and the headlights caught a tall, thin, dark man turning away.

I was suddenly wide awake.

I backed away from the door and forced my brain to work. If I went up to him he might run away, or turn on me. If he had a gun or a knife, I could be dead in a second and he could be on the Subte and gone.

I was nine-tenths crazy and didn't consider how far over my head I was getting. He was a connection to Elena and that was all I cared about.

If, as I assumed, he was there to follow me, I had someplace to take him.

I unlocked the door and stepped outside, careful not to glance across the street. I opened my umbrella in the doorway and hoped my hands weren't visibly shaking. I checked the lock and headed downhill at a fast walk, between the gray buildings on the gray sidewalk in the gray rain.

Follow me, you bastard, I thought.

At the end of the block I crossed Tacuari, then crossed Humberto Primo, staying in the open and keeping up the pace. I didn't slow down until I got to Avenida San Juan, where I turned the corner and ducked into the entryway of the office building there. I pressed myself flat against the wall, trying to look casual. I collapsed the umbrella and pretended to be busy folding it.

Come on, I thought, come on.

I couldn't know for sure that he was following. Maybe he was under the delusion that Elena was in my apartment and he was going to wait there for her. Maybe he didn't want to risk the bigger crowds and higher visibility of a major street like San Juan. Maybe he knew I'd seen him.

Suddenly he was there, turning the corner.

I grabbed him by the arm and pulled him into the overhang. Tall as he was, he didn't weigh much. I'd startled him and there was a second where he clearly didn't know what to do.

«Do you see the cop?» I asked. «Right over there, in front of the market?» I jerked my head in that direction. The same cop was there every Saturday, rain or shine, in the same place. «If you don't want him to come over here wondering what's going on, you should act like you're glad to see me.»

«Who are you?» the man said. «Where do you come from? What do you want with Elena?»

«You first.»

«I saw her come out of your apartment last week. She was crying. If you did anything to hurt her, I'll kill you.»

«I didn't hurt her,» I said. «I'm in love with her.»

I don't know which of us was more surprised by that.

«Tell me who you are,» I said. «Did her father send you?»

He stared into my face. He had intense, dark eyes, almost black, with a depth like a clear night sky. They were Elena's eyes.

«I *am* her father,» he said.

And then he started to cry.

•

MAYBE IT WAS BECAUSE I had seen Elena in his face. Maybe I saw my own despair and hopelessness in his tears. I hugged him and said, «My name is Beto. We should get out of the rain and talk, no?»

He returned the abrazo, then slowly pulled away. He sniffed loudly and wiped his nose with his left hand as he held out his right. «I'm Mateo. I could use a cafecito. This weather is shit.»

He didn't have an umbrella, just a black fabric raincoat. His hair and shoes were soaked. I shared mine with him as we walked three blocks to the Arte y Café, a corner bistro where I ate dinner three or four nights a week. We sat at a table by the window and ordered coffee and agua con gas.

«She told me her father was a banker,» I said.

«That's her *adopted* father.» The word "adopted" carried a load of sarcasm and rage, barely suppressed.

I said, «He's going by the name Osvaldo Lacunza?» Mateo nodded. «But,» I said, «I don't think that's his real name.»

«Do you have another name for him?»

«I'm told his real name is Osvaldo del Salvador.»

«Your sources are good. Del Salvador legally adopted her after she was born. Do you know who he was?»

«Yes. And I think Elena just recently found out. Does she know she's adopted?»

«I don't know what del Salvador told her.»

«And her mother?»

«Her mother was named Elena, too. Elena Bianchi. She's dead.»

We sat in silence for a few seconds. His Spanish was fast and inelegant and I went back over it to make sure I'd understood all his conjugations. Then I had so many questions I didn't know where to start. Finally I said, «Are you going to talk to her? Are you going to tell her who you are?»

«I don't know. Three weeks ago I didn't know she existed. Do I have the right to walk in now and destroy her life? Maybe she's better off not knowing what I have to say.»

«Her old life is destroyed anyway. I don't know her well—»

«You don't?» he interrupted. «You said you were in love with her.» There was a fierceness now to those eyes, a readiness to attack any weakness they might find.

My face heated up. «—but I know she cares about the truth more than anything. That's why she moved out of her—out of del

Salvador's house, because he deceived her. Do you know that she's disappeared? She quit her job, quit dancing, she's vanished.»

He thought it over before he answered. Finally, very quietly, he said, «I know where she is.»

I had thought I was all ashes inside. There turned out to be a coal or two still alive.

«If she thinks like you,» Mateo said, «that I'm a spy from del Salvador, she'll never talk to me.»

«She does think that,» I said. «You won't get near her. Not unless I'm with you.»

He didn't want to believe me at first. He knew that it was after leaving my apartment in tears that she'd gone underground. I tried not to let him see my desperation, only my hurt.

«When we get there,» I finally said, «you can ask her. Ask her if I ever hurt her, if I ever did anything to her that she didn't want me to.»

«You remember what I told you?»

«That if I hurt her you would kill me?»

«Exactly.»

«I'll take my chances.»

It was not quite noon. I paid for the drinks and we caught a cab. I was still in my old clothes, unshaven, eyes bloodshot. I wasn't willing to risk a stop at my apartment, not when it might give him time to change his mind.

It was a long trip and Mateo gave the directions in stages, first sending the driver toward the Primera Junta train station, far to the west of the microcentro. Then, a few blocks from the station, he gave the driver street names. He said nothing to me, except to mention that Elena had left her apartment Sunday night carrying a suitcase and come to this place, the home of a friend.

«Girlfriend?» I asked. «Or...» My throat closed on the word.

He looked at me with what might have been disappointment. «A girl,» he said at last and turned to look out the window.

Eventually we pulled up in front of an apartment building that would have fit in an upscale neighborhood in the States. I felt insubstantial, like I was in a dream. The trip had been good because I was moving toward hope. Now I was seconds away from the possibility of despair.

Mateo left me to pay the driver, 60 pesos plus tip. The rain came down like it could go on forever. I followed Mateo into a courtyard with potted plants, then up a stairway to a row of apartment doors. He stopped at number 29.

There was no bell. I knocked on the glass outer door. I counted to 20 and knocked again, harder.

«Maybe they're out,» I said. The thought robbed me of the last of my energy.

He reached past me and pounded on the door with the flat of his hand. More seconds passed and I started to turn away.

The inner door opened.

It was a woman who could have been Elena's age, though she looked younger, due to the reddish purple highlights in her short black hair, the tiny purple stud in her left nostril, and the heavy liner around her eyes. She was tall and well-built and she wore a man's striped shirt over hip-hugging plaid pants.

She looked at me and then at Mateo, then at me again. Her voice, when it came, was muffled by the glass. «You must be Beto.» I wanted to believe I heard sympathy there. «And who is this guy?»

«His name is Mateo. He's the guy that's been following her.»

Her eyes widened at that.

«Is she here?»

«Beto, you know she doesn't want to see you.»

In my peripheral vision I saw Mateo give me a menacing look.

«Would you please tell her? Tell her that I'm here, and who this is with me. Tell her she needs to listen to what he has to say.»

She searched my face and then stepped back and closed the door. Which meant Elena was there. The idea of her being so close made me dizzy.

Enough time passed to account for considerable back and forth inside. «I hope you haven't fucked this up,» Mateo said. «Why doesn't she want to see you?»

«She won't tell me.»

Mateo grunted.

I reminded myself to breathe, then a minute later I had to remind myself again.

When the inner door opened, it was the same woman. She un-latched the glass outer door and held it open. I felt giddy.

When we were inside, she offered her hand. «My name is Adriana.» She shook hands with Mateo too. «This is the deal. Both of you go in there and sit on the couch. Don't get up, don't go to her. Okay?»

«Okay,» I said.

«If she says leave, you leave immediately.»

«Okay.»

She looked at Mateo. «You too. You agree?»

«Yes, fine.»

There was an entranceway in off-white linoleum, living room on the right, kitchen straight ahead. The furniture was new, sand colored, with an elegant simplicity that said taste and money. Above the low sofa was a large canvas that showed stylized human bodies and a pattern of bright colors. A window opened on the walkway and the opposite wall had oak bookshelves. Across from the couch, to our left as we walked in, was a TV on an oak chest of drawers. Next to the TV was a chair that matched the sofa. Elena was in the chair.

She was hunched over, holding her knees, her feet tucked under her. She had deep shadows under her eyes. She looked like hell, which is to say, she was heartbreakingly beautiful. She was wearing sweat pants and an oversized T shirt.

And the turquoise necklace I bought her in Plaza Dorrego.

The sight of it made me weak with relief. It was hard not to go to her, but I kept my word and sat on the couch. Mateo sat next to me. He was so tall he had to fold himself two or three different ways to fit.

Elena glanced up, met my eyes briefly, looked at Mateo, and then at the floor again.

«Before we start,» Mateo said, «I have one question. Did this guy Beto hurt you in any way?»

Elena had the grace to stare at him as though he was crazy. She looked at me again for an instant, as if she couldn't help herself, and there was tenderness there. «No,» she said. «Beto is a caballero. A good, sweet man.» Then she shook her head as if to say, *And that is the problem.*

«Bueno. First, I need to know how much you already know. You know the real name of the man who raised you, no?»

«The man who raised me? You mean my father?»

Mateo looked at me. «Well, that answers that question.»

«Do you work for him?» Elena asked.

Mateo laughed. «I'm his worst enemy. His worst nightmare.»

That was the moment when, at last, I became truly afraid. What
had I let into Elena's refuge? I had no proof of anything he'd said.
And twice he'd promised to kill me.

Elena said, «The answer to your question is, I was eight years old
when we changed our name. We never said the name del Salvador
in the house again.» She rubbed her nose. «Except once. So I always
knew his real name was Osvaldo del Salvador. What I didn't know,
until six months ago, was who he was, what he'd done.

«It was because of the repeal, all the talk about the trials. I heard
him on the phone, talking to Cesarino. And I put it together.»

«Why couldn't you tell me that?» I said. «Do you think I would
have held that against you?»

She shook her head and looked at Mateo. «Why did you say, 'the
man who raised me'?»

«Because he's not your father.»

Elena closed her eyes. I could not imagine the force of the emotions going through her, though I saw flickers of them come and go.
Gratitude, maybe? Confusion, betrayal, certainly. What I didn't see
was any resistance or doubt.

«Tell me,» she said.

«Beto says you want the truth, even if it hurts.»

«Yes.»

«This is worse than you can imagine. I want you to know that
before I start.»

«You don't know my imagination.»

«Bueno. This is going to take a while. I suggest we make ourselves
comfortable. I would like to get these wet shoes off. Maybe you
could find me a cafecito.»

UN MONTÓN MEANS "a heap" or "a lot," and the story is that the
first montoneros were indigenous tribes, attacking Spanish outposts
in overwhelming numbers. The name passed on to the rural guerillas in the civil wars that took up much of the nineteenth century
in Argentina. But the montoneros that everyone remembers are the
ones from the 1970s.

They started as the left wing of the Peronist party, the party of
Juan Perón, who'd been forced into exile in 1955 by the military. So
overwhelming was the love of the poor for Perón that government
after Argentine government declared his party illegal, not just the

military dictatorships, but also the hapless civilian governments in between, all of them struggling in vain to hold the country together. In 1973, when the party was allowed on the ballot again, the new Peronist president quickly resigned in favor of Perón himself. More than three million people showed up at Buenos Aires's Ezeiza airport on June 20, in the depths of winter, to welcome him home.

One of them was Mateo, 22 years old and fresh out of college, his head full of Karl Marx and sudden new hope for his country. He came early and saw friends from college there, friends who were members of the montoneros. He was standing with them when Perón's plane landed. They had a huge banner with the word MON-TONEROS on it, and they unrolled it and moved toward the stage. There was a struggle going on for the soul of the party, someone had just explained to Mateo. The right wing, who wanted to open the country to foreign investment, was determined to get Perón on its side at any cost. The montoneros and the Perón youth meant to show him how strong they were, that the future of Argentina lay with them.

Mateo stood aside and let them push forward, because it was not really his cause, not his struggle.

Then the shooting began.

Mateo could make no sense of it at the time. Afterward he learned that snipers hidden on the platform and in buildings on both sides had opened up on the montoneros and the Perón Youth. At least 13 people were murdered outright, at least 300 more wounded, though the actual numbers were probably higher.

Mateo only knew the terror of lying on the ground, the bullets hissing and whining above him like willful, poisonous creatures hungry for death. He felt them pass in the crawling of the skin along his back, heard the ugly wet thud as they buried themselves in human flesh, smelled the butcher-shop stench of blood in the cold air, not knowing if the blood was his own.

Eventually the shooting stopped and the chaos became total: the screaming of the wounded, the weeping of the survivors, the shouts of outrage, the police sirens, the panicked noise of the impenetrable crowd.

At the first sound of gunfire, Perón had ordered the hatch closed on his airplane and refused to come down. Later, he blamed the leftists for the massacre. In fact, it had been carefully planned and

executed by the leaders of the right wing, including Perón's
own personal secretary, José López Rega. The snipers came from
the inner circle of López Rega's secret police, the Argentine
Anticommunist Alliance, the infamous Triple A, and these were the
first shots in their war of extermination against the montoneros.

For Mateo, it was the moment that changed him from bystander
to soldier.

The montoneros were not pacifists. They had already kidnapped,
tried, and executed former Argentine president Aramburu and killed
a handful of others. After Ezeiza, they gave up all pretense of limits.

The violence repelled Mateo at first. Then, after he saw the extremes of the Triple A, he convinced himself it was necessary.

At the same time, he was unable to give up his other true love,
which was tango. He would steal away from training exercises to go
to milongas. That was where he met Elena Bianchi.

His first impression was that she was too beautiful to be trusted,
that she was superficial, bourgeois. Her passion for tango was undeniable, however, and when he finally talked to her, he found her in-
telligent, compassionate, and well read. She supported the montoneros in principle, she told him, although she opposed the extremes of
their violence. This before she knew that he was a member.

He fell hard for her and she was seduced by the danger that he
lived in. She never relented in her opposition to violence and refused to actively participate in any of his missions. Neither did she
reproach him for his beliefs or ask him to change.

Perón died in 1974 and his widow took over. López Rega now
had a completely free hand. They called him El Brujo, the Sorcerer,
because of his occult obsessions. His hatred of communism made
him popular with the United States, and US companies began to
set up in Argentina and drive out local businesses, something Perón
had bitterly opposed in his early years. The Triple A moved into
the open and began killing suspected montoneros on the streets, or
kidnapping and torturing them. All the techniques that the Videla
dictatorship would later make universal were perfected under
López Rega.

Mateo was forced underground. He visited Elena at most once a
month. The last two days they had together were in November of
1974 and they spent them dancing to the record player in her flat,
making love, making plans to get out of Argentina.

In January of 1975, in the damp heat of summer, the Triple A caught him on his way to Elena's flat. A traitor in Mateo's cadre had informed on him. The task group waited for him in the lobby of Elena's building, four of them, wearing bits and pieces of police uniforms, carrying M16s the United States had provided for them. They hooded him and beat him and took him out to the street. As this was before the era of the Ford Falcon, they only had a borrowed police car. They threw him in back and drove off with the siren blaring.

Elena saw them carry him out and called Mateo's emergency contact in the montoneros. Mateo's contact had two men and some guns and they were not far away. They made their best guess as to the nearest detention center and intercepted the police car. There was a gun battle in the streets. Two Triple A men were killed and the other two wounded. Mateo's contact and another montonero were killed. Mateo's right knee was shattered by a bullet and he was also hit in the thigh and the left forearm. The bullets from an M16 are 5.56 mm, about the size of a .22, with such enormous muzzle velocity that all three bullets went completely through Mateo's body.

The remaining montonero got him away from the scene and drove him to one of the doctors who was sympathetic to the cause. The wounds in the thigh and forearm were not terribly serious, but there was little the doctor could do about Mateo's knee. The organization smuggled him out of the country, to Mexico and then to Cuba and back to Mexico again. It was there, a year later, that he heard Elena was dead.

The men who killed 30,000 were pardoned, while Mateo was still wanted for murder because of the two dead kidnappers. He drifted around Central America for 25 years, teaching school in Guatemala, working in the oil fields in Venezuela. Never married, never stayed in one place more than two or three years.

It had been three years since he came back to Buenos Aires. Very slowly he had reached out to some old friends. Some didn't want to know him. A few did what they could for him, a little money, a little food, a rental apartment in a rough part of town.

One of them was a tango teacher from the old days. Though Mateo could no longer dance because of his knee, there was unexpected pleasure in talking about the music and the old times.

Three weeks ago the teacher had called and said to meet him at

Salon Canning. Mateo was walking to his old friend's table when he saw her for himself. Elena, not in her fifties as she would have been if she'd lived, but Elena as she was the last time he'd seen her. Her nose was different, something about the eyes, but her mouth, her hair, her body, the way she carried herself, the way her head went back when she laughed—it was her.

Mateo did the math. If his Elena had gotten pregnant the last time they'd been together, the child would be the same age as this woman.

All he knew was that his Elena had been taken by the Triple A, that she had died in the Club Atlético detention center. Someone who'd survived six months there had seen her, and later heard she was dead. The news passed to the few montoneros left after the coup in March of 1976 and they had gotten word to Mateo in Mexico.

After seeing the young Elena, Mateo had contacted Las Madres de la Plaza, and their organization had searched their files. They didn't have a lot of information, but it was enough.

ELENA INTERRUPTED HIM. «Ay, Dios mío,» she said. «Oh my God. Oh my God.»

Mateo scowled at her. His eyes were red and he looked to be on the verge of breaking down. «At the Club Atlético she told them she was pregnant. They tortured her and raped her and beat her anyway, but somehow she didn't lose the baby. They took the baby away after it was born and then they disposed of Elena. Probably the usual way—they probably dropped her, still alive, out of a helicopter over the Atlantic Ocean. After slitting her belly open so she wouldn't float back up.

«The man who tortured her and murdered her—»

«Please,» Elena said, «no...»

«The man who killed her took the baby home to raise as his own. He named her Elena, I guess in tribute to her mother.»

WHEN MATEO FINISHED, it was utterly quiet in the room. Elena cried in silence, her face in her hands, tears dripping onto the knees of her pants and leaving dark blotches.

Mateo sniffed and wiped his nose with his left hand, as he had earlier. He leaned back into the couch. His eyes focused on something far away.

Adriana had slowly settled onto the floor while Mateo talked. She seemed to be in shock. She slowly recovered herself and knelt next to Elena, pulling her into a hug. Elena sobbed onto her shoulder. I wanted it to be me that held her. The chances of that ever happening did not look good.

Elena whispered to Adriana, who looked at Mateo. «That's everything, yes? No other revelations?»

«That's all,» Mateo said.

Adriana nodded. «Elena says to thank both of you very much and asks if you would go now.»

Mateo took a piece of paper out of his pocket and put it next to his empty coffee cup. «That's my phone number. She can call me if she wants. I...I would like...» He couldn't finish. He put on his wet shoes and stood up.

It seemed impossible that I would simply walk away from her. Adriana escorted us outside and handed me my umbrella. She locked the glass door behind us and then shut the inner door. We were out on the balcony again, in the rain, which had not stopped.

We had to walk four blocks to find a street big enough that there were taxis. I memorized the apartment number, the street, every landmark I could find, even as I knew in my heart that I would never get to use them.

In the cab I said, «Is Mateo your real name?»

«More or less.»

«What does that mean, 'more or less'?»

«We all had code names, noms de guerre. Mateo is the name I've always used.»

I was comfortable with his speech patterns now, getting at least the gist of everything he said. «And the name you were born with?» I asked.

«You don't want to know. It puts me in danger and you in danger.»

A few minutes later I said, «What happens now?»

«Tonight, tomorrow? I can't tell you. Sometime in the next few days or weeks or months, I will bring Osvaldo del Salvador down. I will have my revenge, and I will make sure he knows who I am and what he did to me. And after that? It doesn't matter. Nothing matters after that.»

He asked the cab driver if he could smoke and the driver shrugged and said, «Open the window if you do.»

He rolled the window down and lit a cigarette. It smelled like a fire at a garbage dump. A drop of rain appeared on his glasses.

He glanced at me and said, «You can help, if you want.»

«Me?» I stopped myself before I asked if he was crazy. «I don't think so.»

We rode in silence while he finished his cigarette, then I said, «Do you want me to drop you somewhere?»

He shook his head. «I'll take the Subte. I've got time. I've got nothing but time.»

«If she calls you...»

He looked at me. His eyes were black, empty, desolate. «Yes?»

«Will you let me know?»

He found another piece of paper in his pocket, a Xeroxed flyer for tango classes that he'd picked up at one of the milongas, and we traded phone numbers.

I had the cab drop us at the San Juan Subte stop. Halfway down the stairs, Mateo turned and raised one hand to me. I waved and he disappeared into the station.

I WALKED DOWN to the supermercado on Calle Bolívar to finish the shopping I'd set out to do hours before. When I got back, it was four in the afternoon. I got out of my wet clothes and showered and shaved in the futile hope that it would inspire me.

I sat on the bed and listened to the rain echo in the airshaft. My thoughts were drastic. What if I turned all my money into cash and got on an airplane? Maybe to someplace tropical, like Puerto Rico?

I stretched my pecs and forearm muscles, did some yoga to control my breathing. The pain in my head was no worse than a three. Restless and bored, I went to the locutorio down the street and checked my email, then read about the montoneros online. I didn't see Mateo's name, but everything that I read supported his story.

In 1976, Videla and the other generals specifically cited the mon- toneros as one of the major reasons they seized power. It was true that the montoneros had gotten out of hand in the days of López Rega, with one bloody assassination after another, making it seem for a time that the government could no longer guarantee the safety of its citizens. More importantly, they couldn't prevent the kidnap and ransom of foreign businessmen, which was the way the montoneros raised money. Big business—US business—demanded that their government partners eliminate the problem, or step down in favor of someone who could.

The loss of control was merely temporary. In fact, the Triple A was incredibly effective and by the time of the coup the montoneros were all but wiped out. By kidnapping and torturing anyone suspected of leftist sympathies, Videla's death squads ensured that there would be no new recruits.

After a while I had to stop reading. When I first learned about El Proceso, I couldn't believe the lack of attention it got in the history books. The number of the dead was considerably lower than in the European Holocaust, but the level of brutality was comparable. The main difference was that the US was complicit in El Proceso, from the money we put in the government treasury to the CIA advisors we sent to teach torture techniques.

The torture was the worst. How could one human being do that to another? How was it possible to listen to someone scream, and keep on inflicting pain? To know that humans were capable of it, to stare at the undeniable evidence of it, was more than most people could stand. So they looked away and I did too.

On impulse I took the Subte to el Obelisco, changed to Linea B, and rode to the Callao station. From there I walked back east on Corrientes through the district of book and record stores. It didn't take me long to find a copy in Spanish of Jorge Amado's *Tienda de los Milagros,* Elena's favorite book. I started it a few minutes later over empanadas at a tiny three-table restaurant.

I couldn't face the thought of a milonga and I didn't want to go back to my empty apartment. Nobody showed any interest in my table, so I lingered for an hour, reading, then moved to another café for agua con gas, and so on down the avenida, staving off my loneliness with the noise of the crowds until after 9, when the dinner rush filled every restaurant in the district.

Back in San Telmo, I undressed and read in bed until midnight, long past the point where I'd lost the sense of the words and my eyes were closing on their own.

•

I WOKE TO a buzzing noise. I was disoriented and it took me long seconds to realize that someone was ringing for me downstairs. I stumbled to the intercom and said, «¿Quíen es?»

«Beto...»

It was Elena.

«Hold on,» I said.

In a frenzy I put on a pair of pajama bottoms and a clean T-shirt, started out the door, ran back for my keys, and sprinted down the stairs.

I could see her in the rain, a taxi waiting at the curb behind her. My throat had closed tight and my heart was hammering so loudly I was afraid of a stroke. I got the double lock open and still she hesitated.

«Beto, is it okay—»

«Of course, get inside, get out of the rain.»

She waved to the taxi driver and he drove away, squealing his tires on the wet pavement. I reached for her and she held out her hand to stop me. «Beto, we have to talk.»

«Sí, claro, but come inside.»

I let her past me and locked the doors again. She looked like a wet kitten, her eyes sunken deeper than ever. We climbed the stairs side by side and I motioned her into my apartment.

«Beto, you have to stop leaving your apartment door open.»

I was in no shape for a clever comeback. I took her blue vinyl raincoat and hung it on the tiny balcony outside the kitchen. «Let me get you a towel.» I brought her a clean bath towel to dry her hair and sat her at the dining room table so she could take off her wet shoes as well. I got her a pair of dry socks, knowing I was fussing over her too much and not caring.

«Do you want some coffee or juice or something?» The coffee was a bluff, being that I was the only person in Argentina who didn't drink it.

She shook her head. «Talk first. I haven't been able to sleep. I have to tell you the rest of it, to get this over with.»

I didn't like the sound of the words "over with." I gestured at the couch and said, «Do you want to—»

She shook her head again. «Can we just sit here?»

I sat down across from her. She was in the same sweat pants and T-shirt she'd had on that morning. The necklace was still around her neck.

«I'm just going to talk, okay? Is that all right? I'm not going to ask how you are because I can look at you and see that you're not sleeping either, and when I'm done you will be able to say to yourself, okay, she was right, I don't want anything to do with her, and then you'll be able to sleep again.»

«Elena...»

«Shhhh. It's...it's all under pressure, you know?» She pantomimed shaking a bottle with her thumb over the neck. «It's got to come out, just get out of the way and let it happen.»

SHE'D BEEN WATCHING TV in the den on a Sunday night. She was on her way to her bedroom when the phone rang in her father's study. She'd never heard it ring before, never realized it was on a separate line. She was ten feet from the door when her father picked it up. There was a silence and then he said the name Cesarino. There was something about the way he said it, a kind of terrible resignation, as if it were some long-lost girlfriend that he didn't want to remember, only worse, vastly worse.

She glimpsed his back as he closed the study door. He hadn't seen her. The tone of his voice made her do something she had never done in her life, which was put her ear to the door and listen in.

She was in time to hear her father say, «Suarez? You're sure?» The name meant nothing to Elena at the time. After a long silence, he said, «Information? What kind of information?»

Another pause, then he said, «Yes, the 'transactions.' I know.» Then, «Files? You mean computer files?» and a second later, «What do you want me to do?»

Cesarino talked for a long time. Her father said, «What do you mean, 'example'?» and then, «Like the old days, you mean.»

It was like her father had become a completely different person, a cold, scary person. That was when she knew, without knowing how she knew, what was going on.

Her father said, «Dios mío. I'm too old for this.»

Cesarino must have threatened him then, because her father said, «No. No, I understand. I can't talk here. I'll call you later.» The last sentence came out with a bitterness she had heard before, but never in a context like this.

She heard her father hang up and she ran to her room. She was a child of privilege, with a laptop and a fast Internet connection, and she stayed up late that night. The information was sparse and it took her a couple of hours to fit the pieces together. Once she linked the name Cesarino with the name del Salvador, she knew it was the thing that she'd feared, that her father had been a soldier in the Dirty War.

There were no pictures online of del Salvador. She lay awake until dawn, failing to convince herself that it was another del Salvador and not her father. After that she imagined going to him with what she'd found. The thought terrified her. She wanted to get away, as far and as fast as possible.

He'd turned into a stranger. If he even suspected she'd overheard Cesarino's phone call, she didn't know what he'd do. So she waited and pretended nothing had changed, and kissed his cheek as she always did for three long weeks. In the end she didn't have the courage to confront him. She went to her mother instead and said that she needed to move out, letting her believe it was because she'd met someone.

Once she was out of the house she broke all contact with her parents, quitting her job at Citibank and changing her cell phone. And that had been the end of it, until Suarez disappeared and she happened to see the story in the paper.

She knew her father was guilty of murder and that he would get away with it unless she did something. The paper said that Suarez worked for Universal Systems, and she figured that was where she would find the computer files her father had been talking about. She didn't know much about computers, but people at Universal did and she was sure someone there would take pity on her.

That was what she was trying to do, with no luck, when she saw a man on the other side of a glass wall smile at her and ask if he could help.

I FELT COLD. I couldn't speak. I stood up and walked into the bedroom and got a flannel shirt and put it on and then I went back to the table.

Elena was crying. She didn't seem to be aware of it. I pushed a packet of tissues toward her and she didn't notice them either.

«Then I saw you at El Beso,» she said, «and I decided to seduce you. Not seduce you, not really, just to see if I could get you to like me, maybe even love me a little, enough that you would help me.»

I sat back in my chair and folded my arms. My own eyes stung and the inside of my stomach was colder than ever. I had to make a conscious effort to make my shoulders drop. «You did a good job,» I said. «You succeeded beyond what you could have dreamed.»

«I deserve your hatred. I did what all those other people did that I hate. Using other people. Deception. No lies, at least. I never lied to you.»

«So what happened? You lost the courage to go through with it?»

She was quiet for a long time, the tears continuing to run down her face. Then she said, «Do you remember the first time we danced? Do you remember how that felt?»

«How do you know how it felt to me?»

«How do you think?»

«What, are you saying...» I shook my head. «You were using me.»

«It started that way. Though I have to say, it was very, very easy. I didn't have to pretend. All I had to do was let myself be impulsive, let myself say the things that came into my head and not worry about whether I was leading you on. I wish...I wish I'd never seen you at Universal. That we could have just danced together and felt what we felt and it could have happened on its own.

«Last Sunday, Beto, when we went to Plaza Dorrego and you bought me this beautiful necklace, and I saw the way your friends looked at you, the way Don Güicho looked at you, and the way you listened to me, and then we danced en los adoquines, and then you kissed me and I didn't ever want you to stop, and then I remembered what I had done and I felt so ashamed. And this business that I'm involved in, you heard it today from Mateo, it's not a joke. It's dangerous. And I couldn't bear the thought of you being hurt, or the thought of what I had done and how I had ruined everything, and so I ran.»

She folded her own arms across her chest, as if it were the only way to keep them from reaching out, and we sat there, two closed off people, and she said, «I'm not saying this because I think there's a chance that you would forgive me, I don't say this for my sake at all. Please believe me, I say this because I don't want you to think that there is any way in which this is your fault, or that you are anything but what I said earlier today, a good, sweet, wonderful man.»

She was crying hard now, her nose running, sobbing to get her breath. She reached down to take off the socks I'd given her and was

fumbling for her shoes. «I should go. I'm sorry, that's all I can say,
I'm sorry, I'm so sorry—»

By then I had come around the table and pulled her to her feet
and taken her in my arms. She clung to me and I held her while she
shook and cried herself out. Eventually her arms relaxed and she put
her head on my chest, as if we were about to dance a tango.

«Beto. I haven't slept for days. But I could go to sleep right now if
you held me. Beto, I can't make love to you, I'm all inside out. Can I
stay here and just go to sleep in your arms? Just for tonight?»

SHE DRANK SOME WATER and I gave her a brand new tooth-
brush to use, and we each took a turn in the bathroom like an old
married couple. Then I turned off all the lights and brought her
into the bedroom and we lay down together on our sides, her facing
away from me, my left arm under her neck, my right arm between
her breasts, her holding it there where I could feel her heartbeat, her
entire body pressed against the length of me. I could smell the spice
and citrus of her skin and hair and I was as hard as a rolling pin.
She didn't seem put off by it. She sighed and said, «Beto,» and she
was asleep.

I thought I would lie awake for just another hour or so and drink
in the smell and touch of her. Instead I fell asleep too.

I woke up a couple of hours later with her pushing and prodding
me. «Turn over,» she said sleepily, and I extricated my numb left arm
and rolled over. She curled herself against my back and I was asleep
again immediately.

THE NEXT TIME I woke up it was light out and I was alone in
the bed. The rain had stopped. The clock said 8:33. I sat up sharply.
«Elena?»

I heard the toilet flush and I relaxed. A minute later I saw her sil-
houette in the doorway. I lay on my back, that hollow, early-morn-
ing not-enough-sleep feeling giving way to warmth at the sight of
her. She curled inside my left arm, her own left arm across my chest.
We lay that way for a while and then, in the half light, I saw the
whites of her eyes as she looked up. I smiled and her hand came up
to touch my face.

Then, so slowly that she hardly seemed to move at all, she slid on
top of me. I watched her face come toward me, her eyes locked on

mine, her lips apart in a knowing smile. She paused with her mouth
an inch from mine, and I smelled toothpaste and felt the warmth
of her breath on my lips. We were on the threshold. I could feel her
relish the moment. Then we couldn't wait any longer and we fell
into a kiss like falling into deep water, down and down, endlessly.

She tugged at my T-shirt, pulling it over my head, and then we
were undressing each other. Elena was laughing, I was in awe, and
then we were naked.

«I have...condoms, in the drawer...»

«Do we need to?» Elena said. The laughter was still on her face.

«No, I'm healthy...»

«Me too. And I'm on the pill, so you don't have to worry about
that.» Another of her instant mood changes, and she held my face
with both hands, her eyes focused first on my right eye, then my
left, searching. «With me it is all or nothing, my Betito. You can back
out if you want.»

«Nunca,» I said. «Never.»

We dozed afterward until hunger got us out of bed. I made
goat cheese omelets, three eggs each, and sliced an avocado. Elena
wore my flannel shirt and drawstring sweatpants with the legs rolled
up. As we ate I would catch her smiling down at her eggs, or her leg
would find mine under the table, or our hands would entangle in
the open space between our plates.

As I washed the dishes she wrapped her arms around me from
behind. «Beto,» she whispered, and kissed my ear. «Betito...» I turned
and picked her up and carried her into the bedroom.

She was the most passionate lover I had ever known. My chest
and back and neck were covered with tiny marks where she had
nipped or scratched or sucked on the skin. She was playful and
unselfconscious and knew her own body, as eager to show me how
to please her as she was to know what I liked, where and how I
wanted to be touched.

It was only later, my mind floating free from my body, relaxed
and totally satisfied, that one dark thought crept in. It was small
and easily dismissed, asking softly what it would be like if she had
not stopped using me after all, asking if I would be able to tell the
difference.

•

WHEN WE WOKE again, we talked, some parts of our bodies always in contact. I told her about growing up on Greyhound buses criss-crossing the country, my nose always in a book. Getting a degree in English at NC State in Raleigh, drifting into programming when I couldn't find any other work. She told me about Catholic girls' school and her parents' dream that she would become a nun. «I guess that didn't turn out too well,» she said.

The gulf between our ages and cultures was easy to forget when we were dancing or making love. It seemed strange to her that I didn't eat meat. I had a grown son and she had a vague desire to have kids someday. I was not religious, and she was torn between hatred of the Catholic Church and the pull of her upbringing. I didn't care about sports, and she loved the Boca Juniors. «I'll take you to a game,» she said. «You'll change your mind.»

«Maybe I will.» Anything seemed possible.

There were books she wanted me to read, films she wanted to see with me. I mentioned a couple of my favorite writers and said that I didn't know if they were available in Spanish.

"Is a chance," she said, in heavily accented English, "for me to get better my English, no?"

I was startled and embarrassed by the way her broken English made her sound. All her grace and sophistication seemed to evaporate.

She misread my reaction. "I surprise you, no? We all study a little English in school."

«It's just funny,» I said, «how strange English sounds to me now.»

She switched back to Spanish. «Maybe it's *my* English. Your Spanish is much better.»

I wondered how much better it was, wondered how my imperfect language skills made me seem to her. I saw then the terrible power we had to hurt each other, how careful we both would have to be. «Not at all,» I said. «I just think Spanish is more beautiful. I always have. It has more poetry and passion. Like you.»

She answered the compliment with a kiss, and I saw we had steered ourselves away from the edge of something. I took the op-portunity to change the subject. «We should go to Don Güicho's milonga tonight.»

«Oh, Beto, can we? But I don't have any clothes, no shoes...»

«Let's get a cab and go to Adriana's apartment. You can pack all your things and bring them over here.»

The idea was plainly crazy. She hesitated, as she should have.

«You said all or nothing, Elena. You're safe here. It's small, it'll be crowded. If it doesn't work out, you can leave any time. But I want you here with me.»

«Oh, Beto...» Tears came up in her eyes.

I held her and then we were kissing again and then we were making love again, tears and laughter and physical pleasure so intense it crossed into pain, smells of sex and citrus and vanilla, my heart full and overflowing, reckless, ecstatic, and, somewhere deep at the bottom of it, afraid

WE SPENT THE AFTERNOON getting her moved out of Adriana's place, and we went by her other apartment for a few more things. The risk of what we were doing hovered over us, full of potential awkwardness, and we kept it at bay through talk and physical contact, as if letting go would allow one or the other of us to fall back into common sense.

Her own apartment was cluttered, full of half-read books among discarded clothes. She apologized repeatedly for the dirty dishes in the sink. While she packed a bag, I looked at her furniture, beautiful oak pieces in bad repair. My hands itched to work on them. I promised her that as soon as I could get some tools and space to work, I would fix them.

There was enough daylight left for a walk in Parque Lezama, and there I let go of the last of my doubts. It was enough to be with her in the spring air, to listen to the birds and feel the sun on my face, to be completely in the moment, the pain in my head nearly gone, a milonga to look forward to, and then Elena in my bed.

DON GÜICHO LAUGHED when he saw us together. «Bravo, Beto, I must have taught you something after all.»

Brisa slapped his arm. «You should be ashamed. Beto, after you have a tanda with your friend, come dance with me.»

I danced two tandas with Elena because I didn't want to let go. Then I danced with Brisa and between tangos she said, «I see the way she looks at you, Beto. I think she is in love.»

«So am I.»

«I'm so happy for you. And a little jealous.»

«Brisa, I didn't know you cared.»

Now it was my arm that got slapped. «I wouldn't want you, boludo, you're much too old. I'm jealous of being in love.»

After the tanda, Elena ran up to me and threw her arms around me and spun me around. «I danced with Don Güicho! Oh, Beto, what a dancer!»

«Ah, well,» I said, «at least we had our one day together before he stole you from me.»

«I made so many mistakes, he'll never dance with me again. Besides—» She put her lips close to my ear. «—I think I'm too old for him.» Then she bit me on the earlobe and laughed. «Dance with me, Betito, I'm so happy. I haven't been happy in such a long, long time.»

IT WAS ALMOST more than I could do to get up in the morning and go to work. Elena walked me downstairs. We'd agreed that she would take the keys and get copies made while I was gone. I didn't want to let go of her. «Don't worry, Betito,» she laughed. «I'll be here when you get home.» I wanted to tell her that this was Buenos Aires and nothing was certain. Instead I kissed her one last time and stepped out onto the sidewalk.

I called my landlady from the office and told her there would be two people staying in the flat for now.

«Your wife has come back?»

The question made me see myself with double vision, one of me completely finished with Lauren, the other feeling exposed and guilty. «A friend,» I said. «A very close friend.»

«Ah,» she said. «Congratulations, Beto. I hope to get to meet her.»

When I got home, Elena had made dinner—vegetarian, easy on the dairy, with wine for her and agua con gas for me. There were candles on the table and Hugo Diaz played softly on the stereo. I was speechless.

«Beto, has no one ever taken care of you before?»

«No,» I said. «I never let them.»

«Well, you take care of me, so I will take care of you. You will have to get used to it.»

Over dinner I tried to explain. My parents had divorced when I was 5, and at first I stayed in Virginia with my father while my mother went to live with her sister in Phoenix. Then, after a year, my father met somebody and packed me off to Arizona. They traded me back and forth for holidays, summer vacations, every time they started a new relationship. I learned to stay out of their way, hoping that if they didn't notice me they wouldn't send me away again.

«They both had the same sayings, clichés in English. 'If you want something done right, do it yourself,' that was their favorite. That and 'Children should be seen and not heard.'»

She nodded and took my hands in both of hers. «Here we say, 'Flies don't enter a closed mouth,' and 'God helps those who get up early.' I got so sick of hearing it. Growing up like that can make you hard, but I think it was the opposite for you and me.»

She took one hand away to wipe at a tear. «It's like I don't have any skin anymore,» she said. «I'm so sensitive, it's crazy.»

«It's not crazy,» I said.

«Are they still alive, your parents?»

«My father died of cancer. I guess it was eight years ago, now. My mother died in February. She had...a disease of the lungs.» I didn't know to say Chronic Obstructive Pulmonary Disorder in Spanish. «I found out from my cousin that my mother was dying, and I called her and told her I was coming. I got on a plane the next morning and she was dead before I landed. She couldn't even wait long enough to say goodbye.»

«She was dying, Beto, I'm sure she couldn't help it.»

«People do it all the time,» I said. «They hold on. If they want to bad enough.»

She gave me a few seconds and then said, «You can cry for her if you want to.»

«I want to,» I said, «but I can't.»

I ate some more food. Even with Elena, it left me sour and tired to talk about the past.

She seemed to sense it. «And speaking of being responsible for yourself,» she said, «I need to find another job.»

«They'll take you back at the shoe store. Your boss thinks you're wonderful. Just like everyone else does.»

«Do you really think so?» Then it hit her. «So you went there? Looking for me?»

«Yes. I was desperate.»

«Beto, I'm sorry I hid from you.»

«It doesn't matter,» I said. «Nothing matters now.»

•

ON TUESDAY ELENA went to Abasto and got her job back on the spot. She wanted to celebrate by practicing tango at the apartment. «Then we can go out tomorrow and be perfect.»

I brought empanadas home and after dinner we pushed the furniture against the living room walls. I showed her a few of Don Güicho's moves, then we just danced, stopping when things didn't go like they were supposed to. She was reluctant to correct me at first, until I convinced her that I was serious. She was gentle and sweet and surprised me with her technical knowledge.

Wednesday after work I called Sam. I failed to keep my excitement from showing and finally admitted, "I've met somebody."

"If she's the reason you looked so bad last week, I have to disapprove." Though he'd never said it, I knew he hadn't let go of the hope that Lauren and I might work things out.

"How do I look now?"

"D, you're my parental unit. It is totally repellent to even think about the probable reason you look the way you do. So are you going to tell me about her or not?"

I gave him the high points, trying not to sound like a lovesick teenager.

"D, she's closer to my age than yours."

"You guys wouldn't work out, you don't tango."

"Gross. How serious is this?"

"It feels pretty serious."

He slapped himself repeatedly. "My stepmother! My stepsister! My stepmother! My stepsister!"

"I could bring her along next time I call."

"Let's wait a little. Maybe you'll come to your senses."

Much as I wanted him to talk about what he was really feeling, serious was not Sam's style. He deflected me with a sideways reference to Lolita, and I let him go.

That night I took Elena to La Nacional. Tango etiquette made it awkward at first. Because we'd come in together, no one was supposed to dance with Elena until I danced with someone else, and for half an hour no one made eye contact with me. Then my German friend from La Ideal arrived and set Elena free.

Nothing should have shaken my confidence at that point. Still I felt twinges of jealousy when I saw her with men who were younger than me, better looking than me, better dancers than me. I was smart enough not to let it show. At one point she had just finished a tanda with one man when another one came up to her at the edge of the floor and said something that made her laugh, then took her off for the next dance. I recognized him as Miguel Autrillo, the former student of Don Güicho's that I'd met at El Caburé. I had to admit that he was an amazing dancer, as dramatic as a silent movie star, with an arsenal of advanced moves that he deployed in perfect time with the music, all while making her look as poised and graceful as a ballerina. I sat out the tanda to watch them.

When she came back to the table she said, «You know what a piropo is, no?»

I nodded. It was the kind of overblown compliment I had used on her myself.

«That guy said, 'You have to dance with me, or your boyfriend has to kill me.' Then he says, 'Either way I'll be in heaven.'» She laughed again at the memory of it. She was utterly at home in this world, and I thought how happy she would have been in the thirties and forties when tango truly ruled the city, when 12-piece orquestas typicas played cavernous dance halls every night. As much as I loved tango, I would never belong here the way she did and the thought gave me a pang.

«What I didn't say to him was that I hope there are dance teachers in heaven, to teach him not to try so hard.» She laughed harder and took my hand. «Come, Beto, dance with me.»

Thursday I brought her to my lesson with Don Güicho. He was harder on me than he'd ever been, maybe feeling he needed to bring me down from my cloud. He was hard on Elena too. The difference was that Elena thrived under the pressure and got visibly better, more precise and balanced, by the minute, as I lagged behind. She was floating as we left class, asking if we could go home and practice instead of going to El Beso. She didn't care that I was struggling to keep up, I told myself, so why should I?

Friday she had to work late. When she got in I gave her a massage and we ended up not getting out of bed.

Saturday she did a day shift while I caught up on my sleep, and she called me at lunch. «Would you mind if I went out after work and had dinner with Adriana and a couple other girlfriends? We can go dancing after.»

«Of course I don't mind. I can fix myself something here.»

«Listen, why don't you come with us?»

«Are you sure that's a good idea? You guys are old friends, it would be weird to have a stranger there.»

«I want to show you off a little. Are you embarrassed to be seen with me?»

I couldn't be completely sure that she was kidding. «You know better than that.»

«You don't have to come if you don't want to.»

Somehow the conversation had drifted into no-win territory without either one of us intending it. «I would love to meet your friends,» I said.

«We're all going to meet up at the store at six. Is that okay?»

«Perfecto,» I said.

IT STARTED BADLY and went downhill from there. Elena was tied up with a customer until 6:30. Adriana still hadn't shown up by then and I didn't know which of the other young women circling around the store were Elena's friends. I took my cues from Elena and she did the same with me. The result was an awkward hug, under the suspicious stare of the woman in the cat-eye glasses, who was clearly trying to remember where she'd seen me before.

We ended up at a McDonald's in the cavernous Patio de Comidas on the top floor. I had to go off by myself to find some empanadas de verduras. At first the conversation was as uncomfortable as I'd feared, with Adriana and Elena making an effort to include me, then before long they were all talking at high speed about people I'd never met, laughing hard and using slang that completely eluded me. I followed as best I could and kept smiling, while unable to think of anything except how terribly young and alien they all seemed.

When we left, after nine, the others were headed to a movie and I felt the sadness in Elena. «We don't have to dance tonight,» I told her. «If you want to go with your friends, I promise you it's okay with me.»

She shook her head. «I don't want to have to choose between you and my friends.»

Clearly she did have to choose, and it felt like my fault.

We rode the escalators down through the glittering mall toward the exit to the Subte station. «You hardly said anything all night,» she said. «It couldn't have been much fun for you.»

All I could do was shrug.

The Subte car was crowded and it was impossible to talk. Elena held my hand but didn't look at me. My thoughts were grim. I pictured us back at the apartment, Elena finding an excuse not to go dancing. More silence, and separate sides of the bed. There had been too many nights like that with Lauren.

We squeezed off the train at our stop and climbed up to the street. She hadn't looked at me in a long time. She said, «You must feel like a canguro. Like a—»

«I know the word.» Babysitter.

I stopped her and turned her to face me. We looked at each other until I gathered her in and kissed her and kept kissing her until she melted into me and kissed me back.

«Ay, Beto, I get so scared sometimes.»

«Tell me about it.»

«I don't want to drive you away.»

«You're not going to drive me away.»

«You're so different from me. So old and frail, one foot in the grave...»

«And you, barely out of secondary school, your whole life ahead of you...»

Her laughter was like the highest notes on a piano. «Can we change our clothes and go dancing now?»

«Right now? Here in the street?»

She made a face. «Sí, claro, here in the street.» She grabbed my hand and took off toward the apartment at a run.

For her it was over that quickly. I continued to brood, but by four in the morning, when we finally staggered out of El Beso and into a cab, I was too tired to wind myself up anymore.

WITH THE AFTERNOON half gone on Sunday we were still in bed. We'd made love and dozed and we were lying naked in each other's arms, the bed full of her fragrance, a faint breeze from the airshaft tapping the blinds against the window and drying the sweat on my chest.

«Beto.»

«Mmmmm.»

«Beto, I have to figure out what to do about my father.»

«How do you mean?»

«Those files that he was talking about. I have to at least try to do something.»

At some level I had known that the last week had been an interlude, a reprieve, and at the same time I had wanted to believe that it could go on forever. The very things that had brought us together in that tiny apartment, that had allowed me to become her lover, were destined to drag me back into the train wreck of her past.

«You mean look for them,» I said.

She heard something in my voice. «Oh, Beto, mi amor, you don't have to be part of it. This is something I need to do for myself.»

«What did you call me?»

She raised her head to show me her mischievous smile. «Mi amor.» My love.

«I don't think you ever said that to me before.»

«Didn't I? Does it scare you? Maybe just a little?»

«No. I've been in love with you since the first time I danced with you.»

«Another piropo?»

I shook my head, too emotional to speak, and she was serious again in a fraction of a heartbeat, the endless darkness of her eyes burning into me. «I love you, Beto.»

«I love you too. I'll check around tomorrow, see if I can find anything out about the files.»

«Oh, Beto...»

«Todo o nada,» I said, and then in English, "All or nothing."

And then she was kissing me and there was nothing else in the world, not even the fear.

FOR TWO HOURS I sat at my desk, doing no work, pumping up my courage, getting my story straight, anticipating the things that could go wrong.

At 11:30 I looked again at our instant messaging system. It showed that Bahadur was still at his desk, like he had been the last six times I'd checked.

I told myself that the thing I was going to ask him was perfectly reasonable. If he said no, I told myself, I would simply walk away.

I stood up, suddenly light-headed. Just this one thing, I thought. Then you can tell Elena that you tried and you'll be done.

Bahadur was senior enough to rate an office. I knocked on the door, which was open, as always. «Adelante,» he said, without looking up. His turban that day was a muted green.

I waited while he finished a line of code and considered it, his hands poised above the keyboard like a magician in the middle of a mystic pass, then he spun around in his chair.

I looked into his brown eyes, which were gentle and glad to see me, and I couldn't speak. Elena hates liars, I thought. This is wrong.

"Rob," he said, "what the hell is up with you, man?"

"Sorry. I'm kind of dead on my feet."

Bahadur shook his head. "You are much too old for this nonsense." I had of course told him about Elena. He had pretended to disapprove, looking wistful even as he told me I was squandering my spiritual strength.

I'm sorry, Elena, I thought. I don't know how to do this without lying. And I don't know how to not do this for you.

"Listen," I said, "can you give me the combination to the lab? I want to come in some night this week and run a few stress tests when there's nobody else around."

Bahadur looked unhappy. "They really don't like letting that combination out. Can't you run them remotely?"

"The error messages only show up on the client monitors. If I telnet into them it'll affect the performance results."

"Oh, hell, I can't imagine anyone is going to complain if I give it to you. Don't write it down anywhere, yes?"

He went through it with me, these two buttons together, then these one at a time, these last two together. I nodded and he sent me to try it out.

My hands shook so badly the first time that I botched it. I went through it again, slowly, and the handle turned. I let the latch slip back into place and returned to my desk.

It doesn't matter anyway, I told myself. The cops took it all, the computer, everything in the drawers. It was nothing more than a gesture, to prove something to Elena and to get myself off the hook.

ELENA HAD BEEN grocery shopping. It was her day off and she'd found a recipe online for squash and sweet potato soup. We cooked it together in the tiny kitchen while I told her what I'd done.

When I finished, she held my face in both hands and kissed me. Then she said, «Can we go tonight?»

«We?»

«I want to go with you. If it's dangerous, I have to take the risk with you.»

It was probably more dangerous, and harder to explain, to have her with me. There was no explicit rule against her being there, though, and I liked visualizing her in my cubicle, knew that I would remember her there the next day. «If you're really sure,» I said.

«Totally sure. When can we go?»

«After ten, I guess. There shouldn't be anyone around by then.»

«Okay.»

«Remember that there are security cameras all over the place. So we have to look like we only came in to start my tests.»

Elena looked disappointed. «So we can't make love on your desk? I wanted to make sure you would remember me at work.»

«Elena who?» I said.

She grabbed me by the hair with both hands and kissed me. "This Elena," she said.

WE SPENT THE EVENING on the couch reading, wrapped around each other. Elena's love of physical contact woke a need in me that I'd always stifled before. At first I'd been afraid to hope that this affair was anything more than a passing, incredibly generous impulse on her part. Now I was afraid to think that it would someday end.

I dozed off and she woke me at ten, stroking my face and kissing me. «Beto, it's ten. Are you awake?»

I got up and washed my face. I couldn't think of an excuse to call it off and she was clearly not going to offer me a way out. Her eyes were luminous with excitement.

We walked to Avenida San Juan in search of a cab. The night was warm and still and dusty-smelling. Everyone we passed on the crowded sidewalks seemed to scrutinize me. I told myself it was only because of Elena.

«Your hand is so cold,» Elena said. «Are you nervous?»

«Not nervous,» I said. «Afraid.»

«I'm scared, too,» Elena said. «But I've been thinking about this ever since that man, Mateo, told his story.»

«Do you believe him? Do you believe he's your father?» We had carefully avoided the subject for over a week.

«Probably. I can't think about him yet. I have to think about

Osvaldo, about what I'm going to do. I want him to stand trial and go to jail. I wish we had the death penalty. I wish we could sentence him to torture for the rest of his life. I wish there was some way to make him pay for what he did.»

There was nothing to say. I squeezed her hand.

She said, «The only way I know to even start is to find those files.»

«You know there's not much chance of us finding them. The police have looked. They have his computer.»

«I know.»

«If we don't find the files, maybe Mateo could testify against him.»

«Mateo has no proof. And in order to testify he would have to give himself up.»

I flagged a cab and we got in. I gave the driver the address. After a minute she slid over in the seat and rested her head on my shoulder and we rode that way in silence.

All too soon the cab pulled up outside the office. I paid and we got out. It was 10:30, and this close to the microcentro the crowds were even heavier than in San Telmo: tourists, families coming from the movies or a play, office workers hurrying to catch the last train, young couples headed to a late dinner. Waves of sibilant Argentine Spanish broke all around us.

I reminded her of the cameras in the lobby, in the lab, and in the open area where my cubicle was. The lab camera was on the wall above Suarez's desk, so the desk itself was out of its range. I talked her through what we would do, and I watched her nervousness turn back into excitement.

I used my key to get in the front door of the building and we rode in silence to the sixth floor. I saw my face in the chrome of the control panel. My expression was empty and dead, the right eye bloodshot.

A second brass key opened the door to the reception area. I paused long enough for the present to superimpose itself on my first memory of her. It gave me a fleeting rush of something like joy.

My Universal ID badge took us past the next set of glass doors and into the break room. There was a set of cubbyholes there, labeled with our names, for physical mail. Suarez's slot was empty.

The next stop was my cubicle. Her face fell at the sight of it. «It's so sad and small,» she said.

I booted up my computer. Paranoid and driven by my need for

control, I had cobbled together an actual test script. I sent it over the network to the controller in one of the test beds.

I looked over to see Elena holding my garnet crystal. It was unpolished, reddish purple, about the size of a golf ball, with five-sided facets. «What is this?»

I had memorized the word in Spanish. «Granate,» I said. «My massage therapist in the US gave it to me. It's supposed to be for the root chakra, at the base of the spine.»

«And how is it supposed to help you?»

«It's supposed to help the feeling...» I was about to choke up. I shoved the weakness away. «The feeling of not having a home,» I said. «If you believe—»

«Yes, yes, if you believe in that sort of thing. Do you?»

«Not really. But it feels good to hold it sometimes. The weight of it.»

«What *do* you believe in, Beto? Not in God. Not in crystals. Do you believe in us?»

«Is hope the same as belief?»

«No.»

«I hope,» I said, «that someday soon I will come to believe in us.» I got up and started to move past her.

«Wait,» she said. She put her arms around my neck and very slowly moved up against me. «Remember this when you're in this sad, small place and feel like you don't belong anywhere.» Then she kissed me with such tenderness and passion that it cut through all the sadness and numbness and fear, and I was alive again and fully in the moment.

In the circumstances, I wasn't sure that was a good thing.

FOR AN AWKWARD SECOND I thought I'd forgotten the combination. It was a recurring nightmare, standing at my high school locker without a clue, bells ringing for class, panic rising.

I dried my hands on my pants legs and jiggled the handle to clear the memory. These two together, these one at a time, then two more.

The handle turned. I switched on the row of lights that ran down the right side of the room. I pointed to Suarez's desk in the corner and fed her the line I'd rehearsed for the security camera: «You can sit over there, I just need to look at a few things.»

«Claro,» she said.

She would quickly see that what I'd told her was true, that there was nothing left to find, and then we would have done all we could and we could go.

I switched on the monitor for the controller, loaded the script and fired it up. There were eight client systems in the test bed and I turned those monitors on too. The first error message popped up immediately. «Bueno,» I told it. «Keep up the good work.»

I walked to the end of the row, where I could see Elena. She knelt in front of Suarez's desk, working one of the bottom drawers back and forth, a puzzled look on her face. I felt something cold squeeze my stomach.

She looked at me and beckoned me over.

I crossed the room and squatted next to her. She pointed to her ear, inviting me to listen. She opened the drawer again, hesitating as it was almost all the way out. The drawer was completely empty.

I showed her my hands, palms up. What was she talking about?

She moved the drawer in and out a couple of inches, back and forth. Then I heard it. A faint scraping noise.

I motioned for her to let me in and tripped the release that let me take the drawer all the way out. I turned it around and there, stuck to the metal plate at the back with layers of clear packing tape, was a CD in a Tyvek envelope.

Elena had her hand over her mouth, her eyes wide.

I pulled the tape off, got the envelope open, and took out the CD. It had "contabilidad.xls" handwritten across it in green marker. Accounting.

We were both crouched there, staring at the disc, when the rest of the lights flickered on.

"WHAT THE HELL do you think you're doing?"

Bahadur stood in the doorway, one hand still on the light switch. I was paralyzed, a kid caught with his hand in his mother's purse.

"I asked you a question," he said.

"Bahadur—" I said.

"Talk fast, man, before I call Security."

"Give me five minutes," I said. "I'll explain everything."

"I'm listening."

"Not here." I jerked my head in the direction of the camera above my head.

He held the lab door open. "My office," he said.

We walked in single file. Once inside, with the door closed, I held up the CD and said, "I think this is what got Suarez killed."

«Beto, what are you doing?» Elena whispered.

«We have to trust him,» I said. «He may be able to help.»

Bahadur switched to Spanish, in deference to Elena. «Are you crazy? You're getting mixed up with the Suarez business? Do you have a death wish?»

«She's already mixed up in it,» I said. «Elena, meet Bahadur, my boss.»

«Encantado,» Bahadur said.

«Can you trust me long enough to spin up this CD and see what's on it? Then I'll tell you what I know.»

«Why should I trust you? You lied to me.»

«I didn't exactly lie,» I said. «The test is running. But yes, I deceived you. I'm sorry.»

We stared at each other across the narrow space of his office, then he looked at Elena. «It's easy enough to see why you did it,» he said. «I'll listen, but if I don't like the story, I'm going to have to do something.»

«Okay,» I said. I handed him the CD and he fed it to his computer. When it showed up in his Explorer window it contained a single Excel spreadsheet named contabilidad.xls. I glanced at Elena.

«Open it,» she said.

The file was three pages long. The first column, Date, started in April of 1976 and ran through November of 1982. There was never less than one entry per month and some months had three or four. The second column was Check # and the third was amount. Substantial amounts, generally between 5,000 and 10,000 US dollars. In the Received By column, the name was usually Emiliano Cesarino. The rest of the time it was Osvaldo del Salvador. The Notes column had comments like «Met EC at el Obelisco 1300 hours for delivery—MS» or «EC sent confirmation of contracts—MS.»

Some rows had blank check numbers and the Notes column showed model numbers of Universal equipment, with an estimate of the value under Amount. The equipment alone totaled over a million dollars.

Bahadur was the first to say anything. «This is not evidence, yes?

There was no Excel in 1976. There wasn't even Lotus 1-2-3 or VisiCalc.»

«No,» I said. «He must have copied it from handwritten notes.»

«Let me be sure I understand this,» Elena said. She looked like a kid who'd gotten a French racing bike for Christmas—stunned, excited, and not quite sure what she was going to do with it. «Universal Systems was giving money to the dictatorship?»

«That's what it looks like,» I said. «Money and computers.»

She pointed to the Notes column. «The MS means Suarez was carrying the money himself?»

«Probably,» Bahadur said. «He was the *bag man*.» He looked at me. «'*Bag man*,' yes?»

I nodded.

«If nothing else,» Elena said, «this ties Osvaldo to Cesarino. No?»

«It doesn't do much of anything,» Bahadur said, «except show people where to dig. If Universal really was stupid enough to pay out of their business account and still has the cancelled checks, and the endorsements can be tied to somebody in the government, then maybe you'd have something. But what are the odds that those checks are still around?»

I said, «Most likely they made the checks out to cash and Suarez put the money in a paper bag.»

«Evidently Cesarino thought it was worth something,» Elena said. «It was worth enough to get Suarez killed.»

«Claro,» Bahadur said. «Because Suarez's testimony is what it would take to make this stand up in court. Without it?» He shook his head.

«Which means this is evidence that Cesarino had him killed,» Elena said.

Bahadur shrugged. «Cesarino's trial will be over in a day or two. They'll find him guilty, he'll get house arrest, like Etchecolatz. There's nothing more they can do to him, even if they add Suarez's murder to the list.»

«What about Osvaldo?» Elena asked.

«Why all this interest in Osvaldo?»

«He's her father,» I said. «Her adoptive father.»

That stopped him. "Ah," he said. He thought a little and then he said, "Ah," again.

Elena said, «What do we do now?»

«Unless Bahadur says no, I'm going to copy the original, because it's got Suarez's writing on it. We put the copy where we found the original, in case somebody else is looking for it. Then we go try to get some sleep.»

«Go ahead,» Bahadur said.

«Can you make a couple of extras?» Elena said. «Just in case?»

«Burn one for me too,» Bahadur said. «Because I still haven't decided what I'm going to do.»

WE WENT BACK to the apartment, but not to sleep.

«Are you in trouble now at work?» Elena asked. I lay in bed, holding her. I was in pajama bottoms, she was in one of my T-shirts, which came to her knees. The lights were out and warm, damp air leaked sluggishly through the open window.

«I don't think so. Bahadur isn't a...he doesn't live for the company, you know?»

«If I did something that hurt you, I could never forgive myself. Oh, Beto, I can't sleep, I can't stop thinking about this.»

«You don't have to figure everything out tonight. There's always tomorrow.» I turned my head to see the clock. 1:49. «Later today, I should say.»

«Maybe I should go to the police.»

«The cop who came to the office was named Bonaventura. You could go see him. Me, I don't trust him. I don't know which side he's on.»

«Then I have to go to one of the judges in the Cesarino trial. I have to try something.»

«Do you want me to come with you?» My head throbbed as I said the words.

«No, thank you, but...I think I can do better on my own. A pretty girl, maybe a little helpless...»

In another mood I might have found her charming. As it was I resented her easy confidence in her ability to manipulate men— simple, gullible men like me.

«Oh, Beto,» she said, nuzzling her head into my chest. Her ability to read my moods bordered on the psychic. «I do need you, you know that. And I love you. And right now you must go to sleep. Turn over and I'll rub your back. And then we'll both sleep.»

•

ELENA TOOK LINEA A to Congreso at ten in the morning. She started with a guard outside the courtroom and by noon she had worked her way up to a few minutes with one of the prosecuting attorneys, a very businesslike young woman in heavy black-framed glasses named Dominguez.

It went the way Bahadur had predicted. The evidence against Cesarino was overwhelming, and in comparison to kidnapping, torture, and murder, a little financial corruption barely registered.

«But this shows direct support of the dictatorship by a US corporation.»

Dominguez smiled. Elena described the smile as thin and tight. «I hate to say this, but this is hardly news. Everyone knows this.»

Elena asked about Osvaldo. Dominguez took a printed list out of her briefcase. It ran to five pages, single spaced, and each line had a name and a few words of context.

«I don't have him on my list. You have to understand, just now we are going for los peces gordos, the big fish only.»

«He tortured my mother to death,» Elena said.

That finally broke Dominguez's reserve. She took Elena's hands in both of hers and said, «I'm sorry. I'm so very sorry. There were so many to blame. Fuimos todos, somebody said. It was all of us.»

WHILE SHE WAS at the courthouse I was at work. As a precaution, I emailed a copy of contabilidad.xls to my personal email account. According to the instant message system, Bahadur was in his office. He didn't contact me and I left well enough alone.

Elena was asleep when I got back. I stretched out beside her and went to sleep in seconds. In the States I'd never taken naps. In Buenos Aires they were a necessity of life.

I woke up at 11:30, Elena a few minutes later. We heated some soup and threw together a salad while she told me about her day.

«In the end she took the CD and my name and phone number, probably just to make me feel better.» I held her while she cried a little, then we ate and I said, «Do you want to go out?»

«You mean dancing? Tonight?» The way her face lit up when she was happy, the way her whole body hummed with energy, was the most potent drug I had ever known.

«Why not? Porteño y Bailarin goes late tonight.»

«Oh, Beto, yes. Yes, please.»

•

WE BOTH DRESSED UP and the crowded intimacy of the tiny
dance floor and the scratchy music of another time was in fact exactly what we needed. After the first tanda, as we walked to our table, Elena said, «Just for tonight, would you mind terribly if I didn't
dance with anyone but you? You can dance with other people, but
tonight I don't want to be with strangers.»

I stopped and faced her. «I don't want to be with anyone but you.»

«Then why are we going back to the table?»

We only stayed an hour. The classes and the practice had taught
us to move together better than ever, but they couldn't keep us from
feeling the long day in our feet and shoulders.

In the cab afterward, I watched the pleasure of the dance floor
seep away from her. There is always that moment at the end of the
night, the concession that you can't keep moving forever. More than
that, I knew that time alone was not going to heal the pain she was
going through, that patience and love were not going to be enough.

For all those reasons, I said, «I know what you're thinking.»

«Beto, I'm so sorry. It's been lovely and it's not right to let those
other things spoil the evening.»

«It's not spoiled. I want to help.»

«I know you do, querida.» She nodded toward the cab driver.
«Later. We can talk at home.»

Back at the apartment, we undressed in silence and took our turns
in the bathroom, and as I crawled into bed next to her I thought I
would be asleep as soon as my head touched the pillow. She was in
her favorite orange T-shirt of mine, lying on her side facing me, her
head propped on one•hand.

«There's no one left to go to,» she said. «The judges don't care
and we can't trust the police.»

The thought that had come to me in the cab returned and left
me wide awake.

«Okay,» she said. «There is one other person.»

We looked at each other, waiting each other out. Finally I broke
the impasse. «Say it.»

«Mateo.»

«I think he's crazy,» I said. «He told me he intends to bring
Osvaldo down. I don't think there's any question he means by violence. Even if it kills him to do it.»

Elena's expression didn't change, her eyes didn't blink. «Sometimes I feel that way too.»

The words took all the warmth out of the room. I rolled onto my back.

«You think Mateo's crazy,» she said. «Does that mean you think he was lying about being my father? You never said.»

I saw that I couldn't stop what was going to happen, that the best I could do was to not abandon her, to stay close and do what little I could to keep the worst from happening. «No,» I said. «I believe him.»

«Then I need to talk to him. About Osvaldo, but also to see if I can make some kind of peace with him. While I still can.»

With infinite reluctance I said, «Yes. Yes, I guess you have to.»

«I don't even know what I did with the phone number he gave me, I was in such a state that day.»

I was so dry that my tongue stuck to the roof of my mouth and made a clicking sound as it came loose. «I have his number.»

«Oh, Beto.» She turned my face toward her with one slender hand and made me look into those deep, black eyes. «I can't do this alone. If I meet with him, will you come with me? I don't think I could feel safe otherwise.»

«Yes, of course. There's...I never want to be anyplace but with you.»

She moved over me. I felt the heat and weight of her breasts against my bare chest, the smooth skin of her thigh between my legs. She whispered, «I don't know what I would do without you. I need you so much right now.»

I put my hands in her hair and stroked her scalp and neck. «It's okay,» I told her. «Everything's okay.»

Our physical beings are only the shadows of our emotions. A panicked mother can lift a car to save her child. Despair can kill a strong man in a hundred different ways, from pancreatic cancer to a reckless accident. Twelve hours' sleep can leave us exhausted, and sometimes...sometimes we don't need sleep at all.

She lifted her head to look at me. «Beto,» she said, and her mouth moved toward mine.

I DIDN'T MAKE IT in to work until 11:00. Bahadur arrived at my cube a few minutes later. Obviously he'd been waiting for me to show up on the network.

"I've decided to talk to La Reina," he said.

"Isabel? About Monday night?" I felt hollow inside.

"She was close to Suarez. She needs to know what was in those files."

"You think she doesn't already?"

"The dates on the payments coincide exactly with the period that Jim was working out of this office. He was the director. We have to assume that he was the one making them."

"I don't think it's safe to assume anything. Isabel was here those same years."

"As a secretary, and not even as Jim's secretary. Where would she get access to that sort of money or equipment? And when Jim transferred to Anaheim, the payments stopped."

"And by that point," I said, "the dictatorship was on its last legs."

"Last legs," Bahadur said. "That's a good one. Last legs."

"If you go to her, she's going to ask questions. If she finds out about those extra copies of the file, and that Elena is out there showing it around, she's going to fire me." The thought of being unemployed in Buenos Aires, with no prospects of another job and no more savings than I had, put me on the verge of panic. Sweat broke on my forehead.

"Not if I'm right about her," Bahadur said.

"And if you're wrong? I'm wiped out."

Bahadur didn't bother to point out that it would be my own fault. "All right, I will make you a deal. I will try to tell the truth without getting you in trouble. If you think you are in danger, you can lie about the copies and I won't call you up."

"Out," I said. "You won't call me out."

ISABEL'S OFFICE DOOR had a picture of a crown on it and cut-out letters that spelled LA REINA. She looked at our faces when we filed in and said, «Did somebody die?»

«Yes,» Bahadur said. «A lot of people died.» He flipped the CD onto her desk, a desk that held nothing except a keyboard, monitor, and mouse. The blinds were closed on the window behind her and the room was lit by a pole lamp in the corner.

«What's this?»

Bahadur nodded toward her computer.

«Ave Maria, Bahadur, you've got to stop watching so many

movies.» She took the CD out of the envelope and slipped it into her laptop, which sat on a credenza to one side.

She watched her screen as the disc spun up, glanced at us curiously, then clicked. Light from the monitor played across her face as the file opened. Then, as she gradually realized what she was looking at, her expression became pained. «Ay, Dios mío, Jim, what did you do?»

She looked at Bahadur. «Where did this come from?»

«Rob—Beto—found it behind Suarez's desk,» he said. «He brought it to me.» Not the whole truth, but not an outright lie.

«The MS in the notes?»

«We think so, yes.»

«Is this the only copy?»

«I didn't make any,» Bahadur said.

«Who else knows about this?» she asked.

I tried not to react.

«Who can say?» Bahadur shrugged. «We haven't told anyone. I don't think anybody else in the company knows.»

That seemed to satisfy her. I quietly let out the breath I didn't know I was holding.

«Thank you for bringing this to me. I'm going to call Jim and see what he has to say. I hope he has a damned good explanation.»

«And if he doesn't?» Bahadur asked.

«Somebody needs to answer for this,» she said.

As we walked out of her office, I felt exposed and vulnerable. I didn't get much work done the rest of the day, expecting Security to show up any minute and escort me out of the building.

It didn't help that the sole item on the agenda for that night was contacting Mateo.

Elena got to the apartment a few minutes after me. She did her best to seem affectionate and nonchalant. She didn't fool either of us. After dinner she took me over to the couch and huddled against me and said, «Can we call him?»

I nodded and got the number out of my wallet, where I'd been carrying it since he gave it to me. She dialed it on her cell phone. He didn't answer, not that I'd expected him to.

«Hi, it's Elena,» she said to his voice mail. «We need to talk. I know you have the number, but here it is again anyway.» She recited the digits slowly. «I'm staying at Beto's apartment, so you can call him if you can't get me.»

After she hung up, we lay on the couch holding each other. I was on the edge of sleep when her phone rang. She gave me a sweet, apologetic look before she answered it.

«Hola....Yes, I'm okay, well enough....Tonight?» She looked at me, and I nodded. «Okay, where?» She listened for a few seconds and looked at me again. «He says we should meet at the place where the two of you had coffee in the rain. Do you know what he's talking about? He says not to say the name.»

«Yes, I know it.»

«In an hour?»

I nodded again.

«Bueno,» she said into the phone. «We'll—» I heard the buzz of the dial tone. Running out of minutes on his phone card, maybe.

We lay down again, now unable to get comfortable. Elena said, «I bet you wish you'd listened when I told you not to get involved with me.»

«You make it sound like I had a choice.»

She squirmed and sat up, putting my legs across her lap. «I grew up believing you could tell a priest when you'd done something wrong and then God would forgive you. They told me God could forgive anything. A man like Cesarino on his death bed could beg forgiveness and still go to heaven. Are we supposed to be like God? Are we supposed to forgive anything?»

«I don't know much about it,» I said, «but don't they say that you're not supposed to even judge who's right and wrong? Aren't you supposed to leave that to God?»

«I still believe in God, in some kind of God, but I don't know if I believe in heaven or hell anymore. Other than the heaven and hell we make here in this life. So how can I trust God to make everything okay after we're dead? Besides, even with God, you have to ask for forgiveness, no? Make at least some show of regrets? I never heard Osvaldo admit to being wrong, ever, not in my whole life.»

«Maybe forgiveness is too strong a word. Maybe you could say... letting go of him. So you don't have to always be living in the past.»

«But don't you see? The past is never over in Argentina. The past is alive and walking the streets and kidnapping people and killing them, and the government and the police don't care.»

«I just found you, Elena. I don't want to lose you.»

«Part of me is already lost.» She climbed back on top of me and laid her head on my chest. «I'm sorry, that's so melodramatic. I don't know what I want. We'll hear what Mateo has to say and maybe something will come to me. Yes?«

THE NIGHT WAS COOL, damp without rain. Puffs of wind tugged at my hair and my coat as if a giant oscillating fan was blowing on the city.

As we approached the door of Arte y Café, Mateo stepped out of the shadows and took Elena's arm. «Let's walk,» he said.

He led us away from the noise and life of Avenida San Juan, toward the dark streets around Parque Lezama. For two blocks no one said anything. Mateo stopped at a deserted café and gestured toward an outside table.

Once we were sitting down, Mateo said, «I'm glad you called. I didn't know if I was ever going to hear from you again.»

The petulance seemed like a bad idea, though Elena responded by touching his hand and saying, «I'm sorry. I've had a lot to think about.» It was her first kind gesture toward him and I watched him struggle to control his emotions. «I want to get to know you,» she said. «To start from nothing at all…it's very hard. I don't know anything about what your life is like.»

«I'm a fugitive,» Mateo said, still circling the edge of self-pity. «I live in an abandoned building. There is one other from the old days, maybe a dozen or so younger people who come and go. They have a lot of ideals and energy and don't know what to do with them. Friends from the old days help with money and food.»

«Beto said that you…that you are planning something to do with Osvaldo.»

«We are going to put him on trial.»

«And who's going to judge him?» I didn't hear sarcasm or accusation in her voice, merely curiosity. «You?»

Mateo leaned back and smiled without warmth. «In fact, that's the problem.» He signaled the waiter, holding up three fingers for three coffees.

«No coffee for me,» I said.

Mateo shrugged, not taking his eyes from Elena. «There are so few of us. When the montoneros passed judgment on someone, it had authority. When you have so few, it's more like revenge than justice.»

«How do you know the difference?» I asked.

«I can't tell you that. I don't know who can. When the government condemns a man to death, is that vengeance too? When it's a man like me?»

«I'm not sure I care,» Elena said. «Whether it's revenge or not.»

Mateo leaned forward. They had that in common, the two of them, that intensity. I had seen his heredity in her. «You should care,» he said. «You should care with all your heart. In the end, the montoneros were not about justice anymore. We had become what they said we were, we had become terrorists. We killed too many, too willingly, and we lost the support of the people. And so the people thought it was justice when the Triple A took their revenge on us. And when la dictadura took over, most of them were relieved. At least now we will have some peace and safety, they said.»

«Do you have a plan?» I asked. It wasn't that I really wanted an answer, more that I couldn't leave it alone, like a sore tooth.

«Yes. There is a plan. Two or three of them.»

«And you have guns?» I asked.

«Yes.»

«So you'll kill him if he resists.»

«The guns are to make sure he doesn't resist.»

«But you are professionals. The guns will be loaded, no? You wouldn't carry them unless you were willing to use them.»

«We are professionals, yes.»

The waiter came with the coffee. I waved mine away, but he was paying attention only to Mateo. He left the three cups and disappeared.

«And when you find him guilty,» I asked, «as of course you will, the sentence will be death?»

«What other sentence would there be? Would you have us sentence him to house arrest?»

«So when do you kidnap him? Do you have a date?» I couldn't stop pushing, though I knew I was not winning points either with Mateo or with Elena.

«That depends,» Mateo said.

«On what?»

«On whether Elena joins us.»

We both looked at her, like rival lovers demanding she choose between us.

«There is one other experienced person,» she said, «and the rest are young people? How young? I don't want to risk my life for a fiasco.»

«The youngest is sixteen, the oldest is twenty-eight. One of them built a bomb that did a lot of damage to...a business, let's say. No people were harmed and much property was. Another shot a cop. Another deserted from the army. Others have organized demonstrations. I don't want to die without reason either. When we do the operation, it will be with people I trust.»

I thought seriously about getting up and walking away. It was unthinkable that I could be sitting at that table, involved in that discussion. If I did walk away, it would mean deserting Elena. I looked at her. She would understand. She would not blame me for it.

Everything was unthinkable.

At that moment, without taking her eyes off Mateo, she reached out and covered my hand with hers.

I felt sick to my stomach and there was fire behind my right eye.

As if to spare me, Elena changed the subject. She asked Mateo if he had ever seen Pugliese's orchestra.

«Only once in person,» he told her. He was smiling, grateful for the chance to impress her. Somehow she had known that. We were all as eager as puppies for her approval.

«It was December 26, 1969, at Luna Park,» he said. Luna Park is the huge indoor arena between el Obelisco and the river. «It was a festival in his honor and there were eight thousand of us there, every seat in the place full. I was nineteen years old, I'd been dancing for a year, and I had the fire of the new convert. You would not believe the noise in that place. Everyone yelling, '¡Al Colón! ¡Al Colón!'»

Teatro Colón is the Argentine Carnegie Hall and the legend has it that Pugliese's mother would call out «¡Al Colón!» to him as a kid when he practiced the piano, half encouragement, half prediction. It became a battle cry for his fans and in 1985, after the dictatorship fell, it became a reality when he finally played there.

Elena looked entranced. «So you never saw the red carnation on the piano bench?» When Pugliese was arrested, which was often, his orquesta would put a red carnation, un clavel rojo, on his piano bench and play without him.

«That was before me,» Mateo said. «That was Perón, who hated him for being a communist. By the sixties he was an institution, he was on TV all the time. But he never backed down and people never forgot that. At Luna Park there must have been a million red carnations. His music was brilliant, inspirational, but that's not why those people loved him so much. They loved him for his integrity. That was the lesson.»

I thought he might start crying again. He looked away for a few seconds, then it was his turn to change the subject. «Tell me,» he said, «what happened to your nose?»

It was a question I'd never asked, at first because I didn't want her to think it bothered me, then because I'd ceased to notice it as anything else than a part of her.

«I was nine,» she said. «Old enough that I should have remembered it, but I didn't. My mother always told me I fell playing futbol and I believed that. Then, when I was moving out, she told me the truth.»

«Osvaldo,» Mateo said.

She nodded. «Apparently I said something about the name Lacunza being stupid, and hating it, and that my name was del Salvador, and I would always be del Salvador, and he hit me with the back of his hand. It broke my nose and knocked me out. I don't remember him ever hitting me before or after, and my mother—I mean, Candelaria—said he never did. She said he cried when he saw what he'd done, and he drove me to the hospital himself. That was where he first told the futbol story and after that it got repeated until it became the truth.»

There was something terrible in Mateo's expression and it was all the more terrible because it was not the helpless anger that some other parent might feel. I hated Osvaldo too for what he'd done to her. Not just the broken nose, but the lies and the coldness and the oppressive religion. Like Mateo, I hated him enough to want him dead for it. The difference was I couldn't imagine doing the job myself. Mateo clearly could.

It was Elena who said, «We have to go.» The waiter had brought the check and Mateo had casually pushed it out of his way. We all stood up and I looked at the check and got a ten-peso note out of my wallet.

«No,» Elena said, «let me—»

«It's okay,» I said. «I've got money.» It was courage that I was short of.

Mateo saw my untouched coffee, shrugged apologetically, and drank it off.

«I'll call you,» Elena told him.

«Will you?»

«I promise.»

He stood there awkwardly, wanting, and Elena went to him and hugged him and kissed him on the cheek. I could see that he didn't want to let go. His arms finally fell limp by his sides.

I hugged him too and we kissed each other's cheeks. «Take care of her,» he said.

«I know,» I said. «Or you'll kill me.»

Elena gave me a curious look. Mateo burst out laughing. It sounded like a laugh that had been waiting a long time. «That's right. Or I will kill you. ¡Chau!» He was still laughing as he walked away.

ELENA HAD BOTH ARMS wrapped around my waist as we walked home. «Beto, what's going to happen to us? What happens if I do this thing with Mateo?»

«I'm not going to leave you, Elena. If you want to get away from me, you're the one who has to go.»

«But you don't like it.»

«It makes me afraid. Afraid in general, afraid for myself, afraid for you. I think violence just makes more trouble.»

«Always? If somebody broke into our apartment and was going to rape me or kill me, would you use violence to protect me?»

«Yes.»

She was not one to belabor a point. A minute later she started singing. «Para qué te quiero tanto, si no puedo ser feliz...» Why do I love you so much if I can't ever be happy? I don't think she meant anything by it. All tangos are about heartbreak and betrayal.

Then she said, «You know who Mateo should have on his jury? Your friend Bahadur.»

«Elena, you need to get more sleep. Te vuelves chiflada. You're going out of your mind.»

«I'm totally serious. He seems to have that kind of integrity that Mateo was talking about.»

«Too much integrity to get involved with a kidnapping.»

«Really? Because it seems to me he doesn't care about the law at all, only about what's right.»

I stopped to kiss her. «Maybe you're not chiflada. Maybe you're just perceptive. I'm not going to invite him to join the kidnapping just yet, though.»

I was too tired and too edgy for sex. I lay awake most of the night, holding Elena while she slept, trying to see the future.

THE NEXT NIGHT was Thursday and our regular lesson with Don Güicho. Through an effort of will, I shut Mateo and Osvaldo out of my mind and lived entirely in the moment of Elena's body against mine, the music, the struggle to keep my eje upright and strong.

After class Don Güicho said, «You had good intensity tonight. It was almost like you're beginning to understand tango a little.»

«Thanks,» I said. «I think.»

Elena seemed to want a reprieve as much as I did. We went out for pasta and then home to dance and make love.

Friday she was scheduled to work until ten. All morning at the office I kept remembering what she'd said about Bahadur, until I finally went to his office and said, "Can I buy you dinner tonight?"

"What, I don't rate dinner and a movie?"

"You don't need to see any more movies and I need to talk. Actually what I need is a friend. Am I presuming too much?"

"No," he said. "You don't presume."

We knocked off work at 7:30 and walked over to Corrientes. A couple of miles up the street was a vegetarian buffet, Los Sabios, that didn't open until eight. Corrientes on a Friday night is like Broadway in New York, except that the theaters often have two performances a night to accommodate the crowds. Past the theaters came the bookstores and the iconic cafés like La Paz, the historic hangout for leftist writers. Traffic was bumper to bumper and the sidewalks were packed. It was therapeutic to be surrounded by normal people doing festive things. People who might be worried about paying off their credit cards or losing their jobs, who might be having relationship problems, who were most likely not involved in conspiracies to kidnap and murder.

As I thought that, walking easily with Bahadur in the bright lights and noise and chaos of the start of a weekend, everything seemed clear and simple. Spending the rest of my life in prison in a foreign country was not an option. There had to be an easy way out of the craziness and I was sure I would find it. It felt like waking up from a fever dream.

I started explaining it to Bahadur. I told him that Osvaldo had killed Elena's mother and adopted her in secret, that her real father was a montonero who had returned with a wild scheme to put Osvaldo on trial.

We had to suspend the conversation while we got on the Subte. The rush hour trains were packed beyond anything I'd seen in the States, owing to a more lenient concept of personal space and a sporting willingness to always take on one more person. We squeezed our way out at Estación Carlos Gardel, directly below the Abasto Mall, and I thought of Elena, a minute's detour away.

Instead of taking it, we climbed the long flight of stairs to Corrientes. I said, "When I'm with Elena or this montonero guy, the things they say sound almost reasonable." I hadn't used Mateo's name and was careful not to say anything that might compromise him. "Then I get some distance and wonder what the hell I was thinking."

We came up onto the sidewalk and I oriented myself by the one-way traffic, turning to face the oncoming headlights.

"I don't know how crazy it is," Bahadur said. "Maybe this guy Osvaldo needs to be killed."

I was surprised enough to stop in the middle of the sidewalk and stare. The stranger behind me nearly ran into me. "Are you serious?"

"Perfectly." He motioned me on. "Keep walking, I'm hungry. You come from a country with no history, no wisdom of its own. And so you expect government to do everything for you. You expect the police and the courts to deliver justice. Not here. In Latin America the regular guy in the street knows he must avoid dealing with the police at any cost. And God help anyone who ends up in court. In India it is the same. There we have had civilization for more than five thousand years. Buddhism started there. Hinduism, Sikhism started there. And of course Islam is huge there, we have the second largest Muslim population in the world. We don't look to the government for justice. We all of us look to our own beliefs. If we have to, we carry out justice ourselves. Like with Indira Gandhi."

I shook my head. "I remember that she was assassinated..."

"She was executed. She ordered an attack on our holiest site. It was the last in a long series of betrayals. We were promised our own homeland, Khalistan, and for the crime of reminding her of that, she sent her army to desecrate the Golden Temple. So two of her body-guards, who were loyal Sikhs, executed her."

"Elena was right," I said.

"About what?"

"I'll tell you later. I thought Sikhs believed in peace."

"We are peaceable but not passive. Most of my uncles and cous-ins on my mother's side are soldiers. Sikh soldiers are famous for their discipline and courage. The Guru Granth Sahib, which is our scripture and our teacher, tells us to live in peace with one another. It tells us to work honestly and share the fruits of our labors. And not everyone agrees, but I also believe it tells us not to eat meat or drink alcohol when it says, 'Use only what is necessary.' Above all, it teaches equality, toleration, and justice. Where there is injustice, we are required to take a stand."

He reached into his turban and rooted around there, finally com-ing out with a small dagger in a sheath. The blade was the length of my index finger.

"This is symbolic," he said, "but a very important symbol, yes? It is the kirpan, the strapped sword, that all Sikhs are required to carry. We are soldiers in the army of God. We are charged to actively prevent violence to those who cannot defend themselves and the kirpan is a reminder of that."

As he put the knife away, I said, "Doesn't that mean that if you knew about the kidnapping you would be required to stop it?"

"That depends. If the person being kidnapped is innocent and defenseless, yes. If the person being kidnapped is a violent criminal, maybe I would be required to help."

After a block or so of silence, I had to ask, "How do you reconcile all that with those crime films you love so much? They're nothing but violence."

Bahadur laughed. "Crime films are always about justice. Not the justice of the government, the justice of the individual."

"I'm going to ask you what I asked the montonero. How do you know the difference between justice and revenge?"

"What did he say?"

"He said it's not easy to tell."

"He is not Sikh. I would chant the names of God and that would

free me from attachment to anger or ego or my own personal desires. When I was done, I would see clearly what I had to do."

"I guess I envy you that."

"You have no religious beliefs at all?"

"I don't seem to have the ability to believe in a divine being.
Especially when I look at the world around me. Infants with AIDS.
Enron. War in Iraq. The dictatorship here. Torture. Where is God in
all of that?"

Bahadur touched his chest. "Here. God is in the pain those things
cause you."

LOS SABIOS IS SHORT on atmosphere—fluorescent lights, linoleum floor, two rows of steam tables, signs everywhere warning of
dire consequences if you take more than you can finish. The own-
ers are Asian and they always have several traditional Chinese dishes
like dumplings and fried tofu, but also pizza, casseroles, a row of raw
vegetables, and one slice of lemon meringue pie per person, the pie
closely guarded at the register.

"So what was Elena right about?" Bahadur was on his third plate-
ful while I still picked at my first. My appetite had been mostly
theoretical for days.

"The montonero is short of jurors for Osvaldo," I said. "Elena
thought you'd be good. I told her she'd flipped her wig."

"Wait, I know this one. Flipped her wig is like wigged out, yes?"

"More or less."

"Yes, she was right. I will chant and meditate on this and get back
to you."

"Bahadur—"

"Don't worry. I can't flip my wig, I have a turban to hold it
down."

"This is not your fight. I'm not sure it's anyone's fight. You
wouldn't get involved in a battle you knew for sure you would lose,
would you?"

"Yes," Bahadur said. "But because you can only do that once, you
want to make sure it's truly the right battle."

I WAS HOME before ten. I fell asleep in my clothes waiting for
Elena and woke up when she crawled into bed next to me. I mum-
bled something like, «Did you want to go out?»

«Shhh,» she said. «Stay exactly where you are. I will help you get undressed.»

The bedroom was dark and I was half asleep. Her touch was soft and slow as a dream and it was a long time before I realized that she was naked too, and by then my nose was full of the sweet smell of her hair, which was falling all over me, and she was everywhere, enveloping me with her need. I knew that what drove it was fear and the nearness of death, if not hers, then Osvaldo's. The touch of our bodies was the antidote to the whole wretched list of godless injustices I had given Bahadur, and I wanted nothing more in the world than to keep her out of Mateo's plan.

SHE HAD TO BE at work at 9:30 the next morning. I slept in and forced myself to eat a little breakfast and then I left a message for Mateo. He called back a half hour later and agreed to meet me in Parque Lezama at 1 PM, near the cats.

He arrived in the same clothes I'd last seen him in, and his hair was none too clean. He was freshly shaved, though, and looked fit and rested. I stood up to give him an abrazo and he said, «Let's walk.»

We headed deeper into the park, where the noise of families surrounded us. «I only have one thing to say,» I told him. «If you're her father, and you love her, how can you be so willing to endanger her life? You would risk her being shot by the police, or caught and sent to prison for the rest of her life. What kind of father would want that for his daughter?»

He was quiet so long I began to wonder if he'd heard me. Finally he said, «I've been a father for a month. The rest of my life, since I was in school, it's been the struggle. The one thing I know how to do. The other...I don't even get the chance to learn. I look at her, I can only see my Elena. I don't know who this other person is. My brain is fucked. I can't make sense of anything.»

He stopped and faced me. «That's it? Nothing else?»

«Nothing else,» I said.

He hugged me again and said, «I will call you and tell you what I decide.»

THAT NIGHT WE DANCED at La Ideal, danced beyond exhaustion, into a kind of ecstasy. The glamour and the music and the perfume, the glittering marble and the welcoming arms of all those partners drove everything else from our minds. We slept most of Sunday and danced again at Don Güicho's milonga Sunday night. Monday night we went to a movie at a huge theater on Corrientes, Tuesday night we went shopping at the book and record stores on Calle Florida near el Obelisco, Wednesday night we went to El Beso, all in an unspoken conspiracy to avoid the phone call that we both knew was coming.

Thursday we had class with Don Güicho. Back at home, while I was fixing dinner, Elena's cell phone rang.

I heard her fish it out of her purse. «It's Mateo,» she said. «Should I answer?»

«If you want to.»

«¿Hola?» She brought the phone into the kitchen and listened with one arm around my waist. Then she looked at me. «He says I should tell this to you as he says it...He says he has considered what you said to him on Saturday.» She took her hand from my waist and used it to cover the phone. «This is a conversation I don't know about, so I look forward to you explaining it to me.»

Uh oh, I thought. I felt her missing arm like an amputation.

Mateo was still talking. Elena said, «He says he has a compromise. He wants you to take me to dinner tomorrow night. Nine o'clock. Someplace small in the neighborhood, maybe around Plaza Dorrego.»

«Why? What is he planning?»

She repeated the question and then said, «He says better that we don't know. That way we are not part of a conspiracy. Nothing will happen to us, he says, everything will happen somewhere else.»

«Maybe you could call him back in a few minutes.»

She relayed the message and turned off the phone. She took a step backward, all the kitchen would allow, and folded her arms on her chest, waiting for me.

I rinsed my hands and dried them on a dishtowel. «I called him on Saturday and met him in the park,» I said, not meeting her eyes. «I asked him not to involve you in this. I asked him, because he's your father, not to risk your life.»

She didn't raise her voice. «And you did this without discussing it with me first and without even telling me about it after.»

I felt a wave of guilt so powerful that it made me want to wriggle out from under it. «It was...» I started, and then I said, «The only reason I...»

Finally I put the towel down and faced her. «I screwed up. I'm sorry.»

«I don't need you to be my father. I have at least one too many of them already. I don't need you to protect me or decide what's best for me. I need you to be my lover. For that I have to trust you completely.»

«Okay.»

«I thought you understood that. I thought you understood why that's so important to me.»

«I'm afraid,» I said. «Afraid for you, afraid for us.»

«Without trust, there *is* no us. There can't be any more secrets. No more talking behind my back.»

«Okay. I should tell you that I talked to Bahadur last week. About Mateo. I never said his name, just that he was a montonero.»

«That's different. That's not interfering with my choices. Besides, I trust Bahadur.»

«You were right about him. He would make a good juror for Mateo.»

She nodded, not yet ready to let me off the hook. «What about tomorrow night?»

«I don't want anything to do with it. I don't trust Mateo. He's violent and he thinks with his emotions and not with his common sense. Which is nice for some things, but dangerous when you're committing crimes of this magnitude.»

«I don't disagree with you. But I feel like I have to be a part of it. No, I am a part of it, I was born into it. What Mateo suggests sounds like a reasonable compromise. What harm can come from us eating dinner in a quiet restaurant? As long as I know that I have helped, that will be enough. And I can do it alone. You don't have to be involved.»

«Yes I do. I *am* involved.» I needed to touch her, like needing a drug. I put one hand around her neck and buried my fingers in her hair. She tolerated my touch without responding.

«Beto, I'm not angry, but I'm still a little hurt, do you understand?»

«Yes,» I said. I took my hand away.

«I should do this alone.»

«I feel like you're punishing me for betraying you.»

«I'm not punishing you. Beto, if anything happened to you, I couldn't stand it.»

«I feel exactly the same way. But you won't stay away from this trouble, so there's nothing else I can do.»

We stood there, me telling myself that this was no more than a bump in the road, telling myself not to freak out. It was just that the stakes were so high. The issues came back to the thing that had made her run from me in the first place, the thing that I didn't have the history for.

Agonizing as the moment was, I didn't want it to end. It was ending even as I thought about it. Time was pulling us forward.

«The place we ate that first afternoon,» I said. «When we walked in Plaza Dorrego.»

«When you bought me the necklace.»

«That sounds like what he's looking for. I don't remember the name. It's on the corner of Estados Unidos and Defensa.»

«Should I call him?»

«Call him,» I said.

AFTER THE PHONE CALL, Elena sat on the couch, looking at her hands.

«Do you want to talk?»

«Gracias,» she said. Meaning no, like in tango.

I showered and went to bed. I read for an hour and turned out the light at midnight and lay on my back with my hands behind my head. As a matter of discipline I did not let myself look at the clock. Sometime later Elena got in next to me. She turned me onto my side, facing away from her, and held me tight. «I love you, Beto,» she said.

I fell asleep in her arms.

I NEVER STOPPED thinking about it as Friday wore on, alternating between nerves and wishful thinking. Was there a way out? Maybe nothing would happen, maybe this was only some kind of test.

The thing that worried me most was Mateo's insistence that we sit by the window, that Elena be visible from Calle Defensa. That didn't fit with his assurance that everything would happen somewhere else.

Elena's schedule at the shoe store changed every week. That Friday she was supposed to be off at six, and we were both home before seven. We showered and dressed, with the idea that we might

go dancing after dinner. If in fact the dinner proved as uneventful as
Mateo had promised.

We left the apartment at 8:30, both of us too nervous to sit still. We
had our shoe bags, and an umbrella as a charm against possible rain.

On the street it was hot and still, the end of the first really warm
day of the spring. We crossed over to Calle Estados Unidos and I
saw a fresh graffito, black spray paint on the corrugated steel shutters
enclosing a shop front: Apparición con vida/Julio López.

We walked around Plaza Dorrego, pretending to look through a
box of used books. Everything was blue—the canvas backs of the
chairs outside the cafés, the Quilmes beer logos in the windows, the
turquoise in Elena's necklace, the Boca Juniors futbol jersey on one
of the crafters, the Argentine flag in the window of an antique store.

We got to the restaurant exactly at 9:00. All the tables by the window were taken. We told the waiter that we really wanted to sit by
the window and that we would wait. We spent fifteen minutes at the
bar, long enough for Elena to drink a glass of wine. We both talked
about work. She asked if I had "Poema" by Canaro on CD and said
she wanted to dance it with me. There were awkward silences.

One of the couples near the front door left and the waiter motioned us over. He brought us menus and a basket of bread. The
window was open to the street behind ornamental wrought iron
bars spaced a foot apart. I smelled dust and cigarette smoke. Every
sort of improbable disaster seemed imminent. What if Mateo were
sitting on the second floor of the building across the street, in the
advanced stages of lunacy, with a rifle aimed at Elena? What if he'd
contrived to drop us into a frame-up of some kind to ensure our
loyalty? My stomach felt like it was full of wet cement. I couldn't
imagine putting food on top of it.

I ordered ravioli for show. Elena asked for a salad and chicken
parmigiana, then helped herself to a second roll. She was flushed
around the neck and I realized with sadness that the possibility of
danger had excited her.

It was 9:45. There were not many customers and the waiters stood
talking at the bar. Elena reached for my hand and held it in the
middle of the table. «I know this is hard for you, querida,» she said.
Her voice was so quiet I could barely make out the words. «I know
you're feeling powerless right now. It's the very opposite for me. I've
been in that man's power all my life, and to know that he is now in

danger, that everything is being turned around on him, is so...liberating, I can't tell you.»

I nodded glumly and squeezed her hand.

«You don't even know,» she said, «the damage it does to you until you start to get free of it. It's this shadow over everything.»

Distant car doors slammed. I glanced out the window. The half-dozen people on the street had turned to stare down Calle Estados Unidos, in the direction of our apartment. They were looking at a man running toward us, still half a block away. He wore dark, creased slacks, a white shirt, and a green and yellow knitted sweater vest. He had thinning white hair, combed straight back. He looked ferocious and obsessed, and he was staring straight at me.

No, not at me. At Elena.

She saw my reaction and followed my gaze. The life drained out of her face.

«It's him, isn't it?» I said.

She nodded.

«Something's gone wrong,» I said. I felt like I was skidding across black ice.

Two men chased Osvaldo. They were young, in dark T-shirts and jeans, black hair, one with stubble on his face, the other clean shaven. They were almost to the intersection of Calle Defensa when they caught him. They each grabbed one of his arms. He strained toward us, falling forward, yelling, «¡Elena! ¡Elena!»

A black taxi, all its lights out, squealed to a stop in front of them. The man driving had a red bandana over the bottom of his face, like the Zapatistas in Mexico. It was Mateo. He reached back and threw open the rear door of the cab. The two men dragged and pushed Osvaldo inside, banging his head against the top of the open door.

A woman across the street screamed. The people at the table next to us stood up and pointed. The waiter came over to look as the taxi pulled away, the door flapping.

A young, long-haired man yelled something and chased the cab on foot. The street was dissolving into chaos, more and more people running outside, pointing and shouting to each other.

I threw a wad of pesos on the table and grabbed our things. «Come on,» I said to Elena. Her eyes were filmed over, her lips half-way open. «The cops will be here any minute.»

I led her outside and into the thick of the crowd, which was growing larger by the second. Everyone was talking at once.

«What happened? Who was he?»

«He was shouting a name. 'Elena,' he said.»

«Did anyone see their faces?»

«Call the police. We need to call the police.»

Somebody pointed. «He looked like he was headed for that restaurant, over there.»

A cop ran toward us from the north end of Defensa, talking into his radio.

«Follow me,» I said into Elena's ear.

I let the new arrivals move past us, keeping us on the southern edge of the expanding mob. I waited until the cop had his back turned, looking at the open window where we'd been sitting, and then I led Elena away, keeping my head down and turning away from the Plaza onto a side street, then crossing over to the lights and crowds of Avenida San Juan. When I was sure that we weren't being followed, I took her back to the apartment.

Once we were inside, I double-locked the door and leaned against it. My heart was doing somersaults. Elena hadn't said anything since she'd seen Osvaldo. She stood in the middle of the living room, her back to me, the purse dangling from her hand.

When I had my breath, I went quietly up to her and put a hand on her shoulder. «Elena? Are you—?»

She turned on me. Her eyes were still out of focus, her hands trembling as she reached for me. She grabbed handfuls of my hair and kissed me hard, took my lower lip between her teeth and began to tug at my clothes. I had never seen her so crazed.

The feeling was contagious. I picked her up and carried her into the bedroom as she scratched my back and bit my ear.

AFTERWARD WE WERE both starved. We ate leftovers standing in front of the refrigerator and then we picked up the clothes that we'd scattered over the apartment. Only then did I notice the message light on my cell phone.

The message was from Mateo and it consisted of two words: Lo tenemos.

We have him.

•

ELENA CALLED MATEO BACK. He cautioned her not to use any names. The person in question was in isolation. They would begin testimony the next day. If she wanted to be part of it, he would meet her and take her to the place. She should call him at noon to let him know.

Elena and I talked for an hour in bed, holding each other. My head hurt and I couldn't find a position for my neck that felt remotely natural. I had taken Ibuprofen and was concentrating on my breathing.

The talk was a formality leading to a foregone conclusion. I did what I could to talk her out of it and failed. I warned her that there were limits that I would not be able to go past. I meant participating in the actual killing, but as I finally drifted into sleep I wondered if there truly were any limits left to what I would do.

WE MET MATEO outside the San Juan Subte entrance. He was on the south side of the street, wearing a battered black leather jacket and a flat cap. He gave no indication that he'd seen us, starting down the stairs as we crossed the street. We stood a few yards from each other on the platform and got onto the same car of the northbound C line. At the next stop he got off and we followed him down the long, gray concrete passage that ran under the expanse of Avenida 9 de Julio. We got onto the parallel E line and rode two more stops.

We came up onto the street at the northern edge of San Telmo, another part of the neighborhood that was in transition from slum to tourist attraction. We were two blocks from La Trastienda, a big, US-style rock venue where the Fernandez Fierro tango orquesta had a weekly gig. All around us were neon signs and plate glass windows retrofitted onto nineteenth century architecture, while crumbling buildings stood empty on either side.

Mateo led us into a tiny grocery store with a single aisle of wooden shelves holding canned goods, bread, and aging produce. From behind the register, a heavyset man in a white apron gave Mateo a barely perceptible nod. We walked straight through the shop and out the back door into a small courtyard, open to the blue sky and surrounded by three stories of apartments. The floor was orange tile, and red and yellow flowers stood in pots along the walls. An open stairway led up to the apartments, and under the stairs was a door. Mateo opened it and started down a flight of concrete steps inside.

I closed the door after us and had to stop to let my eyes adjust. What light there was came from two bare, low-wattage bulbs hanging from the ceiling by their electrical wires.

At the bottom of the stairs I saw that we were in a large, bare concrete basement, white paint peeling off the walls. In one corner was another door, this one fitted with an incongruously bright lock mechanism. Mateo opened it with the typical big brass lever lock key that was still in use everywhere in the city and then took an oversized flashlight from where he'd had it hanging inside the waistband of his trousers.

«Watch your step,» he said, herding us inside, and shone the light on a flight of makeshift plank stairs that led still farther underground. We waited on the landing while he locked the door and then followed him down.

We were in some kind of disused tunnel. The roof was a red brick arch fifteen feet high and the uneven dirt floor was thirty feet wide. As my eyes continued to adjust, I saw columns of sunlight filtering down in the distance. It was not a single tunnel as much as a complex of sub-cellars, passages, and galleries.

«What is this place?» Elena whispered.

«It's from the nineteenth century,» Mateo said. «Some archeologists from the university started to restore it during the sixties. When Ongania took over, the government money went away and everybody forgot about it. There are tunnels everywhere in San Telmo. Not all connected, unfortunately. This way.»

I tried to pay attention to the route we took, in case I had to bring Elena out on my own. After a few twists and turns I gave up. I was completely lost and anyway, I had no key to get us past the locked doors. We walked for what must have been two or three blocks, mostly on uneven dirt, sometimes on brick or paving stones, sometimes on concrete walkways next to pools of oily, fetid water.

Eventually we climbed another rickety flight of stairs, passed through another locked door, and emerged into another basement. This one was long and narrow, with a steep ramp that led through massive double doors into a windowless, green-walled room full of giant, rusting machinery. The machines ran along both sides of a beautiful old wooden floor the sandy red color of unfinished mahogany. From the occasional missing chunks, I saw that the floorboards were two inches thick.

«You could tango here, no?» Mateo said. «Maybe later.» I couldn't tell if he was trying to be funny.

I looked up into a twenty-foot-square hole in the ceiling, surrounded by railings. Mateo took us up a set of stairs made of the same rich hardwood. We came out into the room that looked down on the machinery and I stopped to get my bearings.

The roof was another thirty feet above me. The lower windows had been covered in plywood and the upper windows were reinforced with chicken wire and years of dirt, letting in light but no recognizable view.

I counted eight people besides Mateo, Elena, and me, distributed among furniture that had been salvaged from the street—chairs, two couches, a folding card table, and another low table that held a pile of gravel and a stack of papers weighed down by a pistol.

The sight of the gun chilled me, took me out of my numb acceptance and reminded me of what was about to happen.

I recognized the two men who'd been chasing Osvaldo. There were two women, one small, with short curly dark hair, the other with spiky blonde hair and a muscular body. A man with a dark beard and an orange skull cap dozed on one of the couches. A large, older man with a reddish beard played cards with a boy who was clearly the 16-year-old that Mateo had mentioned.

Equally clearly, the last man was one of the surviving montoneros from the old days. He was one of the most dangerous-looking human beings I had ever seen. I guessed him to be in his sixties. His graying hair was shaved nearly to the skull. He had severe acne scars and a scar on his lower lip and chin that was not from acne. His sunken eyes had given up human emotion as a waste of energy. He had a ring in one ear and an ageing tattoo of a crucified Jesus on his right bicep, clearly visible where the sleeves of his T-shirt had been ripped away. He carried a service automatic, butt forward, clipped to the left side of his belt. Because of the tattoo I named him Jesús in my head.

«No introductions,» Mateo said. «Everybody knows more or less who everyone is.»

«Where's Osvaldo?» Elena asked. Her voice had a harshness I'd never heard before.

«We are still letting him figure out what he's made of,» Jesús said.

«What went wrong last night?» I asked. «You promised us nothing would happen anywhere close to us, and Osvaldo nearly came through the window of the restaurant.»

«There were...complications,» Mateo said.

I showed him my open palms in the universal gesture for "what the hell?" He sighed and reluctantly told the story.

ONE OF THEIR newest recruits was the clean-shaven kid that we'd seen chasing Osvaldo. Mateo called him Raul.

Raul had phoned Osvaldo two weeks before. He said he was dating Elena and they were becoming very serious about one another. He said that Elena talked about Osvaldo all the time, and he felt she wanted to reconcile with him, only she wasn't sure how to go about it. Osvaldo had swallowed it and they had talked several more times. Finally Raul had proposed that Osvaldo "accidentally" find them at dinner. He was sure she would be thrilled and take the opportunity to make up with him.

Mateo was convinced this would get Osvaldo out of the house without a bodyguard, at night, when they could ambush him. Elena's job was to be visible from outside the restaurant in case Osvaldo sent someone to check.

But Osvaldo had fooled them. He had forwarded his home phone to the office and taken the call there. By the time Mateo realized it, Osvaldo had a head start. Mateo called Raul and got him and another man outside the restaurant, and even then Osvaldo had nearly gotten away.

I kept my mouth shut, though the sheer amateurishness of the operation made me want to panic. What confidence I had in Mateo was shaken. I wondered when the police would break the doors down.

«So,» Elena said, «what happens now?»

«I'll go get him,» Mateo said. «We might as well get started.»

WE SAT IN awkward silence while Mateo was gone. Jesús had slumped deeply into the remains of a stuffed chair and he stared alternately at me and Elena. There might have been the edge of a smile on the deformed mouth.

I told myself that I was not in immediate danger. The hideout was probably secure enough and I was no threat to anyone. But the guns reminded me that the possibility of mayhem was no more than an instant away. I forced my shoulders down and pushed air into my lungs, told the pain in my right eye that eventually this would be over.

Mateo came back. He too had a gun now, a big-framed revolver that he held to the back of Osvaldo's head. I couldn't see Osvaldo's face because he wore a hood that had been improvised from an old navy-blue sweatshirt. He had been left to piss in his clothes, and he smelled of that and sour sweat. His hands were cuffed behind him and his feet were tied together with a short rope that forced him to take baby steps.

I looked at Elena. Part of her had needed to see this humiliation and part of her, I was relieved to see, was shamed by it. Her mouth was a hard line and her hands clutched each other in her lap.

Across the room, the red-bearded man looked uncomfortable too, as if he hadn't been prepared for the reality of what he'd signed up for.

Mateo put Osvaldo against the railing, facing away from the hole in the floor. He unlocked one cuff and relocked it so that the chain passed through the railing, then he picked up the papers from the low table. Through all of this, Osvaldo was silent and docile.

I saw then that the furniture was arranged in a rough semicircle to face the point where Osvaldo stood.

«Osvaldo del Salvador,» Mateo said.

«My name is Lacunza,» he said, with quiet dignity.

«No,» Mateo said, «it's not.» He began to read from the page. «You are accused—»

Osvaldo interrupted him, his voice again soft and clear. «Can you take this thing off my head? Can I at least see you?»

«No,» Mateo said.

Jesús said, «Justice is blind, old man.»

«Then you should be wearing the hood, not me.»

Mateo, annoyed, looked as if he might slap Osvaldo, except that between the papers and the gun, his hands were full. Instead he read, «You are accused of human rights violations including, but not limited to, conspiracy to kidnap, torture, and murder the following citizens of the Republic of Argentina.» He read a list of ten names, ending with Elena Bianchi. Even through the hood I saw Osvaldo react to that one.

«Is this supposed to be a trial, then?» Osvaldo said. «When do I get to consult with my defense counsel?»

Jesús said, «Your viewpoint will be heard. That's more than you gave your victims.»

Mateo read out the details of the accusations. They were like the summaries in *Nunca Mas*: This name kidnapped on this date, taken to Club Atlético. Tortured for this many days, months, years. Beaten. Raped. Starved. Died from shock. Died from injuries. Died when dropped from a helicopter into the ocean. Shot and buried in a mass grave.

Somewhere in the middle of it Elena reached for my hand. When Mateo got to the last name, she began to squeeze.

«Elena Bianchi. Kidnapped 19 January, 1975. Taken to...taken...»

He struggled to control his emotions and failed. Tears streamed down his face. Jesús went to him, hugged him, and took the papers from his hand.

Osvaldo had stood with his head high during the other nine accounts. When Mateo spoke Elena's name, Osvaldo's head fell forward. Then, when Mateo broke down, Osvaldo's head came up again.

«Mateo,» Osvaldo whispered. «You must be Mateo.»

JESÚS PICKED UP where Mateo had left off. «Taken to Club Atlético. Beaten, raped, and tortured for eight months. Gave birth in the detention center to a female child. Child stolen and illegally adopted. Subject killed and body disposed of by unknown means on or about 1 October, 1975.

«All of these crimes were committed at the orders of, or under the direct supervision of, or by the hand of the accused. Osvaldo del Salvador, how do you declare yourself, guilty or innocent?»

«This is not a trial,» Osvaldo said. «You are nothing more than kidnappers yourselves. And murderers, if you 'execute' me.»

Mateo had himself under control again. «When the state is unwilling or unable to deliver justice, then the people must do it for themselves.»

«The people? What people? You? How many of you are there? Four, five, half a dozen? You call this justice?»

«It is the only justice you have,» Jesús said.

«And you, Mateo,» Osvaldo said. «A murderer, a terrorist, a communist, a subversive, how can you sit in judgment on anyone? And how can you begin to claim objectivity?»

«I urge you to take advantage of this opportunity,» Mateo said.

«Regardless of what you think, we are not savages. You will be given every chance to account for your actions.»

«I have nothing to say to you,» Osvaldo said.

Jesús shrugged, apparently ready to get it over with. Mateo looked stunned. The rest of Mateo's group shifted in their seats, disappointed at not getting the high drama they'd bargained for. The silence dragged on and as Mateo was about to end it, Elena said, «Papá, you must speak to them.»

Inside the hood, Osvaldo's head swung around in the direction of her voice. «Elena? Dear God, you're part of this?»

«Talk to me, Papá. Tell me why you did it. Tell me why you killed my mother.»

The strength went out of his legs. He slid to his knees and then the strain of his arms, chained in place at the hands, pushed his head and shoulders forward until his forehead touched the floor in a kind of pained yoga pose.

He lay that way for an endless time, until Elena said, «Give him a chair.»

Mateo brought over a ladderback wooden chair. He undid Osvaldo's cuffs, repositioned him with the back of the chair against the railing, then cuffed him to the chair so that Osvaldo's arms were behind him and he could sit more or less normally.

Mateo came over to perch on the arm of the couch next to me. Osvaldo convulsed a couple of times and I realized he was choking back sobs. Finally he began to talk.

«I was 23 years old,» he said. «I was recruited for the Triple A from the Army. I wasn't given a choice. My commanding officer recommended me because I was disciplined, patriotic, and a devout Catholic. We believed then, all of us, that there was no greater danger in the world than Communism. We looked at it the way you would look now at AIDS or syphilis. It was an infection that corrupted and destroyed healthy minds. It was filthy, and so were many of the people who practiced it, with their beards and long hair and sores on their faces, their dirty, shabby clothes. Our officers told us they were no better than animals and we believed it.»

His voice was like a radio announcer's, his Spanish precise and easy to follow, the opposite of Jesús's, which I could barely understand. But the golden voice had run dry. In the silence I pictured him licking his parched lips, forcing himself to swallow.

«There were those of us who enjoyed the work. You could see that. The ones who enjoyed it too much were transferred out. I don't know what happened to them and I don't want to think about those men. I didn't like the work, mi Elena. I believed it was necessary. There were men from the CIA who trained us and they made us feel important, like we were psychologists—»

Jesús said, «Fucking hell! Psychologists?»

Mateo shook his head. «Let him talk.»

«After the first time I interrogated someone,» Osvaldo said, «I thought I would feel something. Shame, disgust, sympathy, something. I felt nothing. Nothing at all. It was a job.

«We learned skills. You had to know the background of the person to know how to best approach him. The idea was to take him back, through repeated shocks, to a childlike state. Until you became his parent and he gave all control to you.»

Jesús let us all see that he was disgusted, but didn't interrupt again.

«There was no...there was no normal. There was only the daily reality of the detention center, of the work. We all did it, we all pushed each other on, we made jokes, we competed with each other, we got drunk together afterward. We never talked about it to our wives, to our families, not to anybody who was not one of us.

«Even so, there were things I would not do. Raping the women. Even in the altered mental state of that place, I knew that was wrong. I accepted it, I didn't try to stop the others who were doing it. I looked the other way, and I ask God's forgiveness for that. But I never did it myself.»

His head turned inside the dark blue hood. I understood that he was trying to look at Elena. «I know you will think me contemptible for saying this. I know you have lost your own faith. Still, it is the truth. At the time I believed I was doing God's work. As the Jesuits had, as the Inquisition had. And God's work did not include rape.»

Mateo said, «But it did include torturing women.»

«I interrogated some women—»

«Tortured them, you mean.»

«—but not Elena.»

Mateo jumped up and stood over him, fists clenched. «How can I believe you, old man? Why should I?»

Mateo had left his gun on the couch. It was a foot away from me.

I could have picked it up and used it, if I'd had any idea of what to use it for.

Osvaldo said, «I'm not talking to you, Mateo. I'm talking to my daughter.»

«She's not your daughter, old man. She's mine.»

«I raised her,» Osvaldo said. «All you did was put your seed in her mother.»

As did so many others, was the implication.

I thought Mateo would kill him then. If he'd still had the gun in his hands, he might have. Osvaldo must have known the risk he took, but it didn't show in his posture.

Mateo drew his right fist back and then hesitated, long enough for Elena to go to him and gently take hold of his arm. They stood that way for a few long seconds, then Mateo let the arm fall to his side.

«Go on, Papá,» she said. «Tell me about my mother.»

«She had already been badly beaten when they brought her in. They took her to one of the cells and...»

«Raped her,» Elena said.

«Yes. It made me sick, in spite of my conditioning, even though I had let it happen to so many others. The other women, I could tell myself they were whores, they were criminals, communists, murderers.»

«But not my mother.»

«Not Elena. No.»

«You're a liar!» Mateo shouted. «You'd say anything now, to save your miserable life.»

«Would I?» Osvaldo said. «Then kill me right now. There's no one to stop you and I certainly don't care. Not anymore.»

Mateo turned away. He walked around the opening in the floor to the far side and stood with his back to us, leaning against the railing, mirroring Osvaldo.

With his arms cuffed behind him, Osvaldo could only gesture toward Elena with his head. «Look at her,» he said, though he couldn't see her himself, or see that Mateo was no longer looking. «Only a monster could torture someone who looked like that. I have done bad things, terrible things in my life, but I am not a monster.»

Jesús said, quietly, «How ugly does somebody have to be? For it to be okay to torture them?»

Mateo, from the far side of the hole, said, «Who did it, then? Who was the monster who did it?»

«No. I will not tell you his name. That's all over now.»

Mateo turned toward us. His face was hideous with rage. «It's...not...*over!*» he screamed. It was so loud that it must have been audible on the street.

Osvaldo ignored him and continued to point his head toward the last place he'd heard Elena's voice. «I tried to talk to her. I pleaded with her to tell them anything, everything she knew. She swore she knew nothing. We knew she was Mateo's lover. We wanted Mateo more than we wanted anyone else in Buenos Aires, because he had escaped us, because of the men he killed, because he was a ruthless and implacable enemy.»

Jesús said, «When did you know she was pregnant?»

Mateo turned his back again.

«She told the task group when they arrested her. They told the rest of us when they brought her in.»

«And you tortured her anyway.»

«Me personally, no. But yes, she was interrogated. If Mateo hadn't escaped, if he hadn't been in hiding, we would never have touched her. But as it was—»

Jesús walked up to Osvaldo and backhanded him. He did it without apparent anger and with terrible force, putting his whole body into it, and Osvaldo, who could not see the blow coming, was knocked completely out of his chair and his arms were jerked nearly out of their sockets by the handcuffs.

«Do not,» Jesús said calmly, «ever again, attempt to justify your atrocities by putting the blame on someone else. You are responsible for what you did. No one else. That's the reason we're here.»

It took Osvaldo a full minute to recover. Then, with infinite patience, he untangled himself, struggled to his feet, fumbled for the chair, set it back on its legs, and sat down again. He was trembling, and from the upright, even arrogant position of his head, I sensed he was embarrassed by that show of weakness.

Jesús said, «At what point did you decide to steal her baby?»

When Osvaldo didn't answer, Elena said, «Please keep talking, Papá.»

«She asked me...Elena...» Osvaldo was slurring his words and his concentration seemed shaky. The blow had been strong enough to loosen teeth and split his lips. «One night she said to me, 'You're going to take the baby, aren't you?' There was no way to keep the prisoners from talking to each other—in fact, we counted on it, because it made them more confused and afraid. So she had heard stories.

«I told her yes, we would take the baby, we couldn't let her keep it there, and we couldn't let her go until we had Mateo. And she said... she said, 'Please see that he gets a good home.' She was so sure it was going to be a boy. She was going to name it...»

He shook his head. «I felt like she was asking me to be responsible. So I took the baby myself. I think she would have wanted it that way.»

Jesús said, in a very reasonable tone, «I think she would have wanted not to be kidnapped, not to be separated from her lover, not to be raped, not to be tortured, not to be killed. That's just a guess.»

Osvaldo still showed no sign of having heard him. «I raised you the way I would have raised my own daughter. I gave you every advantage, a good home, the best schools, the best of everything—»

From across the pit Mateo said, «You gave her a broken nose, you shit.»

Osvaldo hesitated. After a second, he said, «An accident. She fell—»

«I've heard enough,» Mateo said, cutting him off again.

Osvaldo sat back stiffly in his chair.

In the silence, Jesús said, «Are there any other questions for the accused?»

He looked at Elena and Elena said, «Papá, did you kill Marco Suarez?»

If the question surprised him, it was not obvious through the hood. «No,» Osvaldo said. «Cesarino found out Suarez was on a witness list and was afraid he would talk. He wanted me to make him disappear, like the old days. I told him I was too old, that I had put that behind me. He threatened me and I put him off and put him off, and finally he sent some of his policemen to do it.»

«Do you know where the body is?» Elena asked. «For the sake of his family.»

«I've told you everything I know. I refused to have anything to do with it.»

Elena looked at Jesús, shrugged, and looked at the floor.

Jesús said, «Anybody else?» He pointed to me and I shook my

head. Then he pointed to each of the others in turn, and they all passed except for the small woman with the short dark hair.

She said, «Was it worth it?»

«I don't understand,» Osvaldo said.

«All the people you tortured. Did you get the answers you wanted? Did it make a difference in the end? I'm not asking what you thought then, I want to know what you think now, today.»

Osvaldo didn't say anything for a long time and when he did, he only said, «I think—» and then he changed his mind and said, «I don't know.»

Jesús looked at Mateo. Mateo reached into his pocket and took out the keys to the handcuffs. He threw them across the gap in the floor and Jesús grabbed them one-handed out of the air.

Macho, grandstanding assholes, I thought. I was sick with fear.

Jesús unlocked the cuffs, disentangled Osvaldo from the chair, and cuffed both wrists behind his back again. Osvaldo tried to keep his dignity as Jesús marched him out of the room, but he was still shaking and the rope tied to his ankles made him stumble.

The two women talked in hushed voices with the Middle-Eastern man. Mateo had turned his back again. I still had hold of Elena's hand, but I couldn't look at her.

Jesús came back alone. «Discussion?» he said.

«Let's vote,» Mateo said.

«Any objections?» Jesús asked. No one raised a hand. «You guys would never have been montoneros in the old days,» he said. «In the old days we would argue all night long. There would be shouting and tears and at least one fistfight.»

«Fuck the old days,» Mateo said. «Let's do this.»

Jesús went to the pile of small stones and began to count them out. «Bueno. There are ten of us, counting Elena, so it will take six votes to convict.»

«Eleven,» Mateo said. «Beto votes too.»

I said, «I don't—»

Mateo cut me off. «He's at risk as much as the rest of us. Besides, we're supposed to represent the people. Everyone votes, or it's not justice.»

«You want to give Osvaldo a vote too?» Jesús asked. Mateo glared at him and Jesús shrugged. «Bueno, eleven, then. It still takes six votes to convict.» He walked around the room, handing out stones to each of us in turn. «Put both hands behind your back. Bring one hand out with the fist closed. If it has a rock in it, you're voting for death. Empty, you vote to acquit. Like declaring high or low in poker, no? Nobody shows until everyone has decided. No changing your mind. Rock means death, empty hand is life. Clear?»

He handed me a stone and I rolled it around in my hand. It was the size of a marble, made of quartzite, cloudy white, its edges rounded from centuries in a river somewhere. If I voted, did that make me responsible when the others condemned him to die? I couldn't concentrate, couldn't keep from being distracted by trivialities. Where did the rocks come from? Who had gone out looking for them? Were any of them original montonero rocks from the 1970s? Had they voted this way back then?

Jesús was in good spirits now that we were getting close to the killing part, as if it really were no more than a poker game and he was winning. How many times had he done this? How many men had he condemned? How many had he killed with his own hands?

Mateo took a stone from Jesús and went to stand by the railing.

My hands shook as I put them behind my back.

Elena was still staring at her rock. Everyone else had their hands behind them.

«Elena?» Mateo said.

She looked up, startled, then took the rock behind her back.

Jesús waited until all eyes were on him, then he said, «Ready?»

There were nods and murmurs. I felt my pulse in the constriction of my throat, hard and erratic. We each held out a fist.

«I'll go first,» Jesús said. He produced the rock like a magician revealing a red foam ball and tossed it on the pile, where it clattered in the stillness. «That's one,» he said.

He pointed at the 16-year-old, who held his closed hand straight out and slowly opened it to show the stone.

«Two,» Jesús said.

He pointed to the red bearded man, who suddenly looked like he wanted to change his mind.

«What?» Jesús said. The red bearded man wouldn't meet Jesús's eyes. He slowly opened his empty hand, then sat back in his chair with his head down.

Jesús shook his head in disgust. «Next?»

The small dark woman showed an empty hand. The spiky haired blonde showed a stone.

«Three,» Jesús said. He pointed to the man in the skull cap. When his hand came up empty, Jesús stared at him for long, agonizing seconds, as if expecting an apology. Finally the man in the skull cap looked away.

Jesús pointed at Raul. A stone.

«Four.»

The other man who had chased Osvaldo showed a stone.

«Five. Just one more.»

I showed my empty palm and looked at Elena. Her hand was straight out in front of her and she was shaking, the tendons showing in her knuckles from the strength of her grip. She turned the hand over and opened the fingers.

Empty.

Jesús pointed to Mateo and then started to turn away, taking the final death vote for granted, when Mateo raised his fist to shoulder height and, as if releasing some tiny captive creature into the air, showed his empty palm.

IN THE FIRST, shocked silence, I felt something like relief. Then Jesús exploded. «You fucking idiot! What have you done?»

Mateo shrugged. «I thought, is this the best we can do? To kill this pathetic old man? Is this really the face of evil? Besides, I knew the rest of you would outvote me.»

«Well, you got *that* wrong,» Jesús said. «Now what are we supposed to do?»

«I don't care what we do with him. I suppose we have to let him go.»

Jesús said, «If we let him go, he'll come after us with everything he's got.»

«He's wanted me dead for thirty years,» Mateo said. «Nothing's changed.»

«Everything's changed. He now knows you're alive, that you're here in Buenos Aires, that you're operating again. He knows that Elena knows where you are.»

«He would never hurt me,» Elena said.

Jesús stared at her with burning eyes. «Are you willing to stake your life on that? How about your friend Beto's life?»

«He doesn't know Beto was here,» Mateo said.

«He saw Beto in the restaurant,» Jesús said. «Remember?» The word carried a world of blame.

For the first time I wondered if I'd made a mistake. My vote had saved Osvaldo as much as Mateo's had. I remembered the fierce look on Osvaldo's face as he charged the restaurant, his haughty dignity under the hood, the things he had done at the Club Atlético. He would be a relentless enemy.

But then I would have condemned the father of the woman I loved.

«He would not go after Beto either,» Elena said. «En absoluto.» Absolutely not.

I wished I had her confidence.

«I'll get his word that he will not pursue you, or any of your friends,» Mateo said to Elena. «I'll make it clear that it's a condition of his release.»

«His *word*?» Jesús said. His voice was getting louder by the minute. He stood in front of the low table with his arms folded and legs spread wide, his right hand inches away from his gun.

«He will honor it,» Elena said.

«Can you not bring me into it?» I said.

«Don't worry, Beto,» Mateo said. «We are not complete boludos.»

«How the fuck would he know that?» Jesús said. «Judging by last night's fiasco and today's 'trial'?»

«Let it go!» Mateo shouted at him. «What's done is done. If you want to go ahead and kill him anyway, if that's what your idea of justice has become, go ahead and do it, I don't give a shit.»

The two of them stared at each other, and I wondered if Jesús would get his fistfight after all. Or if one of them would reach for a gun.

Jesús looked away first. «So what do you want to do,» he said, «dump him in the countryside somewhere?»

«No. Wait until late tonight and leave him at his house. If he doesn't have to ask for help, if he doesn't have to go around explaining what happened, maybe...?»

«Maybe,» Jesús sneered. «Maybe.»

«I'll do it myself. None of the rest of you have to be involved.» He looked around the room, staring into each of the faces in turn. Nobody spoke.

«Bueno,» he said. «It's settled, then.» He turned and gestured to Elena and me to stand up. «Let's go.»

HE TOOK US out the way we'd come in. Elena held my hand without speaking, tears still running down her face.

«What happened up there?» I asked Mateo. «What made you change your mind?»

He pointed to Elena. «Seeing how much he loved her. How much he loved her mother. Once you see yourself in your enemy, you're lost.»

«I can't forgive him,» Elena said. «I don't think I ever will. But I kept thinking of something Beto said to me. And I realized that I can't pass judgment on him. I have to leave that to God.»

«God,» Mateo said. «God is behind in his work.»

MATEO LEFT US in the courtyard behind the market. He hugged us both, holding on to Elena for a long time. «Each time I let you go,» he said, «I don't know if I'll ever see you again.»

«You'll see me,» she said. «Why wouldn't you?»

Mateo shook his head and disappeared through the door under the stairs.

When we were on the street, Elena kissed me, a sad, exhausted kiss. «I owe you, Beto. I will never forget this. When you need something from me, you only have to ask. Anything, you understand? Anything.»

I put two fingers to her beautiful mouth. «You talk as if I had a choice. Let's go home.»

«Yes, please. I want to sleep all day and then go out and dance until the sun comes up again.»

ELENA SLEPT, but I couldn't. I should have been grateful to be home and safe, to be no more than an accessory after the fact to a kidnapping rather than an active party to conspiracy and murder. If Elena was right, I had nothing more to worry about.

In fact I felt like there was an icepick in my right eye and my neck had been wrung like a wet towel, twisted into a knotted, lumpy mass.

I untangled myself from her sleeping body and did some yoga in the living room. I ate and then read for a while on the couch. When I did finally doze off I dreamed it was me that was running up Calle

Estados Unidos, terrified, footsteps pounding behind me and getting closer by the second.

WE DANCED at El Beso until five in the morning, mostly with each other. By the end I was in an altered state of consciousness where the music blew me around and around the dance floor like a paper sailboat on a sun-drenched lake. Only when "La cumparsita" finally played and we changed our shoes and found ourselves in the street did I think to look behind me.

We ate the traditional post-tango breakfast of medialunas and got home as the sun was coming up. We slept all day and only got up to go to Don Güicho's milonga Sunday night. Afterward we showered and made love for what seemed like hours and when we were both completely spent, she said, «It's going to be okay now, Beto, wait and see. It's over.»

I ENDED UP at work Monday morning with my internal clock completely confounded, my nerves frazzled, and my head hurting. I was profoundly grateful to have a series of clear, understandable tasks in front of me that no lives depended on.

For lunch I took Bahadur to a tiny café up the street. There, over empanadas, I told him quietly how I'd spent my weekend. I left out specifics about the tunnels and the abandoned building and didn't describe any of the montoneros.

"You should have called me," Bahadur said. "I could have been on your jury."

"Would you have voted to kill him?"

"Since I wasn't there, it's hard to know for sure, but probably, yes."

"You say that so easily."

"He was a torturer and a murderer. Just because he was one of many, or because he maybe had a soft place for Elena's mother, does not excuse it. We are each of us responsible for our own actions, we each make our own decisions. Not God, not our commanding officers, nobody but ourselves."

LATE THAT AFTERNOON, Isabel, La Reina, dropped by my cubicle. «I just wanted you to know that I emailed that file to Jim and asked him for an explanation. I haven't heard back from him yet. As soon as I do, I'll let you know.»

«Thank you,» I said.

I finished work at seven. Elena had phoned to tell me that she was making a special dinner. I thought I would read for a while afterward and have an early night.

I took the Subte home as usual, and my legs hurt as I climbed up to the street. I remember stopping at the top of the stairs to take it all in: the last, fading light of the day, a cool, traffic-flavored breeze from the direction of el Obelisco, a woman's laughter from somewhere behind me, a splash of red and yellow from the magazines at the corner kiosk, and I remember thinking that it was truly beginning to feel like home.

THEY WERE WAITING for me as I turned the corner onto Humberto Primo. Four of them stood by the car, a late model Ford, and though it wasn't a Falcon, it was green and my brain made the connection. I was instantly terrified.

The men wore the kind of pretend-soldier clothes favored by militia types in the US—camo pants and jackets, white or olive-green T-shirts, baseball caps and dark glasses. They had sidearms and automatic weapons and they were all looking at me.

The fifth had apparently followed me from the Subte station. Before I could turn to run, he put the hood over my head and threw me to the sidewalk, skinning the palms of my hands. Somebody kicked me in the ribs and I made myself go limp, knowing I was hopelessly outnumbered, not wanting to show any signs of resistance. No one seemed to care. A hand grabbed me by the back of my shirt and I heard the fabric tear as he yanked me up and threw me into the wall. I hit on my right shoulder and the pain was a white light that paralyzed my brain. I bounced off the wall, flailing, and got punched and kicked again as I fell onto my back on the concrete.

There was laughter and then somebody said, «¡Apurate!» They threw me onto the floorboards behind the front seat, and the car doors slammed, and the engine fired up. Somebody cuffed my hands behind my back, making me cry out because the cuffs were too tight. The tires squealed as we pulled away and all I could think of was Elena in the apartment waiting for me, watching our special dinner, which I would never taste, slowly grow cold.

•

IT WAS A ROUGH RIDE. I was totally disoriented by the hood, as I was meant to be. I tried to count seconds and never got to more than a minute or two before a sharp turn or a sudden stop threw me off. I was lucid enough to notice that even though I was terrified, I hadn't slipped into a panic attack. I was breathing hard but not hyperventilating, nauseated from the blind turns, but not throwing up. There's no time for panic when the worst is already happening.

We must have driven for close to an hour, even allowing for the time distortion caused by my state of mind. When the car finally stopped and the engine shut down I was torn between gratitude that the nightmare ride was over and the knowledge that they might be about to kill me. Instead they took me inside a building. I felt thick carpet underfoot and smelled dust and mildew. We passed through a second door, then a third, and then the floor was linoleum.

They began to strip my clothes off and that was when I finally understood what was going to happen.

They made a game of it. They tossed me from one man to the next, tearing pieces of clothing away as they shoved me. Someone had a knife and now and then he would cut something away. They didn't stop until all that was left was the hood and the handcuffs, and then they threw me in a closet and I heard a padlock close on the door.

The closet had a linoleum floor also, cool at first against my bare skin, warming quickly to my body heat. The air was hot and stale and smelled of industrial disinfectants. I carefully felt my way around the space with my feet. It was empty except for a metal bucket. The chemical smell came from the liquid in the bottom of it. The closet was almost long enough for me to stretch out in, and half as wide. The walls were grooved and I pictured fake wood paneling with a hard plastic finish. A faint glow showed through the fabric of the hood, telling me that a light had been left on.

Working with my hands behind my back, I put the bucket by the door and sat up against the opposite wall and listened. I heard low murmurs and then the sound of doors closing and then silence.

My hands were numb. I could massage one wrist with the other hand and I spent a few minutes trying to work blood back into them. Then I bent forward and moved my chest from side to side to figure out how badly I was hurt. My palms burned from scraping the sidewalk and one of my ribs was either bruised or cracked. Otherwise I was okay.

Not that it mattered, because I knew they were going to torture me. And there, in the emptiness and silence, the panic finally came.

I managed not to throw up, knowing that even if I didn't choke on my own vomit and die, I would still be trapped in the hood with it. I focused on my breathing and got it more or less under control. I did the pulse counting trick and it helped a little, then suddenly it was vitally important that I be standing up. I struggled to my feet and paced, as best I could, around the narrow space. I did it past the point that my bare feet hurt, did it until I finally got tired and then I crouched, and sat, and lay on my side.

I remembered the cognitive therapy advice to notice things, to observe, to be scientific. I tried to quantify my hunger, which was eating the lining of my stomach, and my thirst, which was not as bad, though my mouth was dry. I needed to piss, and the more I thought about it the stronger the urge became, until I knelt in front of the bucket and relieved myself, managing not to spill any even though I couldn't use my hands. I failed to find comfort in that small victory.

I sat against the far wall again. There was no doubt in my mind that Osvaldo had betrayed me. If he'd made any effort at all to keep tabs on Elena he would have known about me and assumed that I knew where to find Mateo. I cursed Mateo and the red-bearded man and the man in the skull cap and the dark haired woman and most of all I cursed myself for not condemning Osvaldo to death.

Eventually I fell into something like sleep. I woke up not much later, knowing at some level where I was. As soon as full awareness returned, the panic came with it. After a minute I began to scream. The screaming felt so good, I kept it up until my throat tasted of blood and no more sound came out.

After that, I thought maybe I could bring the handcuffs around in front of me, and if I could do that, I might be able to get the hood off. I had to pull on the cuffs to bring them around my backside and the pain was terrible, and then I imagined myself getting stuck halfway and the panic started to take me again, so I gave it up.

Eventually I slept some more and woke. The room had gotten cold and I tucked my legs into my chest and slept again, and I woke to voices outside the door.

Maybe they had just been trying to scare me. Maybe they would

take me back home now. I tried to think of anything I would not
do to make that happen.

I heard keys in the lock and then footsteps. Somebody took me
by one arm and turned me on my stomach and took the cuffs off.
I rubbed my wrists and felt the first prickles of returning life in
my numb and swollen fingers. A foot pressed me into the floor and
hands struggled with the binding on the hood, then it came off and
light dazzled my eyes.

«Sit up,» said a voice, and the foot went away. I rolled onto my
side and then into a sitting position, my back to the wall, using one
hand to shield my eyes. Somebody put a paper bag into my lap. I
stared at it in confusion for a second before I realized what it was by
the smell. It was from McDonald's. Inside was a hamburger, an order
of fries, and a large Coke.

«I'm a vegetarian,» I said.

Someone laughed. My eyes were still watering and I couldn't
make out any faces. There was one man in the closet with me and
another in the doorway. A bank of fluorescents in the room behind
them put out a glaring backlight that washed out the details.

The man closest to me said, «This is what the boat brought in.
Take it or leave it.»

I was half crazy from fear, sick with hunger, and also childish and
petulant. This is what they mean, I thought, by adding insult to in-
jury. «Leave it,» I said, and handed the bag back to him.

By that point my eyes had recovered enough to see the rage
contort his face. «Fucking ungrateful piece of shit,» he said. I saw his
hand coming and succeeded only in deflecting it a little. It knocked
me over and he kicked me in the ribs and backside until the other
man pulled him off.

They took the food with them and locked the door. They hadn't
put the handcuffs or the hood back on. I didn't know if that was a
good sign or not.

The floor of the closet, I saw, was bluish-gray. There had been
shelves all the way around at one time and they'd left scars in the
fake wood paneling where they'd been ripped out.

Outside the door I heard boxes being unpacked, metallic banging,
voices cursing. It went on for what must have been more than an
hour, long enough for me to drift off again.

I curled up on the floor, head on my arm, but my fear wouldn't let me sleep. There was only one thing they could be building out there and it was not a home theater system or a recumbent bicycle or a set of monkey bars.

I began to shake.

Eventually they opened the door and two of them came in for me. They each took an arm and when I was slow getting up, they punched and kicked me. My mind emptied. I couldn't think about what was going to happen next. All I felt was my own lack of control, my complete helplessness. The muscles in my back and neck had twisted tight and I was panting, unable to get my breath.

The closet must have once been a pantry because it opened into an industrial sized kitchen, with stainless steel countertops, now rusted, and a black and white checkered floor. There were no windows, no traces of the world outside. I had no idea of what time it was, or even what day it was.

In the middle of the floor sat a steel table, eight feet long and four feet wide. Wide leather straps emerged from slots in the surface, positioned to hold a body spread-eagled.

Two more men stood on the far side of it. One wore a mechanic's navy blue coveralls, the other a white shirt and yellow tie. The one in the coveralls said, «Bienvenidos a la parilla.» Welcome to the grill.

My knees quit supporting my weight and I stumbled. The two men holding me dragged me to the table and manhandled me onto it. I wasn't resisting, I was incapacitated by fear and it made me clumsy and difficult. They strapped my arms and wrists down first, then my legs, then they put a final strap around my forehead.

I closed my eyes, then I had to open them again. The darkness and not knowing made the helplessness worse. The assistant thugs went out of the range of my vision. I heard the scrape of a match and smelled a lit cigarette.

The man in coveralls was older than me, in his mid-fifties. His hair was gray and he had a small mustache and black-rimmed glasses. He looked like an accountant who'd had to take a job in a garage.

He was holding a metal box the size of a pack of cigarettes. He had latex gloves on. Two long wires came out of the top of the box, ending in alligator clips, like miniature jumper cables. A heavy gauge wire ran from the other end to a lunchbox-sized transformer that was plugged into the wall. It had a US-style plug and was connected to a converter for Argentine current.

The man in the tie was also in his fifties, tan and clean-shaven, with buzz-cut hair. He touched the shoulder of the man in coveralls and said something into his ear, pointing at parts of my naked body. I made out enough of the words to tell that he was speaking Spanish with a US accent.

CIA, I thought. Stupidly, the idea gave me a half second of comfort. Surely he understood that I was from the US?

The man in the coveralls walked counterclockwise halfway around the table, then back the other way. He poked at the bruises on my ribs and shins, hard enough to make me cry out. My voice was still hoarse from the screaming.

«Bueno,» he said at last. «No questions just now. First we give a demonstration only, to let you know we are serious. Another time we will have questions. No?»

He pinched little rolls of flesh on my stomach and attached the alligator clips to them. The whole apparatus looked like it came from an electric train and that image kept me from being as frightened as I might have been.

He twisted a dial on the little box and the pain was instantaneous. It felt like he was using a blowtorch on my stomach and I hallucinated the smell of burning meat as the shock arched my back up off the table and jammed my face against the forehead strap. The stomach muscles jumped and twisted even as they burned with pain and I felt the current all the way to the hair on my head and the ends of my toenails. It was the kind of intense pain that you can only really feel for a second, except that this pain went on and on, kept growing, until I was convinced that the wires were burning completely through my stomach and into my spine, causing grotesque, spectacular damage that no human body could survive.

I began to vomit. There was no food in my stomach, so all that came up was thick bile. I couldn't turn my head or control my breathing, so it went down into my lungs and choked me. I knew that I was dying then and didn't mind. Better now than to keep on enduring this kind of pain, only to be dropped out of a helicopter in the end.

When the current finally stopped, my stomach muscles continued to jump and heave. I couldn't see through the tears to know who it was that unstrapped my head and right arm, turning me on my side and slapping my back repeatedly until I choked and spewed bile on the floor. Then I lay on my side and shook.

I was less than one minute into my first torture session.

I looked down and could not believe that my stomach showed no sign of the damage they had inflicted. Before I could fully process what I saw, one of the thugs grabbed my free arm and strapped it down again. I tried to resist and found out I had less strength than an infant. He pulled my head back and tightened the strap across it.

The man in coveralls took the clips off my stomach. The "I" inside my head was gone, the voice that commented on everything it saw, that made plans and sifted through memories and always wanted to fit things into narratives and patterns. In its place was an animal who only knew pain and the absence of it, and when there was no pain, that space immediately filled with mindless terror of the pain to come.

He attached the first clip to my left testicle. I was making noises, small whimpering sounds. He attached the second clip to my right testicle.

There was a second or two without pain. Then there was nothing else. It felt like I was ejaculating burning gasoline. At the same time my balls were on fire and white-hot shrapnel cut and burned the rest of my body in all directions.

I dimly sensed my body flopping like a drowning fish as the convulsions shook me. There was a point at which I thought I literally couldn't bear any more pain. That was a ridiculous idea, of course. What does it mean to think, "I can't bear it," when you have no choice, no control, no alternative? The pain went on no matter what I thought about it, tearing, burning, shredding, destroying me.

And then there came a point where my nervous system shut down and I could no longer feel anything and after that I passed out.

I was not out long. When I came around, the current was off and the shit and piss that I had involuntarily let go of were cooling between my legs. The chill was faintly soothing.

«Wash him,» said the man with the coveralls. Someone filled a bucket at the sink and sluiced the mess off the table and mopped it up.

«Now I'm going to show you why we call it 'the grill,'» he said. He did something with the electrodes and just before the current went on I realized he had attached them to the table itself.

Each kind of shock was the same and each one was different. This one was like being thrown into a pit of fire and also like a full body seizure. My heart was not beating so much as it was stopping dead and then starting again, lurching drunkenly against the waves of electricity. I understood that they had not killed me before and knew that they surely would now.

This time I passed out more quickly and I think I was out longer. When I was half-conscious again, he attached the electrodes to my gums.

I felt every nerve in every tooth scream, needles of agony that went straight from my jaw into my brain. It was like lightning striking my head, over and over, until the darkness came and stayed.

I WOKE UP in the closet. I was still naked. They had given me an old, green wool Army blanket, musty and moth-eaten. My hands were free and they had taken the hood away. The single naked light bulb burned overhead.

I'd only been awake a few minutes when the pain returned. It was like my body had saved the sensations for me while I was unconscious so I wouldn't miss any of them. It started with my teeth, which first ached and then burned. Then my testicles, which had swollen to the size of tennis balls. Finally my stomach convulsed and I crouched over the bucket, venting gas and a little foul-smelling liquid.

There was no paper to wipe myself with, so I used a corner of the blanket.

I lay down and covered myself and begged for sleep to come. All I could think about was the door opening and them coming back for me. A headache smoldered in my right eye and I pulled the blanket over my head to shield myself from the merciless light.

It had been like this in the first days of the headache. Then, I could find a position on the couch with all the lights off where I could hold perfectly still and keep the pain at bay for minutes at a time.

It was more difficult on a linoleum floor, with my entire body bruised and burned. Still I managed tiny slivers of sleep, one of them long enough that I fell into a dream, and in the dream they were taking me into a room with black and white checkerboard tiles and a metal table. I woke up with a loud grunt and huddled against the wall and shook.

And waited.

I tried to imagine what it would look like to fight back. I could picture myself doing violent things to all of them, chopping them to pieces with an axe, machine-gunning them against a wall, smashing their faces with a big rock. What I couldn't see was how to get there from being naked and exhausted and terrified and hurt and locked in a closet.

When the door opened I started to cry. It was one of the thugs. I shrank from him, expecting him to reach for me, but instead he set a brown paper bag on the floor and left.

I had lost my sense of smell and for a while I didn't understand what the bag was. Then I remembered the McDonald's bag, and then I saw that this was a different kind, small and brown and plain. I looked carefully inside and saw a banana and two mandarin oranges.

My hands trembled as I picked up one of the oranges and tried to peel it. My fingers were weak and clumsy. Eventually I got my thumbnail under the skin and tore a piece off. I could smell it now and it made my saliva come so forcefully that the drool ran down my chin. I almost had the peel off when the door opened again and one of them grabbed my arm and the other knocked the orange out of my hand and they dragged me into the kitchen.

There was no CIA man this time, just the two thugs and the man in the coveralls. They were in the same clothes as before, as if no time had passed. The thugs strapped me to the table. The metal was freezing cold and I shivered as soon as it touched my skin.

The man in the coveralls didn't have the electrodes this time. He had a small wooden paddle, the size of the sticks they used to give away at paint stores to stir with. He was slapping it against the palm of his other hand and it made me think of the ruler my father used to spank me with when I was little. It should have been a stupid, trivial thought. Instead it made me feel scared and guilty and desperate for a way out.

When I was strapped down, he hit me on the bottom of my right foot with the stick, then hit me again and again and again. The blows were not that hard. They stung, though it was nothing like the explosive pain of the electroshock.

They didn't stop. He moved up and down over most of the sole, the stinging giving way to burning, the burning turning into spears of hot pain that stabbed down my legs.

First I tried to will myself to black out. Then I remembered hearing about people who had detached their consciousness from their bodies and floated above themselves. I couldn't get there because the pain kept calling me back.

Once when I came back I realized the man in the jumpsuit was saying something. I couldn't see his face because of my head being strapped down and at first I couldn't understand him. He spoke in a sharp rhythm that matched the rhythm of the blows.

«Where. Is. Pablo. Nuncio. Where. Is. Pablo. Nuncio.»

«Wait!» I said.

He stopped asking the question. The beating also stopped for a few seconds and then started again, harder. The man in the jumpsuit was suddenly beside me, leaning over me and I realized he'd given the paddle to one of the thugs.

He started talking again in time with the slaps. «Where. Is. Pablo. Nuncio.»

«Who?» I couldn't keep the desperation out of my voice.

«Pablo. Nuncio. Where. Is. Pablo. Nuncio.»

«I don't know who you're talking about!» It came out as a squeak, all my ravaged throat could produce.

«Tell. Us. Tell. Us. Pablo. Nuncio. Where. Is. Pablo. Nuncio.»

«Who is Pablo Nuncio? I can't tell you something I don't know!»

His face went away and the beating moved to my left foot. The right foot felt huge and red and throbbing. A cartoon foot. I tried to laugh at the image and started to cough and the cough turned to dry heaves. The entire time the beating continued.

He chanted the question again. There was a pause while they changed thugs. I was wearing their arms out, I thought.

And then I thought, they are destroying my feet. I will never dance again. Even if I somehow live through this, I will never dance with Elena again.

"Noooooo!" I cried. It sounded like gargling. I arched my back and fought against the straps that had no give in them, and all the while the beating went on, rhythmic, indifferent, unstoppable.

They moved back to the right foot, which was sore as an open wound. The gentle touch of a finger would have been agony. They were hitting it, pounding it to jelly.

I screamed again and again and finally I lost the feeling in my feet and then lost my way in my head. I found myself in a nightmare from childhood, from the time I was 9 years old and fell down a hill and broke my arm, and they'd given me ether while they set the fracture. In the dream I was strapped to the inside of a giant metal spiral, slowly turning through infinite space and infinite cold. I was completely alone and completely helpless and trapped there for eternity.

WHEN I CAME TO, I was still on the table. I smelled cigarette smoke. The room was quiet.

The man in the coveralls came into my vision. He was staring at my groin. I felt his hand gently move my penis to one side. Then I saw his right arm come up. The stick was in it. He slapped my testicles with it and pain went up through my stomach and chest and into the back of my throat.

«Pablo. Nuncio. Where. Is. Pablo. Nuncio.»

"Please," I said. I was so disoriented I was speaking English. "Please stop. I don't know. I don't know who you're talking about. Please, just, please, stop. Please."

«Pablo. Nuncio. Where. Is. Pablo. Nuncio.»

By the time his arm was tired and he handed off to one of the thugs, I was already going numb, a numbness like death, a hopeless numbness, the numbness of the irreparably broken.

WHEN I WOKE UP in the closet, the fruit was still there.

I moved very slowly, rolling up the blanket and putting it under my ankles to keep my feet from touching the floor, then lying carefully on my side, my knees as far apart as I could hold them to ease the pressure on my swollen testicles. I ate as slowly as I could and then I crawled on hands and knees to the bucket and tried to piss. All that came out was a few drops of blood.

I lay on my back, one arm over my eyes to block as much light as I could. Pain pulsed in waves from my feet and groin. I was completely exhausted, but any imagined sound in the other room would bring me wide awake, heart pounding. Finally, in desperation, I refolded the blanket and managed to get my legs extended up the wall, blanket under my buttocks, my head lowest of all, against the blue-gray linoleum. The yogis call it Deep Lake Pose and it's supposed to bring serenity. Serenity was too much to ask, but it did take the blood away from my feet and balls. The bad news was that it brought that blood to the icepick pain in my right eye.

I put my left arm back over my eyes and used my right hand to push the hair away from my forehead, massaging the tenderness in my scalp that came with the headaches. Over and over, until my arm ached, and then I traded arms and used the left to rub my head. By this point my legs were sliding off the wall, so I curled into a fetal position, the blanket over my head and my feet radiating pain from the points where they lightly touched the floor.

I went in and out of a restless sleep. Thinking about Elena was unbearable, so I tried to imagine Sam there, sitting next to me. "D, these guys are such losers," I heard him say. "I don't want you hanging with them anymore."

"Okay, Sam," I said. "I won't."

The door opened. The two thugs came in and without a word pulled the blanket off me and jerked me to my feet. I couldn't stand up, so one of them held me while the other hit me, punching me in the ribs and stomach and face, over and over. At one point I leaned over to spit out a mouthful of blood and there was a tooth in it. They hit me some more and then threw me on the floor and left.

I found the tooth later, lying in a patch of dried blood. It was a canine from the left side of my mouth and it looked so sad, yellow and worn and abandoned, the root broken off midway down, that I put it in the bucket so I wouldn't have to look at it anymore.

The sequence of things began to get confused. The door opened at some point and there was another bag of food, not fruit this time, another McDonald's bag. This was a different time than the first time because I didn't say anything and nobody hit me and they left me alone with the food.

The Coke was too sweet to drink. There was still some crushed ice in it, so I fished the ice out with my filthy hand and ate that. I ate the French fries and I ate the lettuce and pickles off the hamburger. I couldn't eat the cheese, which tasted like wax. I picked at the bun and by then the sweet smell of the meat had made me sick, so I wrapped the remnants up and put them by the bucket. Then I crawled to the far corner of the closet and spent an indefinite time trying not to throw up.

I was on the table again. The man in the jumpsuit had attached the electrodes to my ears. The CIA man must have told him he was using too high a charge because this time I didn't go into convulsions. Instead it felt like high powered belt sanders were ripping the flesh from my skull.

Later he attached the electrodes to my little toes. He gave me a small dose of current, like I might get from a light switch that had shorted out, enough to make my battered feet blaze with pain. Then he sat on a stool next to me. I knew he was going to ask me about Pablo Nuncio. The tears were already rising in my eyes.

«Mateo,» he said. «Tell me about Mateo.»

I FELT A RUSH of gratitude. I knew that name. I could answer this one. «Mateo,» I said. «Mateo is Elena's father.»

He twisted the dial. The shock picked me up and rattled me like a dried bean in a jar. After he dialed down, I lay panting and convulsing in a pool of my own urine.

«Mateo is no one's father,» the man said. «Mateo is a criminal, a murderer, a kidnapper. He is an enemy of Argentina. I know you are not from here, but I know you love this country. Mateo hates it, and he wants to destroy it.»

«No,» I said, honestly wanting to correct his mistake. «It's not like that. He—»

The man twisted the dial again and the pain went straight up my spine, the way the yoga energy is supposed to do, only this was a path of white-hot destruction. At the end of it my teeth were chattering and my legs were shaking in the restraints.

«Mateo is a very bad man,» he said. «Do you understand that?»

What I understood was that he wanted me to say yes, so I did. It took two attempts to get my tongue to behave and speak the word.

«Good. That's very good.» He turned away from me and said, «Water.»

Later he had a water bottle in his hand. He had undone the strap around my forehead and was holding my head so that I could take a little water in my mouth. «Slowly,» he said. «Slowly, so it doesn't make you sick.»

I was lying on the table and he was saying, «It is very important that we find Mateo. You want to help us with that, don't you?»

This was hard. I knew the answer that he wanted and I didn't think it was the right answer. If they found Mateo, they would strap him to a table like this one and hurt him too. That didn't seem right.

The electrodes were on my testicles again. The pain was unbearable and I knew I couldn't stay conscious, but somehow I did and it kept coming. I was making noises and the noises were numbers. They were something like the numbers of Mateo's cell phone, except I didn't remember the order.

He asked me for the number again and I gave him one, but it was not the same. I realized that and so did he and he sent the current into me again.

When he stopped I said the number again, the same as the time before, and I told him yes, I was sure, and I said the number yet again, and then I said the numbers to myself, over and over, so I would be sure to get them right the next time.

He put the electrodes on my nipples. I said the numbers I had memorized and he shocked me anyway, not a convulsive shock but a pain shock that went straight down to my penis and testicles. «Where is Mateo? Where is he now? How do I find him?»

It was too many questions and I couldn't decide which one to answer so he hurt me again.

Later I was talking, or my voice was talking, without my knowing where the words came from. I couldn't even understand them, they were babble, only they were about the little market and the stairs and the tunnels, the old factory. He was writing things down and saying, «Good, that's very good,» and there was no pain except the pain from before that still hurt. And another pain inside that was not physical, that was shame and hating myself for what I was doing.

Then I was telling him about the others, about Jesús and the small dark woman and the Middle Eastern man and Raul and all the others and the stones and the votes.

«Stones? Votes? What are you talking about?»

I tried to explain about Osvaldo. Osvaldo was the reason I was here. My tongue wouldn't make sense and I wound up speaking English because I was delirious. He shocked me again to make me speak Spanish, but it was too much and I passed out.

I was in the closet and they were coming to get me again. I must have slept because it didn't seem like that long since I'd been on the table the last time. Only it didn't feel like I'd slept, it felt like I had sat against the wall with my eyes closed and my hands pressing against them, thinking about the fact that I had told them everything they wanted to know, that I had betrayed Mateo, who was

Elena's real father, and now they were going to kill him too and she would have no one.

They had brought fruit again. I couldn't eat it because I didn't deserve to be fed, didn't deserve to live. I didn't want it because it was a reward for betrayal, it was thirty pieces of silver, and I was sure I hadn't slept.

One of the thugs was hitting my feet with the stick and the man in the coveralls was asking me for the phone number again, and I was sure I said it right, and I must have because he stopped hitting me. Then he wanted me to say the directions again and at first I didn't want to, but then he was hitting me in the testicles with the little stick and it didn't matter because I had already said them once and saying them again would make the pain stop.

He was holding a map of the city in front of me and my right hand was free and I was using it to point to where I thought the grocery was.

He was asking me to describe the others. I did, and that was when I saw there was another man next to the man in coveralls. He had white hair and a low forehead and a patchy gray mustache. I knew I had seen his picture, and then I recognized him. Emiliano Cesarino, the one who had run the detention centers and killed Marco Suarez. Osvaldo's boss.

I was in the closet. There was an Egg McMuffin with no meat on it, so it must have been breakfast time. Was it only the morning of the second day? It was not possible that I had been there less than three or four days. There was orange juice and water. Marco Suarez had loved the smell of oranges. They made him think of the tropics.

I ate all the food, tearing it with my hands and putting it deep in my mouth to avoid my missing tooth, and then there was nothing.

I used the bucket to piss blood and expel some diarrhea, which was mostly noxious gas. I slept a little, I sat, I did Deep Lake Pose. I thought about Sam, but Sam had nothing to say to me because I had not stopped hanging with these losers like I said I would and because I had betrayed Mateo.

They were doing this on purpose, I realized. They were breaking any possible sense of rhythm to my days, to the meals, to the sessions, to wipe out my internal clock, to leave me with nothing, nothing at all.

I was alone in the closet for so long that I wondered if they were finished with me, if they had left me to die. I tried the door to make sure it was locked, and tried it again later, and again after that.

I was afraid to be alone. At the same time, I knew that if they came back they would torture me. It was an impossible choice that I could not stop thinking about. The more I thought about it, the more my head hurt, a spike going straight through my right eye and deep into my brain, hurting so much that the pain in my feet and my testicles and my chest and mouth could not compete with it.

Then I was on the table again and they were beating me with the stick, and I wanted to tell them it was time for the shock, not the stick, except that I was no longer sure, and I didn't want the shock either.

«What is he planning? Mateo. What is he planning, eh? He has a plan. He is up to something. What is he doing?»

Too many questions again. I tried to explain that Mateo had no plans, or if he had plans I didn't know anything about them.

The next time I was on the table there was no shock and no beating. This time there was only a pair of pliers.

«Mateo. What is he planning?»

«I don't know.»

«Beto, I am very disappointed in you. Just like your father was disappointed in you when you were a boy, back in Virginia. Do you remember?»

He'd wanted me to play basketball. He'd never been good enough to play in college, so he wanted me to succeed where he'd failed. He'd put a hoop above the garage and sent me outside to practice every afternoon. He would come out to check on me, never to play with me, and he would find me sitting and daydreaming, or chasing an escaped ball down the twilight street. Disappointed in you, he would say.

How did they know that?

«You must try again, Beto. Tell me what I want to hear.»

«But I don't know—»

He took hold of my left hand. Then he had just the index finger, pushing it down onto the metal table. I felt something touch the fingernail. It was the jaws of the pliers. The pliers began to pull on the fingernail.

«Try again, Betito.» His voice was kindly and patient. «Tell me what Mateo is planning.»

«I don't know! I swear to you I don't know!»

The pain started in the tip of the finger and then the whole finger and then the whole arm. I couldn't see what they were doing and that made it worse, because I knew what they were doing and I was even more powerless because I couldn't see it. The pain was terrible and cold, an absence, an unbearable loss. I thought of my sad yellow tooth on the floor of the closet and now this. My entire forearm vibrated with agony and then, mercifully, I was gone again.

In the closet. I was afraid to look at my finger. Eventually I had to. It was swollen to twice its normal size, fat as a sausage, and where the fingernail should have been it was puckered and covered with dried blood. Moving it through the air made it hurt, a pounding, savage, devastating ache. I cradled it with my right hand and curled my body around it and lay on the floor without moving.

On the table. The stick again. They had barely started when I nearly choked on the smell of cigarette smoke. One of the thugs stood over me, laughing. He took a drag from his cigarette and the end glowed bright red, like molten steel in a foundry, like the setting sun. He took the cigarette by the filter and brought the hot end down toward my face. It looked like he was going to put it into my eye. With that thought I realized that I had still been holding on to some hope of coming away from this alive. I let that hope go.

He put the cigarette out on my left cheekbone. The smoke from the cigarette and from the burning flesh made tears stream down my face.

The man in the coveralls loomed over me from the other side, the right side, the side with the eye that I could still see out of. «Mateo,» he said. «What is he planning?»

The thug lit a new cigarette with a wooden match. He shook the match out and dropped it on my chest. I remembered a joke from when I was little: Want to see a match burn twice?

«Don't be difficult, Betito. You have been doing very well up to now. Tell me what Mateo is planning.»

The thug blew smoke in my face, took the cigarette out of his mouth, and pointed it at my chest.

«A bomb,» I said. I knew what he wanted. That was more important than the truth, he had showed me that.

The thug hesitated.

«He's making a bomb. Una bomba de tubo.» I'd seen the word for pipe bomb in the newspaper one day.

The man in the coveralls waved the thug away. «Good, Beto. What is he going to do with the bomb?»

«Citibank. He's going to put the bomb in Citibank.»

«When?»

«I'm not sure.» I hadn't thought ahead. It had been the day before Halloween when they took me. How long ago was that?

I was too slow with the answer. The thug burned me where the skin was thin over the center of my collarbone, pulling the cigarette back before it went out and then puffing on it so that it filled the room with the stink of burning meat. I was throwing up again and they had to release me enough that I could vomit onto my own left arm.

«Christmas,» I said, gasping and choking. Surely it wasn't Christmas yet. «The bomb will go off at Christmas.»

«Where?»

«Citibank, I told you. Citibank!»

«Which one?»

«Calle Florida. Where all the shopping is.»

I was in the closet, because I could move my arms and legs, though I was sorry when I did. I couldn't remember anything after Calle Florida. I didn't know what they'd done to me to make me pass out. There was a burn on my face and one high on my chest, neither of them where I could see them. They both felt like the coal from the cigarette was still there, still smoldering. My right eyelid had drooped more than halfway down and my left eye was swollen nearly shut from the burn, making it hard to see. It was just as well, because I couldn't bear to look at my finger, which was swollen and crusty and an inflamed red at the edges of the dried blood.

On the table. Electrodes on my testicles. I didn't remember getting there. I didn't remember the question. I could no longer differentiate where the pain was coming from. I heard faint voices that could have been in another room.

My eyes were barely functional, but something made me look at the face of the man with the coveralls. I was staring at him when the most amazing thing happened. His eyes started to pop out of his head. Then his forehead bulged, like it was made of soft clay and someone was poking it from the inside. Then big pieces of the

forehead flew out, scattering bits of red and yellow-gray tissue and
one of the eyes fell out and hung by a string.

Somewhere in there I also heard a loud noise.

I understood that I was making it up, that the last borders between my fantasies and reality had broken down. Yet when his body
collapsed across my chest, it felt real and heavy.

There were more loud noises, three or five or ten of them, and
maybe somebody screaming, which could have been me.

A man's voice, far away, said, «Dios mio, what have they done to
him?» I felt the electrodes come off my testicles, and then the body
of the man in coveralls jerked away from me and landed in a heap
on the floor.

A face looked down at me. I still didn't understand what was
happening. At first I thought it was Cesarino again, but it wasn't,
it was another old man. It was Osvaldo. The only other time I'd
seen his face was in the street outside the restaurant, when Mateo
kidnapped him.

«You,» I said.

He undid the strap holding my head, then the straps on my arms,
then my legs.

«Can you stand up?» he asked.

«No.»

«I'm going to put you on your side. Go slow.»

I curled onto my side and didn't want to move. There were new
smells in the air. Cordite, which I knew from target practice with
my father. And blood. I tried to vomit and came up empty.

«I'm going to sit you up,» Osvaldo said. «We have to get you out
of here.» There was gentleness in his voice. He brought my legs
down and helped me sit up.

The room was a slaughterhouse. The man in the coveralls lay
at my feet, his face gone. The two thugs sprawled against the wall,
dead. There were bullet holes in the plaster above them, stained with
blood and gore. Three men stood with pistols ready, wearing black
police uniforms and caps. I felt a tiny flowering of joy in my heart.

Osvaldo reached for me and I held my arms out to him like a
child. He lifted me up and carried me into the daylight.

I CAUGHT NO MORE than a glimpse of the neighborhood—
a wide, cracked street lined with deserted offices and industrial

buildings. The sky was hazy and the air smelled of car exhaust. I thought it might be afternoon.

He laid me down in the back seat of an expensive car. There was a sheet and a blanket on the seat and I wrapped myself in them to cover my nakedness and because the car was cool from air conditioning.

There were other cars parked behind us. Some of them must have belonged to the dead men in the kitchen. At least one of them must have belonged to the other men who had rescued me, because Osvaldo said something to them, then he shut the door on me and got into the front seat alone.

Once we were moving there was too much noise from the road and the traffic for me to talk. So I lay quietly and every once in a while I would see Osvaldo's eyes in the rear-view mirror as he checked on me.

At some point we got on a freeway. The motion felt good, taking me away from the closet and the metal table, the farther and the faster the better. Sometime after that the car stopped and Osvaldo turned to face me.

"This is the British Hospital," he said in English. "It is a good place. They will help you here. I am sorry I can't come in. I have to leave you here. Maybe you understand."

"Why are you doing this?"

"I do this for my daughter. She loves you."

"She called you...?"

"She called and say she will kill me. I tell her what I tell you now. I do not kidnap you. I keep my word, I tell no one what happen with Mateo. I keep my word in the future, too. But I am able to know who does kidnap you and this I find out. As you see."

"Thank you. But who—" I couldn't say the words "betrayed me." Not after the way I had betrayed Mateo and the others.

Osvaldo didn't seem to have heard me. "Cesarino is a very bad man. I am not finished with him, I think. But that is not for you to worry about. You must go now."

He came around and opened the back door of the car. It hurt when he moved me and I understood that he couldn't help it. I could see the hospital now. I still had my bad memories of the hospital in Durham, but at that moment the British Hospital was very beautiful. There was a new wing that was white with a red and blue logo on it, and grass and flowers. He carried me to the door, wrapped in the sheet and blanket, and set me down gently.

"Be well," he said. "Know that I love Elena very much."

He said something to the guard at the door and then he was gone. A few minutes later two orderlies came with a gurney and took me inside.

I WAITED A LONG TIME before anyone thought to examine me. Once they did, they gave me morphine and I went to sleep. I woke up in a semiprivate room by a window and it was night outside. Elena was there.

She saw that I was awake and started to cry. She pulled her chair next to me and put a hand on my face and one on my chest. The one on my chest was touching the burn and I winced and she took it away. She tried to say something that only made her cry harder. Finally she said, «I did this to you. Beto, I am so sorry, so sorry.» She was crying again.

The IV drip was in my right arm. My left hand was wrapped in bandages. I wanted to touch her, but it was difficult. I put my right hand on her hair. She had clearly not been sleeping much, but otherwise she was exactly the same. She was wearing Dani's necklace and jeans and a T-shirt and one of my flannel shirts. She was so beautiful and I was so broken. It made me a little sick to see her next to me.

«What day is it?» I asked.

«Saturday. They had you for five days.»

«I betrayed them,» I said. «Mateo, Jesús, Raul, all of them. I didn't even wait. I betrayed them as soon as I could.»

«Beto, they tortured you. How can you blame yourself? This is my fault, nobody's fault but mine.»

«Are they dead?»

«Mateo and the others? No, no, they are all okay. I called them when you went missing. They left immediately, went into hiding somewhere. I don't even know where they are.»

«Good,» I said. «That's good.» It didn't feel good. It felt hollow. My guilt was the same, whether they lived or died.

«Beto, I was so afraid they would kill you.»

I said, «It was your father—Osvaldo—who rescued me.»

«I know. He called me as soon as he left you here. This place is only a few blocks from your apartment. I came right away, but they wouldn't let me see you until you were in the room.»

«He said you threatened to kill him.»

«Yes. When I thought he was the one who took you...»

«That was why he came for me. Because you called, because you told him that you...that you...»

«That I love you.»

«Because of that. So it was you that saved me.»

«Mi amor, I have to be able to touch you. To do that, I have to know where they hurt you.»

I let her take the sheet away. I was wearing a hospital gown underneath, so the first thing she saw was my feet, swollen like an elephant's and wrapped in cold packs. She burst into tears again.

I lay with my legs open, feet turned to the sides. I lifted the gown so she could see my testicles, the size of grapefruit, also resting on a cold pack.

«You see what they took from me? My dancing, my sex. There's nothing left for you to love.»

She got into the bed, carefully distributing her weight so she was beside me and on top of me, barely touching me. She kissed my split lip and said, «You must never say that. Never ever say that.»

In spite of itself, my penis stirred. It woke the pain, which made me go limp again. She had told me once that I didn't have the history to be involved with her. Now she was the one who didn't have the history.

«Show me the rest,» she said.

I showed her where the cigarettes had burned me, where the electrodes had been, the missing tooth, the missing fingernail, the bruises from the beatings, and she bit her lip to stop the crying.

«So I can put a hand here?» she asked, touching my right upper thigh.

«Yes.»

«And here?» She put her other hand on the left side of my chest, above the nipple, left of the burn.

«Yes.»

«And my head here?» She laid it gently on my left shoulder.

«Yes.» I could smell her hair. I had thought I would never smell it again. For the moment I refused to think about the hopelessness of it. I rested my right hand on the smooth curve of her waist and fell asleep.

I WOKE UP screaming. I scared Elena, who had drifted off also, and when she jumped she hit the burn on my chest, which made me gasp with pain.

By the time we had sorted ourselves out, the overhead lights came on and a female nurse came in, demanding to know what Elena was doing in bed with me. She was my age, short and squared off. Was Elena crazy, did she not know what I had been through?

«Better than you,» she said. «I knew he needed to be touched.»

I had dreamed I was in the black and white tiled kitchen. Time was running in reverse. The head of the man in coveralls reassembled itself as I watched, and I realized that the rescue had never happened, that it was only one more false hope.

The mood of the dream still clung to me and I found it hard to get emotionally involved as Elena argued with the nurse, who told her that visiting hours were over and she had to leave. Elena insisted she was my partner, my compañera, and that I needed her here around the clock.

«Please,» I said to the nurse. «Please let her stay.»

Finally she relented. «But stay out of his bed,» she said. «If I find you in there again, I'll call Security.»

She turned to me and said in English, "You can have the pain medication again now if you need it."

"Yes, please," I said.

Elena moved a brown vinyl-covered recliner next to the bed, her head by my feet. From there her left hand could reach the bed and rest on my thigh.

The nurse came with the morphine and injected it into a port on the IV. She looked at Elena, who was already falling asleep again, and said, "She is strong for you, this one, no?"

The morphine burned through my vein and the pain immediately faded. "Strong for me," I said. "Yes."

I was afraid to go back to sleep, afraid of the dream. In the end, the drug was stronger. I nodded in and out as the sun came up on Sunday morning.

•

FOR BREAKFAST they brought scrambled eggs. The smell of them reminded me of the Egg McMuffin, nauseating me, bringing back the closet and the green wool blanket and the bucket, and I shifted in the bed, feeling the edges of panic, fighting not to throw up. Elena took it away and found me fresh fruit, strawberries and apples and oranges. The oranges could have triggered something, but they didn't, other than to remind me of Marco Suarez again, whom no one had come to save.

Bahadur arrived at eleven. He brought a bouquet of yellow flowers and Elena propped them in a plastic cup of water. We shook hands carefully and Bahadur said, «You could start a new weight loss program. The Torture Diet. You could make millions.»

I tried to smile. During the night the nurse had helped me to get to the bathroom. There I had seen myself in the mirror for the first time. The right eyelid was at half-mast and the left eye was still puffy from the burn and the beatings. I had a week's growth of beard and my hair was filthy and matted. I must have lost 20 pounds, though I had been thin already. It showed in my cheekbones and the hollows of my eye sockets, in my arms and protruding ribs. Virtually every square inch of skin was mottled with yellowish-red bruises.

«Okay,» Bahadur said, «I will spare you my comedy stylings. I mostly want to tell you that I talked to La Reina last night and this morning and she promises me that she is going to take care of everything. She will put in for medical leave for you, retroactive to last Tuesday, and when that runs out, she says you will have long-term disability for as long as you need it. So you don't need to think about that at all.»

«Okay,» I said.

«She has also talked to someone she knows in the police. They told her there is not going to be any investigation of the three dead bodies found in an abandoned office building yesterday. It has being ruled a drug killing.»

«No investigation? But Cesarino ordered it. He was there.»

«Then you haven't heard?»

«What?»

«Someone got into the apartment where Cesarino was under house arrest. It happened late last night. According to the news report he was shot five times.» Bahadur relished the story, as if he were rehashing the plot of one of his crime movies. «Once in each kneecap, then, some considerable time later, once in the stomach. Then, later still, twice in the head.»

I looked at Elena. She nodded enough to tell me that she knew, as I did, that Osvaldo had done it.

Bahadur said, «No one understands how the killer got in and fired the shots and got out again without anyone knowing. It's all a mystery.»

«He probably got in the same way Cesarino got out to come see me,» I said. I felt churned up inside, elated and triumphant and helpless and sad.

«Anyway,» Bahadur said, «it means you are free to go back to the US.» He wouldn't meet my eyes as he said it.

«What do you mean, the US?» I said. «What are you talking about?»

«La Reina called your wife as soon as we heard you were safe.» He was acutely uncomfortable. «Everything has been arranged. She is coming to get you.»

«My wife...?»

«Correction,» said Lauren's voice from the doorway. «His wife is *here*.»

SHE COULD NOT have been long off the flight from Dulles. Her black linen suit showed every wrinkle from the overnight trip. "You must be Bahadur," she said, walking briskly in to shake his hand. She switched to Spanish as she crossed the room. «And you must be Elena. You are even more beautiful than I imagined.» Her accent was not particularly good, but she had a photographic memory for vocabulary.

Elena's face registered the same shock and hurt that I felt. She, at least, was not in on it. She took Lauren's hand by reflex and said, «Thank you.»

Finally Lauren came to me. In nineteen years I had seen her cry exactly three times. As she gently brushed the hair from my forehead, I was shocked to see her eyes mist over. "Oh, baby," she said, "what did they do to you?"

"Lauren..."

"Hush, baby, don't say anything." She turned to Bahadur and said, "I need to examine him, if you don't mind."

"Well," Bahadur said. "I should be going anyway." His face was still flushed, his posture stiff. "Rob, I'll talk to you once you're settled. I know you'll get the best possible care now."

"Duke Hospital," Lauren said. "One of the top five medical facilities in the entire world."

"And for the sake of your own safety," Bahadur said. "At least until this dies down."

I nodded at Bahadur, feeling betrayed and knowing I had no right to complain, betrayer that I was. He made an awkward attempt at a smile and left.

In Spanish I said, «Lauren. I appreciate what you went through to get here, but I don't want to go back to the US. My home is here now, with Elena.»

Lauren started to lift the sheet, and looked at Elena. Elena said, «Go ahead. I have already seen it.»

She pulled the sheet down and the gown up and gently pressed one finger against the skin at the top of my left foot.

I winced and said, «Lauren, are you listening to me?»

She switched back to English. "Rob, with all due love and respect, I don't think you're in any condition to make that kind of decision at the moment. You've just been through a living hell, you're severely damaged, and you're full of opiates besides. You need world class medical attention and I'm going to see that you get it."

She had moved up my legs and was cupping one of my testicles. "I've got a flight set up for tonight. We'll be in first class. I'll keep you sedated and there'll be an ambulance waiting at RDU to take you straight to Duke."

I began to hyperventilate.

Lauren saw it and punched the intercom. «I need that Ativan in here right now, please.»

I had seen it before. Lauren had only to walk into a hospital and people lined up to take orders from her. A nurse was there within a minute carrying a tiny pill in a plastic cup.

"Put this under your tongue," Lauren said. I was writhing in the bed as the panic took control of me. There were too many people in the room, I couldn't breathe, I needed to be moving, but I couldn't walk, there was no escape, and in a minute I would be throwing up and screaming. I put the pill under my tongue and swallowed the saliva that was flooding my mouth.

"Breathe," Lauren said. She gave me her hand to squeeze and I

was too desperate to refuse. The Ativan worked quickly. In five minutes my heart rate dropped and the pressure around my forehead let
up, the pressure that had been squeezing it like a leather strap.

My vision, which had narrowed to a few feet directly in front of
me, opened up again. Lauren was on the right side of my bed, still
holding my right hand, and Elena was hanging on to my left arm
with both hands.

Lauren smiled at me. "Better now?" She gave me a cup of water to
drink. The Ativan was making me sleepy and I fought to stay alert.

"We need to leave for the airport in half an hour," Lauren said.
"I've got things to take care of and I know you two will need a few
minutes, so I'll give you some privacy." She nodded to the nurse and
the two of them left together.

The panic was still inside me, muffled, like it had been wrapped in
blankets. Elena leaned into me and buried her face in my neck.

«I love you, Beto,» she said. «Maybe this is best for now. They
will fix you up in the United States and then you can come back
to me.»

«Elena...» I couldn't find the words for what I was feeling. That
I'd been tricked again, that the head of the man in the coveralls was
coming back together, that the rescue had been a bitter dream, that
everything was lost after all. «Don't let her take me. Please don't let
her take me.»

«I don't want to cry. I don't want you to go back to the United
States and only remember me crying.» It was too late. I felt the hot
tears on my neck. «Beto, you are so strong. Look what you lived
through.» She lifted her head to look me in the eyes. «You can live
through a short vacation in the United States.» She laughed at that
and I wanted to smile for her sake, but I couldn't.

«I love you, Beto. I will always love you. I will be here waiting for
you. You will call me on Skype and write me long passionate letters
and then you will come back to me and we will dance at El Beso
and La Ideal and make love all night.»

I knew she meant the words as she said them. To me they were a
fantasy, impossible to believe. I closed my eyes so she wouldn't see
the despair in them. This is it, then, I thought. Let Lauren take me,
so I won't be a constant reminder to Elena of what we once had.

She kissed me one last time, with infinite gentleness, and said, «So
long, Betito. I will see you soon.»

I heard her footsteps tick away across the floor and then, in the corridor, she began to run.

LAUREN KEPT ME so full of drugs that I registered only brief moments of the next few days. As they wheeled me out of the hospital I felt the last threads of attachment break. I was leaving the last place on Earth I'd seen Elena. I was seeing Buenos Aires for the last time. Something inside me let go. This is best for now, Elena had said. Best for now.

They took me through the airport in a wheelchair, sitting on an inflated ring, and put me straight onto the plane. I felt a jab of pain in my penis as they moved me into the airplane seat and discovered that Lauren had had me catheterized while I was unconscious.

I'd never flown first class before and I remembered almost nothing of it. I woke up at one point to see Lauren drinking a glass of champagne. She patted me on the arm and said, "How you doing, Rob?" and I went to sleep again.

We arrived at the Raleigh-Durham airport in a cold November rain. I had forgotten it was winter in the US. I had a glimpse of I-40, lit by the blue strobing lights of the ambulance, and the next thing I knew I was fighting claustrophobia in an elevator at Duke Hospital and Lauren was putting another Ativan under my tongue.

Best for now, I said to myself.

When I was conscious again, Sam was there.

"Sammy," I said.

"Yo, D, did you get the number of the Hummer that hit you?" Like Lauren, Sam was not a physically affectionate person. He came over to the bed and squeezed my shoulder. "I was just in the vicinity, thought I'd see if you wanted to toss the old pigskin around." Even Sam, the eternal, unflappable comedian, was having trouble hiding his shock and pain at the sight of me.

"Absolutely," I said. "Just let me catch another couple of winks and we'll do it."

The next day they did a series of CT scans and MRIs and X-Rays, taking me around in a wheelchair with the legs elevated. They had to put me under for the MRI, after the sight of the narrow drawer they intended to put me in triggered another round of claustrophobia and panic.

In between I slept a little and ate a little. They gave me non-steroid anti-inflammatory drugs for my feet and testes, Dilaudid through the IV for pain, and Ativan for panic. Lauren spent an hour with me that morning before she went to work and a couple of hours that night. Sam visited in the late morning and then caught a flight to Boston.

On the second day a parade of specialists came in to tell me there was no permanent damage to the brain, nerves, or renal system. On the third, I woke up with my head reasonably clear. As soon as Lauren arrived, I asked if I could use her laptop.

"What for?"

"I want to check my email." I told myself I just wanted to catch up, but in fact some stubborn part of me refused to give up one last thread of hope.

Lauren saw right through me. "I don't think that's a good idea."

I let it go.

Later that morning the internist in charge of my case came to see me. I was sitting up in bed, paging through a magazine that I was unable to read because of my headache.

She was in her mid-thirties, fit, with short black hair and creamy brown skin. She gave me a quick exam and then pulled over a chair and sat in it backwards.

"Things could be a lot worse," she said. "The hospital in Argentina did a good job of debriding those burns. There'll be some scarring, but plastic surgery could fix that." I made a dismissive gesture and she said, "I would consider it. It might do you good not to have a reminder of what happened staring you in the face, as it were."

"Speaking of my face," I said, "what about my eyelid?"

"The ptosis? Sorry, ten-dollar word for droopy eyelid. We don't know what caused that. It indicates some kind of neurological event. You might have had a mini-stroke. All things considered, that wouldn't be surprising.

"The rest of the facial story is that you lost a canine. Once you get out of here, any competent dentist can fit you with an implant or a permanent bridge.

"Moving down, you've got two cracked ribs, not terribly serious. There's nothing to be done about them—they're already held in place by plenty of muscle and they'll heal on their own, though I know they hurt.

"As to your finger, the root of the nail is still there. People don't realize how deep those things actually go. They think they've lost the entire nail, but it's just the nail plate that typically comes off with severe trauma. It'll take about six months for the nail to grow back. I'm not saying it's going to be pretty, but you'll have a nail.

"Your testes will gradually return to normal size. You may have some loss in terms of sperm generation. I don't know if that's an issue for you at this point in life. There shouldn't be any impairment to your sexual function. So that's good news, I hope. Once you feel up to it, you can get a sperm count and see what the story is there."

I nodded. Reflexively I thought of Elena's desire to have kids, and pushed the thought away.

"It's pretty much the same story with your feet," she said. "I think, in time, they should heal up okay. I don't want to say you're lucky— that would be pretty insensitive in the circumstances. It does work to your advantage that the techniques they used on you were largely intended to not do permanent damage.

"I want to get you up and moving on a walker, though the consulting podiatrist is a little doubtful. The longer you're in bed the more debilitated you'll be, and I'm concerned with your overall condition. They've got some boots with patellar tendon bracing, basically a shoe with a bar on each side that connects to the leg just under the knee. They'll let you walk without putting weight on the bottoms of your feet."

"Will I be able to dance again?"

"That's not a trick question, right? Like the old joke about playing the violin?"

I tried to smile, because she was working so hard for it.

"It depends on what kind of dancing," she said. "If you're talking about flamenco, probably not a good idea."

My throat was dry. "Tango," I said.

"That's mostly sliding the feet around, right? Not a lot of hopping or jumping? In time, a few months, I should think you'll be fine. No promises, you understand."

"Okay," I said. "Thanks."

She looked at me for a minute and then she said, "I'm going to take a guess at what you're feeling. Stop me if I'm wrong or out of line, okay?"

I nodded.

"This is all good news, but in a way it feels like kind of a letdown, am I right? After what you went through, that the physical damage could be so...superficial?"

I nodded again.

"The physical damage is serious, but yes, the human body can be amazingly resilient. Especially with people like you, dancers, athletes, people who stay in good shape. The mind is something else again.

"I have to tell you that you are a prime candidate for Post Traumatic Stress Disorder. It's pretty much a certainty that you're going to have at least some symptoms of it, possibly severe. You should be aware of that."

"What kind of symptoms?"

"Hypervigilance. Anxiety. You will probably have trouble sleeping, and some nightmares. Maybe even flashbacks, where you relive parts of the experience. You'll probably have a lot of anger that will be difficult to control. The thing is, it will sneak up on you and you won't know where it's coming from. It may help you to say, 'I'm feeling this way because I was tortured.' And I strongly recommend you see a therapist of some kind—psychiatrist, MSW, whatever. Sooner or later, you're going to have to trust somebody with some of the hurt you're carrying. That's when you're going to be able to start getting well."

"You seem very kind," I said. "Thank you."

She stood up. "People are not designed to deal with this kind of violence. You have nothing to be ashamed of. It's the violence that's unnatural, not what you're feeling. The violence is literally inhuman."

She was about to walk away, then hesitated. "I have a colleague who studies people who've been in serious auto accidents. He's found that nearly half of them show significant levels of PTSD. Years later their nervous systems are still flinching from the impact. And that's nothing compared to victims of violent crime, or what Iraqi veterans go through once they get home.

"The point is that even as our bodies show this incredible ability to heal, we can't keep up neurologically. Human beings are far more sensitive than we give ourselves credit for and violence does much more damage than we want to admit. It fosters more violence and numbs us to the effects, which fosters more violence yet. It's a disease, and it's contagious."

She pushed her chair across the room. "So that's my wish for you. That we can stop this disease from growing in you, and make you fully human again. Good luck. I'll check on you again tomorrow."

I ASKED MY NURSE if there was a computer with Internet access anywhere in the hospital.

"What you want it for?" he said.

"I want to check my email. Five minutes."

"You guys are crazy. Can't keep away from that shit even when you're in the hospital. Just chill, man. You be back up to your neck in all that mess soon enough."

THE NEXT DAY, they let me sit outside for a while. The sun was bright, the sky a deep and even blue. I wore sunglasses and a blue baseball cap that Lauren had found in my storage shed to protect my eyes from the glare. She'd also found some of my old clothes, and though they hung off me, the familiarity was comforting.

I was able to experience the wonder of it—to be alive, to have my physical pain under control, to inhale the air that smelled of autumn leaves and the chlorophyll in the lawn that had not yet given up for the winter. To know that I was healing and that better days lay ahead. I was sure then that I would eventually dance again and that I would go back to Buenos Aires. I stopped there and did not let myself think about Elena.

I made a list in my head of the things I wanted and that night I laid them out for Lauren.

"I don't need to be here," I said. "There's nothing they can do except give me drugs and I can take those anywhere. They've run every test they can think of. I want to get a place of my own, start working a couple of hours a day remotely, get a massage, see my chiropractor."

"You can't be on your own yet," Lauren said. "You can't drive, you can barely get around with the walker. But yes, there's no reason to keep you here. I'll bring you home tomorrow."

"Home?"

"Our house. Where did you think?"

"I don't know what I was thinking."

"Silly. We are still married, you know." There was something flirtatious in her voice that made me tense up. She kissed me on the cheek and said, "I'll go get the discharge paperwork started."

BY THE NEXT MORNING she had turned her downstairs office into a room for me, complete with a rented hospital bed. It was strange to be in the house again, which seemed enormous—the cathedral ceiling in the living room, the vast, beige-tiled expanse of the kitchen, the multi-tiered back deck. She'd put the rest of the box of old clothes in my room, along with a random box of my books, though my head still wouldn't let me read. There was a TV and a DVD player and a boom box. She had moved her computer upstairs, she said, "to get it out of the way."

I was anxious for her to go to work and trying not to show it. Finally, making sure once more that I had the numbers for her Blackberry, her pager, and her office, she kissed me on the forehead and left.

I gave her ten minutes and then worked my way upstairs. I did it sitting down, lifting my rear end carefully from one step to the next. It took fifteen minutes and left me dizzy and out of breath. I'd had to leave my walker downstairs, so I crawled into her bedroom on hands and knees.

She used a professional cleaning service to keep the rest of the house presentable, but the bedroom was her retreat, where chaos ruled. The bed was unmade, showing mismatched cream and forest-green sheets. The floor was littered with cast-off clothes, the end tables loaded with glasses and books and half-used tissues. The intimacy of it was erotic and my mind, against my will, went back to times we'd been in that bed together.

She'd made enough room on the dresser for a keyboard, mouse, and flat screen monitor, connected to a desktop tower on the floor. I could just reach the keyboard when I perched on one corner of the bed. The system woke up as soon as I touched the mouse, the monitor light turning from red to blue. My hands shook as I loaded up a browser and went to my email account.

I had 53 unread emails. I looked at all the return addresses twice. Nothing from Elena.

I didn't put it past Lauren to have tampered with my email, so I went to the backup on my service provider, a backup that Lauren didn't know about. It had the same 53 messages.

I went through the messages again to make sure Elena hadn't tried to get in touch with me through someone else. I was surprised at how much it hurt. Something in me had wanted to believe, against all common sense.

I tried to write her and couldn't find the right tone, the one that wasn't desperate or accusing or superficial—Dear Elena, I am fine, how are you?

Leave her alone, I thought. Let her deal with this however she needs to. The more I thought about it, the more final it seemed. I heard her telling me it was for the best. I heard her running from my hospital room.

It was easier going down the stairs than getting up them. When I got to the bottom I took hold of the walker and pushed myself into the bathroom, leaning on the counter to stare at my transformed face. The drooping eyelid made me seem sinister, the bandage on the burn made me look hard. My face was gaunt, haggard, old. And she was so young and so beautiful. What could she possibly want with me? I'd been kidding myself to think it could last.

Not to mention the way I'd collapsed, betrayed Mateo, would have betrayed her if they'd asked.

The pain in my right eye felt like it would destroy me. I took two Dilaudid tablets, which did nothing at all, cranked the bed into an N shape, and propped myself up with every pillow I could find. I lay in darkness and fought to stay one position change ahead of the pain. It was a full-time job, but my brain found time to call me names just the same. Loser. Fool. Cripple. Traitor.

ON MY SECOND DAY out of the hospital I called my old manager in Research Triangle Park, and she called Bahadur, and the end result was that Thomas, the hardware guy for my group at Universal, came by the house to drop off a laptop, preloaded with a remote network client.

He shook his head when he saw me. "Hope them sons of bitches paid for doing that to you."

"They're all dead," I told him. There was something in my voice when I said it, a certain relish, that was out of place in Lauren's palatial Southwest Durham home.

"That's good," Thomas said. "I'm glad to hear it."

After that I worked as much was I was able. Some days it was an hour or two, some days five or six. Reading from the computer screen didn't bother my head the way reading from the printed page did, though I had to keep the overhead lights off.

I traded instant messages with Bahadur every day. My initial feelings of distance from him melted over time. I couldn't blame him for not standing up to Lauren. She was a force of nature.

La Reina had told everyone that I'd been in a traffic accident and Bahadur had agreed to go along. No point, he said, in feeding the office gossip machine. I didn't really care one way or the other.

He said that my landlady had put my things in storage and was keeping them until I let her know what to do. He offered to ship them to me and I told him to wait. He said she also wanted to know if she should rent out the apartment.

"Elena's not there anymore?"

"Guess not," Bahadur wrote. "She said it was empty, except for the boxes. I guess Elena packed them for you."

"You haven't heard anything from her?"

"Sorry," he wrote. "No."

This will get easier, I told myself. Somehow I will get through this.

Endless trivial details eroded my will. Canceling and replacing the credit cards that had been in my wallet when I was kidnapped. Getting a new driver's license. Dental appointments, medical appointments, chiropractic and massage. Finding a shrink. Renting audiobooks and DVDs to pass the idle hours because I still couldn't handle the glare from a printed page.

I cut down on drugs. Ibuprofen was all I took for pain after the first few days. I kept my feet elevated and iced them after using the walker. I kept my left hand mostly elevated too, and typed with my right. I had also iced my testicles, ten minutes out of every hour for three days, and they had shrunk to nearly normal size.

One night, after I'd been home a week, Lauren gave me a quick exam. She decided the burns needed only Band-Aids and the ribs were improving. When she got to my groin, she stroked the testicles gently and said, "And how are these little guys?"

My penis stood up in response. There was some pain, not enough to impair anything. Lauren was fresh from the shower, smelling of expensive soap and conditioner, obviously not wearing anything under her damp gray T-shirt and sweat pants. It was hard for me to breathe.

She held my penis with one hand. "Maybe we should have a little function test."

"I don't know if that's a good idea," I said. My voice had a small tremor.

"You're not the doctor here."

She pulled her T-shirt off. It was the body I remembered so well, that I had once loved above all things.

"Lauren—"

"What?" She gave me a mischievous smile. "We're married. It's perfectly legal. Expected, even."

"What about your surgeon friend?" It was the first time I'd brought up her lover.

"Patrick? What about him?"

"Aren't you sleeping with him?"

She shrugged. "On occasion. But he's married too. And this is none of his business. This would come under the heading of recreational therapy. Very healing for you."

"You talk about us like we're still married, but for me that's over. It ended in Buenos Aires."

"Are you talking about your little girlfriend? You're not kidding yourself that there's any future in that, are you?"

I took her hand away. "I think you should go now."

She put her T-shirt back on. She was still smiling, though I could see her feelings were hurt. "I still love you, you know. I wish you wouldn't shut me out."

I nodded and looked away until she sighed and kissed my cheek and went upstairs.

THE ATIVAN was tougher to shake than the Dilaudid. My first night without it, I lay awake all night. The next night I took an herbal sleep remedy and woke up screaming at two in the morning. My stubbornness kicked in and I stayed with it. The third night I tossed and turned and finally got a few hours of decent rest.

The next morning, as I wheeled my way into the kitchen, Lauren was working a crossword puzzle. She smiled and tossed it on the table when she saw me.

My eyes saw the pattern of black and white squares on the page and with no sense of transition I was on the black and white tiles of the kitchen in Buenos Aires. I could feel the hands of the thugs on my arms. Our oak kitchen table was suddenly made of stainless steel.

I couldn't stop screaming. Lauren put her arms around me and I shoved her away, lashing out with my fists. Without the walker to support me, I went down, banging my forehead on the table as I fell.

I thrashed on the floor, flailing out with both arms and legs, then Lauren came back and sat on top of me and forced the little round Ativan pill into my mouth and under my tongue and held my jaw closed, talking to me calmly, saying my name over and over.

"Rob, it's okay. Rob, listen to me. Rob, you're having a flashback. You're okay, Rob. You're in Durham, nothing bad is going to happen to you."

I was still making noises through my nose, blowing snot down my chin, but now I could see Lauren and the real kitchen and I let her hold me while I cried. Then the Ativan kicked in and I went to bed and slept for ten hours straight.

DESPITE THE LACK of apparent progress from one day to the next, I took stock after I'd been out of the hospital for a month and the improvement was clear. I'd been going in twice a week for a medical massage, once a week for chiropractic. The dentist had ground down the teeth on either side of the missing canine and replaced it with a permanent bridge. I had gel-soled shoes that allowed me to get around for short periods with a cane instead of a walker and even to drive. I wore a protective cap over my left index finger.

Every time I checked my email, I held my breath until I saw that there was nothing from Elena. When I lay awake at night I would compose long, passionate letters to her in my head, and in the light of day I would talk myself out of sending them.

I saw an MSW twice a week for psychotherapy. The goal, she said, was to build up enough confidence between us that I could talk about what had happened. She wanted me to "own" my experiences.

I didn't.

One thing got me through the pain and loneliness and fear. That was my increasingly vivid and detailed plan for revenge.

I hadn't told Thomas the complete truth. Not everyone involved in torturing me was dead. If Osvaldo hadn't informed on me, someone else had.

I had a good idea who it was.

•

I TOOK MY TIME. I began to swim laps at the Duke pool, taking advantage of Lauren's connection to the university. I went into the office one day a week, then two. I switched from Ativan to Valium, 10 mg at bedtime only, and after a week I was sleeping again, though not without nightmares.

My feet had recovered from the initial trauma. I had developed some plantar fasciitis as a secondary symptom, tightness and pain in the connective tissue that ran from the heel through the arch of my left foot. Stretching and Ibuprofen kept it under control.

Gradually I was able to read again and, thinking of Bahadur, I lost myself in suspense novels where justice always found a way to triumph.

Lauren replaced the hospital bed with an ordinary double mattress and mentioned, in passing, that I was welcome to move upstairs if I liked. She let me know in other small ways that she was available, from smiles at the dinner table to making sure I caught frequent glimpses of her body. The irony was profound. For years I'd wanted nothing more than for her to desire me. It wasn't like I didn't want her or even fantasize about her. It was just more stubbornness on my part.

Christmas was awkward, relieved mostly by Sam being home for a week. One night he stayed up with me after Lauren had gone to bed and he said, "I made Mom tell me everything they did to you."

I was stretched out on the sofa and he sat in an armchair near my feet. He was leaning forward, his hands clasped, his eyes glistening.

I felt my mind clamp down, refusing to let the subject matter start conjuring memories. I nodded stiffly.

"I can't..." he started, then broke off. "It's so hard to get my mind around it. Things like that, they just don't happen."

I remembered how shattered he'd been in third grade when his bicycle was stolen. I wondered, for the thousandth time, if other parents spent their lives feeling this helpless.

"I guess," I said, "the point is that they do happen. Just not so much in this country, not to people like us."

In a perverse way, it was a good couple of hours. I couldn't remember the last time we'd talked that plainly. Then the next day it was back to the jokes, back to being an imitation of a family, going through the motions.

Not a day, not an hour, went by that I didn't think of Elena. But each day it was easier not to write to her, easier to accept that it was finished.

IN LATE JANUARY, Bahadur sent an instant message to tell me he'd applied for a transfer to Bangalore. A development position had opened up that would mean less pay, but he would be closer to his family.

"And my parents have found a girl they think I might like."

It was one shock on top of another. "Are we talking arranged marriage, here?"

"Not exactly. It would be my choice. But my parents have a good idea of what is suitable."

"How soon?"

"I don't know. A month, maybe?"

The idea of Buenos Aires without Elena or Bahadur seemed grim and lonely. Almost as grim and lonely as North Carolina.

THE SECOND WEEK in February, I called the Executive Assistant to James Watkins, Senior VP, Software Development, at the New York office. I told her that I had some personal and confidential information from Isabel in Buenos Aires that she had asked me to discuss with him, and that I needed just fifteen minutes of his time. His assistant told me how difficult it was to catch Jim in his office and asked if I could put it in an email or possibly talk to anyone else in the organization. I was polite and firm and slightly mysterious, and said I could see him any time, night or day. She told me she would call me back.

She called the next morning and, after one more attempt to talk me out of it, offered me an appointment for the next day, Thursday, at 6:15 in his office. She emphasized that he really could give me no more than fifteen minutes. I said that would be fine and booked a flight for the next morning and a room for that night at the Sheraton where Universal had a discount.

For Lauren I had a different lie. I told her that Watkins had heard what had happened and wanted to meet me in person. I didn't have to come down too hard on what it might mean for my career— careers were something she understood very well. The hard part was talking her out of going along. I convinced her that Watkins needed to see that I was able to get around on my own.

The flight was hellish, delayed for two hours due to bad weather, overcrowded, with nowhere to put my feet up. A mixture of rain and sleet was falling when we finally landed at La Guardia and it continued throughout the afternoon. I dropped my suitcase at the hotel and barely had time to wash my face and ice my feet for ten minutes before catching a cab to the Universal offices on Madison Avenue.

I found myself reflexively comparing the city to Buenos Aires. New York loomed over me, the huge, impersonal buildings dwarfing the dark streets, the grim people shouldering past me in silence. I'm homesick, I thought.

It was my first trip to corporate headquarters and I was not at my best. My suit hung off me, my face was gaunt, and I leaned heavily on my cane. Everyone around me had the right haircut and thousand dollar shoes, and I looked like I'd been tortured.

I wondered how much of the money the company had saved through layoffs in North Carolina had gone into upkeep for the Manhattan offices. Everything gleamed. The amber-lit water sculpture in the ground floor lobby made gentle shushing sounds. The metal detectors that guarded the banks of elevators were so high tech as to be nearly unobtrusive.

I arrived fifteen minutes early, breathing deeply and taking my pulse. Sweat was trying to break across my forehead and the admin stared at me suspiciously. She was in her fifties, brisk and humorless, and she must have taken me for a junkie.

She called Watkins at 6:15 to remind him, then told me, needlessly, that he was running late. She hoped he wouldn't have to cancel. I reminded her that I had flown up from Durham specifically for the meeting.

At 6:25 a large man with thinning red hair and a yellowish suit emerged from the office. One side of his mouth twitched in a nervous tic. He said nothing as he went straight to the elevators and slammed the down button with the flat of his hand.

A moment later, Watkins came out to greet me. He was in his sixties, thin and tan, radiating health and prosperity. His hair was short and intermittently gray. His suit must have cost ten times what mine did and it sat on him as comfortably as jeans and a polo shirt. "Rob?" he said. "Jim Watkins." I felt an electrical energy in his grip. It was not a happy association. "Come on in."

He closed the door behind us. The office was long and narrow, the long wall all glass and looking out over the city as the last light faded. His desk was at one end, a sofa and armchairs at the other. He headed for the couch and sat comfortably at one end, one leg up on the cushions. I sat in an armchair and said, "I hate to ask this, but would you mind if I put my feet up? I'm really not in very good shape yet."

"Make yourself at home. Were you in an accident?"

"Not an accident," I said. "I was tortured."

"In Buenos Aires?"

"Yes."

"Recently?"

"In November."

He looked genuinely shocked. "My God, it never ends down there. Were they caught?"

"By the police, you mean? The police were involved in it."

He nodded somberly. "I guess that was a stupid question on my part. I should have known better. Why did they come after you?"

"I think it was because of the file that Isabel sent you."

"I'm sorry, what file?"

I had retrieved the file from my email and printed a copy, just in case. I took it out of my breast pocket, unfolded it, and handed it to him.

"Isabel was supposed to have sent this to me?" he said.

"That's what she told me."

"Where did this come from?"

"Do you remember Marco Suarez? They took him too, and killed him. He had it hidden in his desk. Obviously he put this together after the fact, but the details are pretty convincing."

He flipped through the pages. "So they did it anyway," he said.

"They?"

He dropped the printout on the coffee table next to my feet. "You obviously know most of this already. If I talk to you about it, it's Universal Systems Confidential. Okay?"

He meant that I could be fired if I talked about it outside the company. "I understand," I said.

"The CIA was very involved in Latin American in the seventies, as I'm sure you know. Castro had them in a panic, and Allende and all the others." He pronounced Allende the Argentine way, ah-*shen*-day, giving me a pang. "They had huge amounts of money available to support anti-communist regimes. They approached me about working with the Videla government to...negotiate some lucrative contracts with them."

"Bribe them, you mean."

"Yes. I was convinced we could do it without money changing hands, so I refused. Clearly they found somebody else who was willing."

"You didn't have any scruples about working with a dictator? With the disappearances and the torture and the murder?"

He took a few seconds to answer. "The military was always careful to maintain deniability. And we honestly didn't know how bad it was. Those were different times. Back then, people thought of communists the way they think of terrorists now. Anything seemed justified to stop them."

"So who was it? Who did the CIA get to?"

He didn't answer.

"It was Isabel, wasn't it?" I said. "That's why she never sent you the file. But how did she have access to the money?"

Not looking at me, as if he were only thinking out loud, he said, "Her first job was in accounting."

Suddenly things started to make sense. Cesarino had taken me because of his obsession with Mateo. Somehow Isabel had known about my connection to him. It wasn't about the contabilidad file at all, which was why the man in the coveralls never asked about it. Cesarino already had it, thanks to La Reina. He'd killed Miguel Suarez to protect her cover, not because he was afraid for himself. She would also have given him details to use in the interrogation, like the business with my father.

I wondered if the CIA man in the kitchen had been one of Isabel's old friends.

My heart was thrashing wildly in my chest and I couldn't get my breath. I got up and paced around the room without my cane. The pain in my feet made my hatred burn brighter.

"What happens now?" I said, as calmly as possible.

"There will be consequences for her," Watkins said.

"What kind of consequences?"

"I appreciate what you've been through," he said. "This is a matter that I will deal with through the proper channels."

"You have no fucking idea what I've been through," I said, gripping the back of the chair I'd been sitting in. "And this is a matter
that needs to be public knowledge."

Watkins had been threatened by tougher customers than a scraw-
ny, beat-up old programmer with bad feet. I hadn't even managed to
annoy him.

"Two things to think about," he said. "One, this is very old news.
Nobody cares about Argentina, or what happened there in the seventies. Two, I believe you're aware of the consequences of violating
company confidentiality."

"So you're going to slap her wrist and hush it up."

"Thanks for taking the trouble to come to me with this." He
stood up. "The brief I got from my assistant said the company
has completely covered all your medical expenses and disability
leave, though it didn't say anything about the cause of your injuries. Anyway, I want you to know we were glad to do it. Employee
loyalty is one of Universal's greatest strengths and we know how to
reward it."

He offered the printout to me and I took it. He could read me
well enough to see that I didn't want to shake hands.

"I wish I had more time to spend with you, but I am literally
booked solid until ten tonight." He walked past me and opened the
door, and there was nothing for me to do except to go. As I limped
past him, he gently touched my arm and said, "I'm truly sorry for
what happened to you."

I stopped to look in his face. I saw nothing there but sympathy
and regret. I nodded stiffly.

"Take care," he said.

Another man in a suit sat in the outer office, waiting to take
my place.

RATHER THAN TAKE A CHANCE that I might lose my nerve, I
flagged a cab and went straight to the *New York Times* building. The
receptionist found a reporter from the business section who was
willing to listen to me.

She was about forty, with short red hair and a round, Irish face.
She listened to the bare outline of the story there in the lobby,
then looked at her watch and said, "I haven't had dinner yet. How
about you?"

She took me to a nearby deconsecrated church, complete with stained glass, that had become a pizza joint. She took extensive notes while I talked and asked a lot of pointed questions. By the time she had the whole story, we'd finished our food and she was rubbing her jaw.

"It's a dynamite story," she said. "Pulitzer material, if it's done right. But there's a problem."

I had already figured this out from her questions. "Evidence."

"Exactly. I don't doubt anything you've said. I mean, no offense, look at you. The problem is, the people who tortured you are dead. The crime scene is cold and the cops have closed the case as drug business. This spreadsheet here, as you've told me, is obviously ex post facto and there's no provenance for it at all. Nobody at Universal is going to talk about this. It's a one-source story with no corroboration."

"So the truth just...disappears."

"The stuff we know that we can't print would curdle your milk. It's one of the many frustrations of this job. Along with watching my entire industry die. Who's going to be left to force these people to keep up even a pretence of honesty?"

She closed her notebook. "I'm going to see what I can find out. It's possible I can jar something loose. But I wouldn't get my hopes up."

"You need to know that there's a danger for me in this. If Universal finds out I've talked to you, they'll fire me. I'm okay with that if the story gets published, but I would hate to lose my job and my pension and my medical coverage for nothing."

"Understood. I can't make any promises, except that I will be discreet."

She gave me her card and took all my contact information. When she left me she said, just as Watkins had, "Take care."

LAUREN WAS DUMBFOUNDED when I told her I was going back to Buenos Aires.

"You're not recovered yet," she said. "You've still got a ways to go physically and you've barely started on the psychological end of it."

It was the first week in March. The Bartlett pear trees had erupted in white blossoms and the redbuds were scattering purple petals all over the ground. Time for change.

I said, "Buenos Aires has more psychiatrists per capita than any place on Earth. And they've got experience in exactly this kind of thing."

"This is about Elena, right?"

"No," I said. "I'm sure you're right. She'll have moved on by now."

"Then why? Why, Rob?"

"I just have to," I said.

MY LANDLADY had rented my old apartment, which was just as well. The memories would have overwhelmed me. She had another place, more modern, a block down Humberto Primo. Yes, she assured me, there were hardwood floors where I could practice my dancing. She would have my boxes there waiting.

Bahadur had still not heard about his transfer. "Maybe it's not going to happen," he said. "And I'll be stuck here. It will be good to have you back. Nobody here speaks English worth two craps. Yes? 'Worth two craps?'"

I wrote Don Güicho when I had my plans in place. I would arrive on Sunday, March 18, going from the end of one winter to the beginning of another. Don Güicho didn't respond, but then he'd never been comfortable with email.

I went to a few tango practicas before I left the States. By this point I rarely needed the cane. I danced for an hour each time and though my feet hurt afterward, it was no different in kind from the pain I always felt after dancing. My old friends and partners were full of questions and I had to tell them I wasn't ready to talk about it yet.

The tangos themselves were amazing, profoundly emotional experiences that sometimes left me blinking back tears. I felt no self-consciousness, only the power of the music moving through me. They were the tangos oscuros that Don Güicho had talked about, an exquisite sadness. I didn't explicitly think about Elena while I was dancing and yet she was an inescapable part of every step.

RIDING FROM EZEIZA AIRPORT into Buenos Aires in the cool of the dying summer, I knew I'd made the right decision. I'd loaded up on Valium for the flight and managed to sleep for much of it.

It was good to hear the music of spoken Spanish instead of the harsh, flat vowels of English, to hear the tango station playing in the cab, to see the familiar sights of the long freeway drive through the decaying perimeter of the city. Despite the foreignness, despite the danger, it was where I needed to be.

The hardest part was going through the boxes that Elena had packed from the old apartment. I imagined she might have left me a note, or some kind of token. Instead I found the shirts she had worn that still smelled of her. I put all the clothes into plastic bags and left them at the laundry around the corner.

La Reina threw a party for me on Wednesday, my first day back at work. My eyes kept returning to her, trying to reconcile this competent, powerful, laughing woman with the betrayal that had destroyed me.

During my lunch hour on Thursday, I stood on the street outside the office and called the Citibank in Calle Florida on my new cell phone. I asked for Osvaldo Lacunza and gave his secretary my name. I didn't know if he would take my call. If Elena had told him that she and I were through, he would have no reason to.

He did pick up. «I can't talk on this line,» he said. «I can meet you somewhere near here for a few minutes this afternoon. There's a magazine kiosk in front of the bank. Can you be there at three?»

This was the shopping district I had come to many times, with Elena and on my own, a pedestrian mall full of high-end stores selling electronics and appliances, books and CDS, shoes and leather coats. That afternoon, as always, it was mobbed—with tourists, with well-dressed porteños, with musicians and hustlers of various stripes, all of them glancing repeatedly at the overcast and threatening sky.

I got there early and Osvaldo came out of the bank at 3:15, prompt by Buenos Aires standards. He looked me over and then embraced me gently. «You look better,» he said. «How do you feel?»

«I have headaches sometimes. Sometimes bad. Other than that I'm okay, thanks to you. I don't want to keep you, and I hate to ask you another favor, but there's no one else I can go to.»

«Ask me.»

«There's a woman named Isabel Salcedo, who is the head of the Buenos Aires office of Universal Systems. I think she worked for the CIA during la dictadura. I think she may be working for them now. I thought you might know, or know somebody who would know, if this is true.»

«It's true. In the seventies she delivered money from the CIA to the government. Or rather, Marco Suarez delivered it for her. It came either to me or to Cesarino. In return, Universal got contracts worth a lot of money. Millions and millions of dollars. That was what we did in those days. Argentina was once one of the richest countries in the world. We put a faucet in that wealth and all the US companies came by with buckets and we filled the buckets up for them and they took the money away.

«Does she still work for the CIA? I don't know. I wouldn't think she's very active these days. However. She came to Universal from the School of the Americas in Panama. You know what I'm talking about? The school for dictators and assassins. You don't walk away from that.»

I said, «I think she's the one who betrayed me to Cesarino.»

Osvaldo nodded. «I had the opportunity to converse with Cesarino before he died.» His casualness impressed me. I wondered if I could ever learn to be that cold. «He said that Isabel called him and wanted him to take care of you and some Indian guy. Cesarino refused. Then she told him that you could lead him to Mateo.»

So there it was. My eyes went briefly out of focus as the anger and fear and memories of pain washed over me.

Osvaldo put both hands on my shoulders. «Listen to me. Now that you know this, it's best if you forget it. Isabel is a very dangerous person. I'm sure she assumes you have learned your lesson. If you show her otherwise, she will find a way to kill you. She might even do it herself.»

«I know,» I said. It would have been less than gracious to say I had no life left, given that I owed him what life I had.

«Bueno,» he said. «If you need anything else, you know where to find me.»

THAT NIGHT I HAD my first lesson with Don Güicho since I'd gotten back. I arrived at Saverio's early, as usual, and refused the usual cup of coffee. Don Güicho held our embrace for a long time. «And how are you now, my friend? Are you okay?»

I shrugged. «I'm okay.» In fact my head was clear enough, the pain no more than a lurking threat.

Brisa gave me a long hug and stroked my cheek, near the burn scar, with the back of her hand. Her compassion made my eyes water and I had to turn away.

In the studio I changed my shoes and Don Güicho put on Pugliese. I took my time finding my embrace with Brisa and waited for the music to tell me when to take my first step. I danced the way I had at the practicas in North Carolina, mostly walking to the music, not doing much of anything fancy. Don Güicho didn't stop me and at the end of the song Brisa said, «You dance differently now. Don Güicho, doesn't he dance differently?»

«You dance like a porteño now,» Don Güicho said. «Congratulations, Beto.»

«The price for that is very high, no?» I said, not without bitterness.

«Yes, for some it's very high. It's not something you can put into words. People find out for themselves or they don't.»

«Well, that's all I want now. I don't care about the ganchos and the back sacadas.»

«You would have to learn the back sacada from Saverio in any case,» Don Güicho said. That was the porteño style, too, to always be ready with a joke. I hoped to regain that someday.

«I just want to learn to move with the music.»

«Bueno,» Don Güicho said. «Now we begin the advanced class.»

The advanced class turned out to be much like the beginner's class, with a finer grain. We started with the walk again, then the doble tiempo, the quick-quick-slow of the ocho cortado and change of direction, this time in terms of how it fit with each style and era of the music. At the end of the hour I saw, with a slow, sinking feeling, that I was still only a short way down the path.

Brisa had to hurry away, as usual. «Come to the milonga Sunday, Beto,» she said. «I want to dance with you some more.»

«She's very sweet,» I said to Don Güicho when she was gone.

«Yes, very sweet. And very young. Walk with me?»

It was 9:15, the night chilled by the rain that had yet to fall. I couldn't stop myself from asking the question, though I knew the answer would tear me apart. «Have you seen Elena?»

«Yes.» He showed no inclination to elaborate.

«Tell me.»

«I think she is maybe involved with a teacher named Miguel Autrillo.»

«I know him. You introduced me once.»

«Claro. She's been performing with him. I'm sorry, Beto. I know this doesn't help you. At least he's a good dancer and a good man.»

«No, no, if she's going to be with someone else, I would want him to be a good man.»

«Does she know you're back in Buenos Aires?»

«I don't think so.»

«Are you going to tell her?»

«We're not...in touch. We haven't been since the hospital.»

We walked on in silence for a while and then I said, «You know Mateo, don't you? From the old days. And you're in contact with him now.»

«Did he tell you that?»

«It was a guess. He told me it was a tango teacher from back then who first recognized Elena. When I was in the US, going over everything again and again, I knew it was you.»

«I'm not a man of action. I couldn't kill anyone. But I support their cause. I did what I could to help then, and I help now.»

«You knew Elena's mother.»

«Yes.»

«Was she very beautiful?»

«She looked just like Elena. Only with a straighter nose.»

«I want you to ask Mateo to call me.»

«Why?»

«I don't want to tell you.»

He stopped and faced me. «They nearly got you killed once. Wasn't that enough? You want to finish the job?»

«It wasn't Mateo who killed me.»

«Beto, you're not dead!»

«Am I not?»

«I watched you dance real tango tonight with a beautiful woman who enjoyed every second of it. If that's dead, kill me now.»

«Please, Don Güicho. I ask you as a friend.»

He held me a bit longer with his stare, then finally turned away. «I'll think about it.»

We came to the Pasco Subte stop and he hugged me tightly and kissed my cheek. «You're not so old, not so bad looking. The scar helps a little, I think, gives you some mystery. You've got a good job and you can dance. This city is wide open to you. Don't do anything stupid. Promise me.»

«If I do anything,» I said, «I will try not to make it stupid.»

•

MATEO CALLED the next night.

It was Friday and I was exhausted. I didn't have the reserves of strength I used to. I'd fallen asleep on the couch reading *Tienda de los Milagros* for the second time. I'd been so deeply asleep that I'd forgotten how to answer the phone. I stared at it for a full three seconds before I remembered to press the Talk button.

«Hola,» I said.

«The usual place, the café. Half an hour. Okay?»

«Okay,» I said.

I got to Arte y Café first and walked slowly up and down San Juan. I expected him to come from the east, from the other side of the airport highway, and was surprised to look up and see him next to me. I stopped and embraced him and he said, «Let's walk.»

We turned away from the lights of San Juan, working our way south and east, away from the river. The first thing I said to him was, «I betrayed you. To Cesarino.»

«Of course you did. Do you think anyone blames you for that? I would have done the same. I'm glad you're alive.»

«You too,» I said. «Everyone got away?»

«Claro. The place we have now is not as nice, not as interesting. A few of the young people quit after Cesarino took you. That's to be expected. The rest of us are all right. Is that why you wanted to see me? To apologize?»

«No,» I said. «I need a gun.»

He looked like he might burst out laughing. «A gun? What for?»

«I'm going to kill my boss.»

Now he *was* laughing. «That's very socialist of you.»

«She's the one who betrayed me to Cesarino.» I laid it out for him: the CIA connection, the payments to Cesarino, the spreadsheet, the confirmation from Osvaldo.

«Then we should put her on trial. If she's guilty, we'll take care of her for you.»

«Then I'm still helpless, still a victim. I'll still have the nightmares and breakdowns. The pain will never stop.»

«You remember that discussion we had? What you're talking about isn't justice. It's revenge.»

«I've changed my mind. I don't care anymore. You said yourself it's hard to tell the difference. You have even fewer people than before. Does your so-called trial have any greater moral authority than the fact that I'm willing to give my life to do this?»

«If I agree to help you, would you know how to use it? Have you ever fired a pistol?»

«My father had a .38. We used to go into the country and shoot tin cans.»

«A can is not a human being.»

«I know that.»

«I'm not sure this is a good idea. I have to think about it.»

After a minute, Mateo said, «I may be leaving soon.»

«For where?»

«Cuba, maybe. I don't know. I can't stand the cold weather anymore and I feel useless here. Tired of running and hiding like a dog.»

«Have you talked to Elena about it?»

He shook his head. «We never talk. I had this vision that I would find her and we would be a family. Stupid, I know, but it's what I hoped for. Every time I see her, I see her mother. When she sees me, she sees a stranger. It's another reason to go.»

«I'm sorry,» I said.

«I'm supposed to be a fucking revolutionary. I'm supposed to be bringing the future and all I'm doing is living in the past.»

We had come to the lights and noise of Avenida 9 de Julio and San Juan. He hugged me tightly. «I'll call you,» he said, and ran down the steps of the Subte.

SATURDAY MORNING he called again. «You know the place in the park where we met before? Be there at noon. Don't speak to me, don't give any sign that you know me. Just follow, keep your distance, and watch what I do. Carefully. Understand?»

«Claro,» I said.

I didn't know which I'd been more afraid of, that he would agree or that he would refuse. Now everything was decided. There was a hard, painful comfort in that.

It matched the terrible pain in my right eye.

I HAD A BOOK in my lap. I wasn't even pretending to read. The park was cool and damp from showers overnight. Two young boys listlessly kicked a futbol back and forth. A dog lay under a tree, curled tightly into himself.

At 12:25 Mateo walked past without looking in my direction. He had a white plastic grocery sack in his left hand.

My heart began to pound.

I gave him a head start, then I slowly got up and dusted off my pants. My hands shook. I put the book under my arm and followed.

We walked north, toward the river that was just out of sight. After a while Mateo stopped and took a plastic water bottle out of the bag. He glanced around as he took a drink, then casually dropped the bag into an open trash can.

I sat on a bench a few feet away and watched the can. The park was empty except for old people, dogs, and kids. Mateo kept walking until he was out of sight and once he was gone it occurred to me that I would never see him again.

I picked the bag out of the trash and walked away.

The bag was heavy. I peeked inside and saw a small bundle wrapped in newspaper.

In my bedroom, I unwrapped it carefully. It was an off-brand revolver, chrome finish, black plastic handle, .38 caliber, with five bullets in the cylinder and an empty chamber under the hammer.

I held it with both hands. The feeling of power was overwhelming. I raised it and pointed it at the mirror.

"Bang," I said. "You're dead."

On Monday I took the gun to the office in my briefcase, a vintage brown leather satchel that I'd bought at the big indoor flea market near Plaza Dorrego. For days I'd been visualizing what I was going to do, imagining having the gun there as I walked through reception and back to my cube, then carefully putting it in my desk. I was amazed at how easy it was. How many other guns were there in this city block? In this building? In the Universal offices?

I put it in the bottom drawer of my file cabinet, all the way at the back. It was wrapped again in newspaper and inside the white plastic bag.

That evening the first serious cold front of the fall came through. The chill went deep into me as I walked home from the Subte. I wondered if I could take another winter.

I hadn't been to a milonga since I'd been back, not even to Don Güicho's on Sunday to dance with Brisa. As much as I wanted to dance, I couldn't bear the thought that I might run into Elena. That

Monday night, like most other nights, I left the apartment long enough to buy groceries, then I cooked a lonely dinner and went to bed, where I tossed and turned all night.

On Tuesday, as soon as I got to the office, I unwrapped the gun and slipped it into my briefcase. I left it there all day and waited to return it to the drawer until I'd shut my laptop down for the night.

It was there in my briefcase again on Wednesday morning at 11:25 when Bahadur called me from Isabel's office and asked if I would join them.

There was a sound in my head, the sound of the wind vibrating a taut wire, a high thrumming. I was so far inside myself that I could barely feel my arms and legs. I nearly tripped on the carpet as I picked up my briefcase and walked toward Isabel's office. I passed two people in the hall and didn't return their nods or hellos.

Words from another time came into my head: all or nothing. The bitterness of the thought helped keep me going.

Todo o nada.

My head throbbed and my right eye burned with pain.

I looked at the golden crown on her office door and remembered how I'd once thought it funny. I knocked and went in.

Todo o nada.

Past Isabel, through the window on the far side of the office, I saw Avenida 9 de Julio swarming with black taxis. Bahadur faced her in a low chair, his back to me. His turban was orange.

I sat in the chair next to him. He finished his sentence. I hadn't registered a word he'd said.

He turned to me and said, «La Reina needs an update on where we stand for a release in June.» He sounded like he was talking in the next room. I could barely hear him. I nodded and tried to smile.

«Beto, are you okay?» Isabel asked. She sounded genuinely concerned. I stared at her. I pictured her picking up the phone and saying, «I have two men I need you to kill.»

Todo o nada.

I looked at Bahadur and said in English, "I think you should get out of this office, now. Hurry."

Isabel said, «Beto, speak up and slow down if you're going to use English. You know I don't follow it so well.»

I bent over and opened the top flap of my briefcase and reached inside. The gun was not where I thought. I began to sweat. I looked down and pushed a legal pad to one side and there it was. I put my hand on it.

At first I thought it was caught on something. It was heavy, was all. Tremendously, unbelievably heavy. I couldn't lift it.

I imagined Isabel's face as she saw the gun point at her. I pictured a black and white tile floor and a steel table. Sweat dripped off my forehead, running into my eyes.

«I think he's sick,» Bahadur said. He got up and stood next to me and switched to English. "Rob, are you okay? Do you need help?"

My whole arm was shaking. In desperation I tried once more to pull the gun out of the briefcase. My hand came out empty. Tears of frustration and self-hatred mixed with the sweat and poured down my face.

«I'll take care of him,» Bahadur said. He took me under the arms and lifted me to my feet.

«Do you need to go to the hospital?» Isabel said, reaching for the phone.

"No!" I said.

«Not yet,» Bahadur said. In English he said, "Rob, can you walk?"

"Briefcase," I said.

He closed the briefcase and picked it up with one hand, as if it hardly weighed anything. He took me under the arm and guided me toward the door.

«Let me know how he is,» Isabel said. «If he's okay, take him home in a taxi. I'll cover it.»

He led me to my cubicle and sat me down. I was crying helplessly. He gave me a handful of tissues and said, "What's in the briefcase, pal?"

I motioned for him to look. He opened the flap, poked around, and said, "Ah." He pulled his hand out and closed the flap again.

I took a long, gulping drink of water and got myself more or less in control.

"Do you want to see a doctor?" Bahadur said. "Or do you want to go home?"

"My apartment," I said. "Let's take that cab."

Bahadur nodded and picked up the briefcase.

•

WE DIDN'T TALK until we were in the apartment with the door locked. We sat at the dining room table and Bahadur laid the gun in front of him.

"Where did you get it?" he said.

I shook my head. "Next question."

"The next question is obvious. What the hell were you doing?"

I went to the kitchen for a bottle of water and glasses. I came back and filled the glasses and said, "It was her. Isabel. She told Cesarino that I knew where Mateo was. She told him because he didn't want to do what she'd asked him to do, which was kill both you and me."

"Rob, do you understand how crazy that sounds? I don't think your judgment right now—"

"Listen," I said. "Just listen."

I told him what I'd learned from Watkins and Osvaldo and what I'd put together for myself. The longer I talked, the farther Bahadur sat back in his chair, as if he wanted to distance himself from the words.

"Have you told all this to your montonero friend?"

"He offered to put her on trial for me."

"You didn't agree?"

"I guess I'm not that impressed with their moral authority. Or their competence. I thought I needed to do it myself. Apparently..." I shrugged, fought to keep from breaking down again. "Apparently I was wrong."

"But you are done with this idea now, yes? It's one thing for me to talk about violence. This is not you."

"No," I said. "It's not me."

I took a drink of water.

"There's only one part of this I don't understand," I said. "I don't know how Isabel knew about Elena and...and the montonero."

Bahadur looked down at the table. "That was me."

I felt a chill. "Tell me."

"We were having a meeting, just the two of us. This was not that long before they kidnapped you. She was asking about you, wanted to know how you were settling in, if you had a sweetheart, that sort of thing. I said yes. She seemed very casual, just interested because she liked you. Was it a local girl? Did she dance tango like you? That kind of thing. I see now that she was fishing. Fishing, yes? She has a way of making you want to tell her things."

"I know."

"So I told her you were seeing this really interesting woman, that she was the daughter of a desaparecido, that she'd been adopted by one of the torturers. I didn't think it was a secret or anything."

"It wasn't."

"But because I told her that, she connected you with this man."

I had to wait for an initial flash of rage and betrayal to pass. "Bahadur, you can't blame yourself. It's not your fault, it's Isabel's." I said it because I had to, but when the words were out, I saw they were true.

"I have my share of it." He looked up at me. "There is so much blame to go around. Enough for everyone."

"Mostly," I said, "for Isabel."

"Is it Isabel's fault? Or is it human nature? Greed is so strong in us. We are all so restless with it. Universal was greedy, so they made a deal with the dictatorship. I am greedy so I work for Universal despite the evil they do. These are the things we settle for. A bigger house, a sports car, the power to hurt other people. All because it's so hard to get what we really need."

"And what is that?"

"Love," Bahadur said. "And justice."

He dragged the pistol across the tabletop with one finger, looked at it, picked it up and hefted it. "This is a real piece of shit, I think. 'Made in Italy.' Not like a Colt or a Smith and Wesson."

"Probably. Beggars and choosers."

"Indeed," Bahadur said. "Beggars and choosers." He stuck the gun into the back of his jeans.

I was suddenly alert. "What do you think you're doing?"

"I will take care of this for you."

"Take care of what? Of the gun, or..."

"First I will clean it carefully to remove all possible fingerprints. Then I will dispose of it." He smiled at me and stood up to go. "Don't worry, Rob. Everything's going to be okay."

I WAS A WRECK. I couldn't remember the last time I'd slept through the night. I was emotionally and physically exhausted, my shoulder and neck muscles like steel hawsers, my headache like a sulphuric acid injection through the middle of my right eye. I swallowed two Valium and took a long, hot shower. I put on a pair of sweat pants and fell asleep in front of the TV. Sometime after dark, I woke up, ate some leftovers, took another Valium, and went to bed.

The next morning, Isabel came by my cube to check on me. I told her that I'd had a flashback, that it had happened before, that I was okay now. She seemed honestly solicitous.

I ate lunch there in front of my monitor and did as much work as I could. Bahadur checked in with me every hour or two via instant message. I longed to ask him if he'd gotten rid of the gun like he promised, and knew better than to put a question like that into the internal messaging system. As I was about to leave he typed, "You *are* going to your class tonight, yes?"

"Not sure," I said.

"It will do you good."

"I suppose."

"Don't suppose. Do it. If you stop dancing, I will have them put you in the loony bin."

"OK," I wrote. "OK."

I WAS WORTHLESS in class, unable to concentrate.

«Beto, this is a waste of time,» Don Güicho said. «You're dancing like a zombie.»

«Some days are better than others,» I said. «This isn't one of the good ones. I'm sorry.»

«Don't be sorry,» Brisa said. «Just take care of yourself, okay?»

I stopped at Arte y Café on the way home to get a tarta de verduras. I was talking idly with the owner when my brain, after grinding away for hours, finally made the obvious leap.

«Can you make that to go?» I said. «And hurry, please.»

I walked home as fast as I could push my tired feet. I switched on CSN, the Argentine news channel, and collapsed at the table with my food still in the bag, my stomach now too twisted up to let me eat.

I sat through a full hour of news, slowly beginning to relax and hope I'd been wrong. My eyes gradually closed and I drifted into a hazy half-sleep. And then I heard Isabel's name.

«Salcedo was the director of the local office of Universal Systems, the giant multinational computer company,» said a woman's voice. I snapped to attention. The blonde news anchor was where she had been, sitting with her laptop open on a bare desk against the blue-lit background of the studio. A banner underneath read, MURDER

ROCKS QUIET NEIGHBORHOOD and POLICE EXPAND SEARCH FOR MYSTERIOUS ASSAILANT. The time was 23:08. «As she walked home on a nearly deserted street shortly after eight o'clock this evening, a man approached Salcedo from behind. Apparently he said something to her, she turned, and he fired two or three shots at close range, then quickly walked away. Only a single witness has come forward, claiming the man may have been Jamaican and describing a knit Rasta cap and a bulky black jacket with the collar turned up. Salcedo was pronounced dead at the scene.»

The picture changed to a reporter on the street with Salcedo's husband. The husband was heavy and balding, dressed in a sky-blue track suit, the color of the Argentine flag. He choked back tears as he said, «I can't understand it. Everybody loved her. We've got three kids, the youngest is only twelve. How do I explain this to them?»

FOUR DETECTIVES ARRIVED at the office at 9:00 the next morning. Three were regular investigators in bad suits and the fourth was Sublieutenant Bonaventura, the one who had confiscated Suarez's computer. They got on the intercom to announce that they would talk to each of the 83 employees individually. Bonaventura arrived at my cubicle a few minutes later.

He sat me down in one of the empty offices and gave me a slow once-over. I didn't necessarily look like I'd been tortured. I could have been mistaken for a terminal cancer patient or an escaped psychopath. Or the accident victim in Isabel's cover story.

«I imagine you have an idea what this is about,» he said.

«I saw the news last night.»

«Bueno.» He had an expensive leather holder for his legal pad. He opened it, then didn't bother to look at his notes. «We have information that you were making some 'wild accusations' against Sra. Salcedo.»

Only one person could have given him that information and that was James W. Watkins in New York. I didn't bother to hide my surprise. «Really? What sort of accusations?»

He picked up the leather folder and read, «That she was out to get you, that she had it in for you in some way.»

It sounded like Watkins hadn't mentioned the torture. It made no sense that he would, since there was no official record of it.

«Forgive me,» I said, «but that sounds a little crazy. Isabel was very

generous toward me. I think everybody here will tell you the same.
There must be some kind of misunderstanding.»

«Can you account for your whereabouts last night?»

«I was at a tango class from 8 to 9. Then at a restaurant.»

«So you're a dancer, eh?» He didn't seem to think much of the idea.

«That's right.»

«You have witnesses?»

I gave him Don Güicho's number, the number of Saverio's studio,
and the name of the restaurant, and he wrote them down in neat,
architectural-style lettering.

«So what's wrong with you?» he said.

«Excuse me?»

«Were you in an accident or something? You don't look too good.»

«Food poisoning,» I said. «I had to leave work Wednesday. I'm still
not a hundred percent.»

«But you were well enough to dance last night.»

«I didn't dance very well. As Don Güicho will tell you.»

He watched me for a while, maybe to see if I would unravel. I
tried to show him a man with nothing to hide. Finally he said, «You
don't have any plans to go back to the US anytime soon, do you?»

«No,» I said. «This is my home.»

That, finally, seemed to get his grudging approval. He sat back and
said, «I grew up on a farm outside Salto. You know it?»

It was a town in Buenos Aires Province, west of the city. «I've
heard it's very beautiful,» I said.

«It was clean. This city is very dirty. But there's something about
it, no? It makes you a part of itself, like it or not.» He stood up.
«Another detective will have some questions for you later. For now,
you may go back to work.»

WATKINS HAD TO have thought that I killed her. I wondered if
he'd been tempted for a second or two to let it go, to not stir up
any more ghosts of la dictadura. In the end, though, he and Isabel
had been friends. And it was not a good precedent to let a software
developer get away with murdering a director. So, like the executive he was, he'd opted to delegate. Turn me in to the cops without
mentioning the contabilidad CD or the CIA or the torture, and let
things fall out as they might.

The detective who interviewed me in the late afternoon looked badly in need of a nap. He went through his photocopied list of questions in a monotone. Did Isabel have any enemies that I knew of? Did she use drugs? Had there been any changes in her behavior lately? Had she said anything to me or anyone else to indicate that she was worried about something?

I gave him the answers that I believed would arouse the least interest. Everybody liked Isabel. We were all in shock. I had no idea who might have done it.

I went to my cube and continued to stare at the lines of code on my screen, as I had all day, without touching the keyboard. I had seen that Bahadur was on line and had said nothing to him.

The police left at six. A few minutes later, word got around that one of the cops had admitted they were stumped, that it was going to be written off as a failed robbery. At six-thirty I sent Bahadur a message: "dinner @ los sabios?"

WE WALKED the entire way. Bahadur looked like he wanted to be somewhere else. As we passed the big theaters on Corrientes, I said, very quietly, "What did you do with the gun? Afterward?"

"What gun?" he said, and gave me a bright, artificial smile.

The dinner conversation was awkward. We ended up talking about my headaches. I'd said that I had beaten them before and I would beat them again. I had an appointment with a massage therapist for the next morning.

"That deals with the physical part," Bahadur said. "But what about the stress?"

I showed him the same false smile he'd given me in the street. "What stress?"

He leaned forward. "All right. Let's make a deal. Tonight only, we talk about this, and then never again. Cards on the table, yes?"

"Deal," I said.

"You have to forgive yourself, Rob. Nobody else can do it."

"For betraying the montoneros?"

"For not killing La Reina. For not taking revenge. For not being a man of violence."

"You think I need to forgive myself for that?"

"Yes. Because you know what I know. That without Osvaldo you would be dead. That if La Reina had not been killed, she might have come after both of us again. That peace is a worthy goal and we all have to work for it, but without the option of violence we are at the mercy of the violent."

"My doctor in the States says violence is a disease."

"Maybe it is. Maybe one day they will wipe it out like small pox, like polio. Right now, it's an epidemic."

"What do you want me to do? Watch more movies, get tougher, so next time I *can* pull the trigger?"

"No. No. That's not what I want at all. I want to keep you as far away from this as I can, which is one of the reasons we will never talk about this again. You can't treat this disease without catching the disease. Do you understand what I'm saying?"

"No."

Bahadur sighed. "Okay. I will say this one thing. Before she died, I looked into La Reina's eyes. She saw the gun, she recognized me, she knew that I knew. She understood everything. You know what I saw there?"

He seemed to need a response from me. "What?" I said.

"Relief."

His eyes were very red. Nobody, I thought, got much sleep last night.

"I was prepared for her to attack me," he said, "to fight until the end. Instead she...surrendered."

He looked at his plate, stabbed a piece of broccoli, then changed his mind and put the fork down again.

"Two days ago," he said, "I would not have understood that. Now I understand it very well."

"I understand it," I said.

"Yes," Bahadur said. "Maybe you do."

"Did you know she had a husband and kids?" I asked him.

"I doubt anybody in the office did. She kept everything in..." He made a box with his hands. "...containers."

"And it doesn't make any difference to you?"

"A snake can have babies."

I considered that for a while. I didn't want to put into words any of the responses that came to mind.

"Tell me," I said at last. "Did you really wear a Rasta cap?"

"Clever, yes? A way to hide my hair and at the same time to throw them off the smell."

"Off the scent," I said.

We said goodbye at the Subte station near the restaurant. I felt a gulf had opened between us that I would never be able to cross. It made me wonder how much more I could stand to lose.

THE MASSAGE ON SATURDAY morning woke up the pain that my body had been hiding. The therapist was in her forties, half German and half Mexican, a large and serious woman with a firm touch that I liked. I made a month's worth of appointments with her and then went to Parque Lezama to sit on a bench in the chilly afternoon.

Something had happened while I wasn't paying attention. If being in that black and white tiled kitchen had changed me, now I felt like a different person yet again. I would never go back to being the man who had first seen Elena in the Universal lobby, but I was no longer the broken husk who had said goodbye to her at the British Hospital either.

The obvious answer was that for the first time in months I was out of immediate physical danger. I knew that was part of it. A bigger part was having had the chance to pull the trigger and not doing it. The thing that had seemed like weakness at the time now looked like something else.

I knew that I had started the chain of events that led to Isabel's death when I got the gun from Mateo. I had as much as put it into Bahadur's hands. I knew there would be long nights ahead when I would lie awake and think about that.

I hoped Bahadur was wrong when he said that without violence there could be no peace. I had no brilliant rejoinders or surefire solutions. All I had was hope.

I felt old and not unpleasantly fragile. The sun warmed my face. The ground was quiet beneath my feet. The pain in my back and neck had faded for the moment. I breathed in and breathed out. There was nothing left to be in a hurry for.

I sat for a long time and when I was ready I walked to the locutorio and sent two emails, one to Lauren and one to Sam, telling them that if they'd seen a news story about the shooting, they shouldn't worry, that I was all right. I told them I would send more details later and then I walked home.

ON MONDAY the new acting head of the office arrived from New York. He was 34, clean-cut, and his Spanish was substantially less than fluent. He immediately looked to me for help and I did my best impression of a grounded, competent company man.

At the end of the day it looked like I still had a job.

On Wednesday Bahadur dropped by my cubicle. "It seems La Reina was sitting on my transfer paperwork. The new boy found it on his desk and asked me why she hadn't put it through. I said I thought she had. He asked me if I still wanted to go and I said yes. And—poof."

"Poof?"

"I start the job in Bangalore in two weeks." His smile was weak, but genuine.

"Congratulations," I said. "I'm going to miss you."

"It's better this way," he said. "You know?"

I didn't know. I was feeling old again, not as much in the body as in the heart. I'd come to be afraid of change, had lost my belief that it was ever for the better.

ALL THROUGH THURSDAY night's class with Don Güicho, I saw looks pass between him and Brisa. When we were done, Brisa said, «Don Güicho and I want you to come to supper with us.»

«I would be honored,» I said.

We shared a cab to La Paz, the famous hotbed of revolution in the sixties. It was a spacious room with two levels, far more elegant than its history would imply, furnished with wooden tables and chairs and linen tablecloths, noisy with clinking glasses and animated Spanish conversation.

After we'd ordered and Don Güicho had made his customary comments about my missing the delight that was Argentine beef, he said, «This woman who was killed last Thursday, she was your boss, no?»

«Yes.»

«The police asked me many questions. I didn't tell them any more than I had to. They asked if you were sick and I said you weren't feeling well. I said nothing about the torture.»

«Thank you.»

«Did you kill her?»

«Directly? No. I didn't pull the trigger.»

«Was it Mateo?»

I held my thumb and forefinger an inch apart. «If my

responsibility is this much, Mateo's is this much.» I moved them half an inch closer.

Don Güicho held out his own hand, thumb and forefinger almost touching. «Which makes my responsibility this much, for telling Mateo to get in touch with you. Who was this woman?»

«She was CIA. She betrayed me to Cesarino. She had me tortured, and would have had me killed.»

Don Güicho sat back in his chair and nodded. «Bueno. Then I am content.»

«Is Mateo still here?»

«Venezuela,» Don Güicho said. «Times have changed so much. Who really believes in a Revolution anymore? All those days have gone, and the old Buenos Aires with them.»

«The Buenos Aires of the tango is gone too,» Brisa said, «the big ballrooms, the big orquestas. I wish I could have seen all that.»

I nodded. «Elena used to say that all the time.» I was going to have to learn to think before I spoke. I swallowed and gave myself a couple of seconds. «Anyway. Where else is there to go? This is the Buenos Aires we have.»

Don Güicho lifted his glass and we drank to our Buenos Aires querido.

Brisa said, «Speaking of Elena...»

«There was another reason we asked you here,» Don Güicho said.

«We want you to come out dancing with us tonight,» Brisa said. «To El Beso.»

I'd been longing to go dancing, feeling myself going crazy in the tiny space of my apartment. So far, I hadn't made it as far as getting dressed. «You're very sweet,» I said, «and I appreciate what you're trying to do, but I don't think I'm ready yet. If Elena was there, I don't think I could take it.»

Don Güicho said, «She'll be there. She's there every Thursday. You have to do this, Beto. It's part of dancing tango. Relationships change, but you still see each other on the dance floor. It hurts, but you keep dancing. You can't hide forever. The first time will be the worst, then it will get easier.»

«Let me think about it.»

«You think too much. You've been that way as long as I've known you and it's done nothing but hold you back. You want the advanced tango class? This is your assignment.»

•

BY THE END of dinner I was sure that Don Güicho was right.
Better to face her, get it over with, and move on.

It was a short walk from La Paz to El Beso and it was eleven
when we arrived. The Thursday night milonga ended at 12:30. I
wouldn't have to endure more than an hour and a half.

I didn't see Elena as we came in. Then again, I was not looking.
The owner made a fuss over Don Güicho and seated us at a front
row table in the couples' section. I didn't look at the dancers, just
bent over and changed my shoes. Brisa strapped on impossibly high
heels. Don Güicho had come empty-handed, ready to dance in his
leather-soled street shoes.

I stayed bent over as long as possible, double-knotting my laces,
putting my street shoes into my shoe bag. Eventually I had to sit up.
The dancers glided by, inches away from us, and I gradually let my
eyes focus. It had been, I suddenly realized, five months to the day
since I'd seen her. I had worn the sharpness off every memory I had
of her, going over them and over them in my mind. Would I even
recognize her? I kept thinking I saw her in the crowd, then a second
or third look, with my heart racing, would show me I was wrong.

At last the tanda ended with a few seconds of U2.

The floor cleared and a scratchy old Osvaldo Fresedo tango, "El
irresistible," started.

«Vamos, Beto,» Brisa said, standing up and pushing at me. I got to
my feet, then looked to Don Güicho for permission, as was proper.
He waved me away.

We stepped onto a dance floor that was already becoming con-
gested and slowly found our embrace. She was a beautiful woman,
she smelled good, she felt wonderful in my arms. It was tango,
something I knew, more or less, how to do. The music was loud
enough that it filled the moment and didn't leave room for anything else.

At the end of the song Brisa gave me a contented smile. «Muy
lindo, Beto. Very nice.» The tradition was small talk, nothing too
heavy, so Brisa talked about her English class and the professor, who
had a thick German accent. «And at eight in the morning, too,» she
said. «There's not enough coffee in the world.»

We danced again and she asked about my head, which was okay,
all things considered. I told her about my new massage therapist and

how she, too, had a German accent, which made Brisa laugh harder than it should have. I hadn't thought that she would be nervous too.

After the next song she told me about her ne'er do well sister, who was back in Buenos Aires after a bad love affair in Paris. Then we danced once more and the tanda was over and we went back to the table.

I didn't see Elena come in. The first I saw of her was when the next tanda started with a romantic Di Sarli tango called "El am-amecer," the dawn. She was dancing with Miguel Autrillo. He wore a dark suit and a bright blue dress shirt and he was very good, centered and light on his feet, tuned into the crowd, into the music, and into his partner. She had her eyes closed and a quiet smile on her face.

I found, to my surprise, that it hurt much more than I had imagined. In fact, I could not bear it.

«Sorry,» I said to Don Güicho and Brisa. I couldn't see them for the stinging in my eyes. I was trying to smile and I suspected the effect was horrifying. «I can't do this.»

I grabbed the bag with my street shoes and headed for the door as quickly as I could without injuring anyone. With luck, I thought, she would not have seen me.

I made it to the hall outside the club and then I heard her voice. «Beto?»

I took out my handkerchief as I turned around and pretended it was sweat I was wiping from my face. You can do this, I told myself. I tried another, gentler smile. «Hi, Elena.»

She was five feet away from me and she stopped there, uncertain of what came next. She wore a loose black cowl-neck sweater and a black skirt below her knees, black stockings and scuffed black heels. She looked like she'd lost some weight too. «I...I heard you were back.»

I nodded. «I don't get out very much.»

«But, your feet—you can dance?»

«Yes. Not for hours at a time yet, but eventually...»

«Oh, thank God. I'm so glad to hear it.» Her smile was so pure that it blinded me.

«And you?» I said. «You're okay?»

The smile flickered and turned into something more complicated. «Yes, I'm okay. Working at the shoe store. Dancing.»

I nodded. «Good,» I said. «That's good.»

There was nothing safe left to say.

«Well,» I said.

«It was good to see you, Beto. I'm so glad you can dance.»

The moment was beyond awkward, into another new kind of pain. I was becoming a connoisseur. At least it was nearly over. «It was good to see you too,» I said, and she smiled sadly and slowly turned away.

And in that moment I saw that I was in danger of learning nothing from what I'd been through. That if I didn't speak, I would no longer exist, that the job that Cesarino and his men had begun on me would be well and truly finished. I was fairly certain that she would not want to hear what I had to say and I understood that I couldn't let that stop me.

«Elena,» I said.

She turned back.

«I love you,» I told her. «I have never stopped loving you for a second since the first time I danced with you. I don't want to interfere with the life that you've made for yourself. I just need you to know that you're the only thing in this world that I want.»

She stared at me like she didn't quite understand what I was saying.

«I'm sorry,» I said. «I know you—»

She put both hands on the back of her neck, under her hair. I stopped talking because I didn't know what she was doing. She slowly pulled a silver chain out through the neck of the sweater, and on it was the turquoise pendant I'd bought her that Sunday in Plaza Dorrego in what seemed like another century.

I looked in her eyes and I saw that she had been waiting, just like I had, too full of guilt and shame and fear to make the first move, both of us sinking deeper and deeper into a mutual despair of our own making.

«Beto, I beg of you. Please, please stand exactly where you are and wait for me. Will you?»

I nodded and she disappeared into the club. Di Sarli's "A la gran muñeca" came on the loudspeakers, with its staccato strings and pounding piano. I had heard it in every tango class I'd taken on that first trip with Lauren and it was inseparable from my idea of tango and Buenos Aires. I felt myself to be in a weird suspension of time between one life and yet another new one, and I almost turned and fled down the stairs because I was afraid of it, afraid of having what I wanted, afraid that it might one day grow old and change again, and I wanted to always be there in that moment of expectation, waiting for Elena, listening to Di Sarli.

But then I saw her, carrying her jacket and her shoes, and in another few seconds I would be holding her and her hair would be in my face, smelling of vanilla and citrus, and then we would be in a taxi on our way to Confitería Ideal to dance on the marble floors under the crystal chandeliers.

I reached out my hand.

AUTHOR'S NOTE

I HAVE TAKEN a few liberties with historical fact here. As in my other novels, I hope it was in service of higher truth.

Marco Suarez is a fictional character, but Jorge Julio López is not. As of this writing, his kidnappers (and, doubtless, murderers) have not been identified, let alone punished.

The role of US corporations in some of the bloodiest repressions in Latin America is well known, but rarely discussed in the US. Universal Systems is a fictional creation; Ford Motor Company, Citibank, ITT, United Fruit/Chiquita, and other corporations are not.

Osvaldo del Salvador and Emiliano Cesarino are fictional. Miguel Etchecolatz is not and the details of his trial are accurate to the best of my knowledge. Mateo is fictional, the montoneros are not, and my account of the massacre at Ezeiza airport is taken from published eyewitness reports.

MY BIGGEST DEBT of gratitude is to Orla Swift and Alicia Rico-Lazerowski. Orla, my partner in all things including dance, was the first to suggest we take tango lessons and then to suggest we vacation in Buenos Aires. She not only read the book in manuscript, but served as a sounding board and did everything she could to make more time for me to write. She is a wellspring of love and encouragement. Alicia, born and raised in Buenos Aires, is a wonderful *tanguera* as well as an astute reader. She gave me an invaluable critique of the first draft, resulting in a new title, a name change for the protagonist, many corrections to my "too Mexican" Spanish, and dozens of other vital repairs.

Other readers of various drafts provided huge help, including Jim Blaylock, Richard Butner, Ralph Earle, Mariana Fiorentino, Karen Joy Fowler, John Kessel, Gary McDonald, Georgene Russell, Carol Stevens, and Dave Stevens.

THE LIST OF PEOPLE who have tried to teach me tango is long. I would particularly like to thank the following:

In Buenos Aires, Pedro "El Indio" Benevente, Osvaldo Cartery, and Alicia Pons; Mario De Camillis, José Garafalo, and Paula Ferrio; Dina Martinez; and Leticia Tulissi. Extra special thanks to Mario, who also made himself available for urgent questions in email.

In North Carolina, first and foremost, Tito Restucha, el maestro porteño; Gülden Özen, with love; and Jason Laughlin, the master technician. Of the touring pros, I owe the most to Ney Melo and Jennifer Bratt.

Other friends on the ground in Buenos Aires were enormously helpful, including Sergio Gaut vel Hartmann, Ethan Earle, and Roberto and Amalia Restucha. Thanks also to Luis Pestarini of La Biblioteca Nacional.

Gurpreet Hothi answered my many questions about Sikhism with patience, grace, and great clarity. For the record, Bahadur's character was fully formed before I ever met Gurpreet and no resemblance between the two should be inferred.

My good friend Barry Harrington provided information about panic attacks while helping me through my own. Lesley Gaspar shared her experiences, read a late draft, and beat the drum for me.

For medical information, a reading of the manuscript, and many delightful tangos, I am indebted to Fran Meredith, MD. Fran also gave me a referral to John P. Miketa, DPM, who was a huge help with issues surrounding foot injuries and their rehabilitation.

AMONG THE MANY books that I used for research, the following were especially important: *The Shock Doctrine* by Naomi Klein, *Nunca Más,* edited by Ernesto Sabato, *Lo Pasado Pensado* by Felipe Pigna, and the 1963 *KUBARK Counterintelligence Interrogation* manual used by the CIA in Argentina.

For more about the history of blacks in Argentina, see Daniel Schávelzon's *Buenos Aires Negra.* The underground complex that leads to Mateo's hideout is based on Schávelzon's *Arqueolgía Histórica de Buenos Aires: Túneles y Construcciones Subterraneas.*

Among the other valuable books that I consulted are: *The Sikhs* by Patwant Singh; *Las Venas Abiertas de América Latina* by Eduardo Galeano; *La Dicatdura Militar 1976/1983* by Marcos Novaro and Vicente Palermo; *At the Side of Torture Survivors* edited by Sepp Graessner, MD, Norbert Gurris, and Christian Pross, MD; and *Paper Tangos* by Julie Taylor.

•

ONCE AGAIN, my bottomless gratitude to Subterranean Press: to publisher Bill Schafer for his unfailing faith in me and support for my work; to my dedicated proofreader, Jenny Crisp; to Gail Cross, for keeping a watchful eye on my fledgling design skills; and to Yanni Kuznia, who keeps everything on track.

GLOSSARY

abrazo "Embrace." Can refer to the tango embrace, or to the hug and kiss on the cheek that acquaintances of both sexes give each other on meeting or parting, or to a romantic embrace.

agua con gas Sparkling mineral water.

apurate "Hurry up."

bandoneón A cousin of the accordion and concertina found almost exclusively in Argentina, but not manufactured there. Technically a 72-button portable reed wind instrument, it is the defining sound of tango and considered one of the most difficult instruments in the world to master.

barbaro "Great!" or "Cool!" Usually an interjection.

beso "Kiss." Can be the quick kiss on the cheek with an abrazo, or a romantic kiss. Members of the opposite sex will casually say «un beso» on the phone or in email as a farewell.

boleo From bolear, to knock a ball around. In tango, a low kick created when the leader pivots the follower with enough force to bring her free foot off the ground.

boludo More or less "idiot," except that it's mildly obscene. Obscene speech is more accepted in Latin America than in the US, but not universally.

caballero "Gentleman." It also carries some of the weight of its historical meaning, which is "knight."

cabeceo Literally a nod, but in tango, the non-verbal invitation that starts with the leader making eye contact, then tilting his head toward the dance floor.

cacerolazo A cacerola is a saucepan and the -azo suffix in this case indicates "a blow with." This is a protest where people create a ferocious noise by banging on pots and pans and pieces of pipe.

calle "Street."

cartoneros The name for the poor and homeless in Buenos Aires who go through the bags of trash that people set out on the sidewalk, pulling out the cardboard (cartón), cans, and other recyclables and selling them to recycling agencies.

chau The Argentine spelling of the Italian ciao, used only for "goodbye" and not for "hello."

chiflado(a) "Crazy."

claro Literally "clear," used all the time to mean "right," "sure," "of course."

club deportivo "Sporting club"—sort of a cross between a YMCA and a sports bar. The name took on sinister overtones after El Proceso because one of the worst detention centers was known by that name and was in the basement of a club deportivo at Avenida Paseo Colón and the airport highway.

colectivo The massive Buenos Aires city buses, which are cheap and convenient, though their routes can be confusing for out-of-towners. They travel at high speed on narrow streets and are a hazard for the unwary.

¿como no? Common expression meaning "of course" or "why not?"

cortina Literally "curtain," a few seconds of (usually) instrumental music played between tandas, or sets, of tangos during which the dancers keep the same partners. Tango etiquette requires that you not dance to the cortina, but instead vacate the dance floor.

dale Literally "give it to me," but in practice an all purpose expression meaning "okay," "hurry up," "let's go," "let's see what you've got." Pronounced DAH-lay.

dictadura "Dictatorship." There have been many in Argentina, but when there's no qualifier, people mean the dictatorship of el Proceso, 1976–1983.

Don Term of respect for a man, affixed to a first name, e.g., Don Juan. The feminine version is Doña, e.g., Doña Juana.

eje "Axis." In dancing, the center you would spin around if you were a top. As with a top, if your axis is not straight up and down, you wobble.

empanadas The national dish of Argentina. A square sheet of pastry dough folded over any of a number of fillings, from ham and cheese to creamed corn, and baked in an oven until crisp. There are chains of fast food empanada stores competing with mom and pop bakeries, and even the bad empanadas are delicious.

encantado(a) Literally "enchanted," but commonly used to mean "nice to meet you." Typically said to the opposite sex; a woman would say «encantada» to a man.

ESMA La Escuela Superior de Mecánica de la Armada, the Navy Mechanics School. One of the most notorious detention centers during the dictatorship of 1976-83.

gancho Literally "the hook," a tango move in which one dancer's leg wraps around the other's.

Gardel, Carlos The all-time Argentine superstar—tango singer, matinee idol, composer—who died at the height of his fame in a 1935 plane crash.

gracias "Thank you." In Argentina, in response to a yes or no question, it means, "No, thank you."

Güicho Nickname for Luis.

igualmente "Equally." Used most often as a reply when someone says they're glad (or enchanted) to meet you.

locutorio A shop lined with telephone booths where you can make long distance calls. More and more of them have desktop computers where you can get more-or-less high speed Internet service for a few pesos an hour.

medialunas Literally "half-moons." Sweet-glazed crescent rolls, served at many of the same places that make empanadas. A breakfast favorite, especially after staying up all night dancing tango.

microcentro Midtown Buenos Aires, the area around the Obelisk. This is the central business district, the theater district, the main shopping district.

milonga A dance party, a dance step, and a variety of music. Essentially a quicker, more staccato form of tango, the milonga step is danced to milonga music, which has a strong habanera rhythm. The events where you go to dance tango are also called milongas, so you can dance a milonga to a milonga at a milonga.

milonguero viejo Literally "old milonga guy"—a term of respect for the old paunchy guys who show up at the milongas, usually in suits and open collared shirts, not doing anything especially fancy, but effortlessly right on the music.

ocho "Eight." In tango, a figure where the follower pivots from one leg to the other, crossing back and forth in front of the leader.

ocho cortado A cut version of the ocho, a mainstay of the Buenos Aires style. Essentially a change of direction to the quick-quick-slow rhythm.

onze "Eleven." Also El Once, an unofficial neighborhood of Buenos Aires. The name comes from the Once de Septiembre (September 11) railroad station, commemorating the date in 1852 when Buenos Aires began a secession from the rest of Argentina that lasted until 1880.

parada Literally a "stop," a tango move where one dancer's foot blocks the movement of his or her partner's foot.

piropo Elaborate compliment from a man to a woman, often addressed to strangers, and often involving wordplay, e.g., «Such curves and me with no brakes.» This is a major indoor—and outdoor—sport in Latin America and the man wins if he gets a laugh, or any other response, from his target.

porteños What the people of Buenos Aires call themselves—the people of the port.

practica A formal tango practice session. Here, unlike at a milonga, it's appropriate to stop and try a move over again, or make a suggestion to your partner, or ask the supervising teacher for help.

principiante "Beginner." The first stage of tango apprenticeship.

proceso Literally "process," but used most often as a proper noun to refer to el Proceso de Reorganización Nacional (the National Reorganization Process), the name the military junta of 1976–1983 used for itself.

qué lindo "How beautiful."

querido(a) Literally "beloved." A common endearment, equivalent to "dear" or "darling."

reina "Queen."

sacada Literally a "taking out"—a tango move in which the leader's foot seems to displace the follower's. The sacada por atrás, or infamous "back sacada," is a particularly difficult heel-first variation.

Subte Short for Subterraneo, or Underground, the Buenos Aires Subway system.

tanda A set of tangos, usually three or four in number, in which you keep the same partner. At the end of the tanda, the DJ plays a cortina to clear the floor.

vals Tango waltz. A tango in three-quarter time, using some of the same moves as tango, with a lighter, more circular feeling.

verduras "Greens" or "vegetables." Typically this means acelga, Swiss chard, which Argentines freely substitute for spinach.

yerba mate The national drink of Argentina, a hot herbal tea containing caffeine and other stimulants. Typically served in a hollowed gourd with a metal straw and passed around on social occasions.

zapateo Literally "tapping the feet"—stomping the feet as a kind of drumming. It passed from the gypsies to the Spaniards to the gauchos of Argentina and thus into folk dances like the chacarera.